MONTANA
HOME FOR

*This chilly season, Whitehorn has more
than its share of troubles.*

*Newsflash: Maddie Kincaid goes down in history
as the nastiest patient ever to be injured. But why,
all of a sudden, is Dr. Noah Martin so determined
to baby-sit this beautiful, bronco-busting banshee?
And what's eating Homer Gilmore?
Join some new and familiar faces for winter wonderland
excitement and, as always, true love!*

CAST OF CHARACTERS

Dr. Noah Martin: Neither storm nor sleet nor rain
can stop this determined doctor from getting the job
done, even if it means taking care of the meanest,
most obstinate, most alluring patient he's ever had
the misfortune—or incredible fortune—to run in to.

Maddie Kincaid: She can fall off her horse and get right
back on, even if it kills her! There is no way Dr. Stubborn
(but oh-so-cute!) Martin can get her under the covers....

Homer Gilmore: The man wanders around town in his
bathrobe and slippers, lost in his own world but carrying
a burden that no one can see. Does he know the person
who's been causing trouble around Whitehorn this
holiday season?

Nurse Connie Adams: What is she doing letting Homer
run loose around town? And why is she making eyes at
Melissa's husband, Wyatt North?

Mark and Darcy Kincaid: This newlywed couple has
some explaining to do.

Dear Reader,

Do I have a sweet lineup for you—just in time for Valentine's Day! What's more enticing than a box of chocolates? The answer lies in the next story, *Cordina's Crown Jewel*, from *New York Times* bestselling author Nora Roberts's CORDINA'S ROYAL FAMILY series. This gem features a princess who runs away from royal responsibility and straight into the arms of the most unlikely man of her dreams!

Another Valentine treat is Jackie Merritt's *Marked for Marriage*, which is part of the popular MONTANA MAVERICKS series. Here, a feisty bronco-busting beauty must sit still so that a handsome doctor can give her a healthy dose of love. And if it's heart-thumping emotion you want, Peggy Webb continues THE WESTMORELAND DIARIES series with *Bittersweet Passion*, a heavenly opposites-attract romance between a singing sensation and a very handsome minister hero.

In *With Family in Mind*, Sharon De Vita launches her gripping SADDLE FALLS miniseries. One Valentine's Day, this newlywed author admits, she wrote a heartwarming love poem to her husband about their first year together! Our next family tale is *Sun-Kissed Baby*, by Patricia Hagan—a darling tale of a new single mom who falls for the man she thinks is her little boy's father. This talented author shares her Valentine's Day dinner tradition with us—making "a heart-shaped meatloaf" and at the end of the pink meal, "a heart-shaped ice cream cake, frosted with strawberry whipped cream." The icing on the cake this month is Leigh Greenwood's *Undercover Honeymoon*, a passionate tale of two reunited lovers who join forces to stay ahead of a deadly enemy and care for an orphaned little girl.

Make sure that you sample every Special Edition delight this month has to offer. I wish you and your loved ones a warm and rose-filled Valentine's Day (and that box of chocolates, too)!

Best,

Karen Taylor Richman
Senior Editor

Please address questions and book requests to:
Silhouette Reader Service
U.S.: 3010 Walden Ave., P.O. Box 1325, Buffalo, NY 14269
Canadian: P.O. Box 609, Fort Erie, Ont. L2A 5X3

Marked for Marriage

JACKIE MERRITT

SPECIAL EDITION™

Published by Silhouette Books

America's Publisher of Contemporary Romance

Special thanks and acknowledgment are given
to Jackie Merritt for her contribution
to the MONTANA MAVERICKS series.

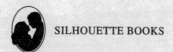 SILHOUETTE BOOKS

ISBN 0-373-24447-9

MARKED FOR MARRIAGE

Copyright © 2002 by Harlequin S.A.

This edition published by arrangement with Harlequin Books S.A.

® and TM are trademarks of Harlequin Books S.A., used under license.
Trademarks indicated with ® are registered in the United States Patent
and Trademark Office, the Canadian Trade Marks Office and in other
countries.

Visit Silhouette at www.eHarlequin.com

Printed in U.S.A.

JACKIE MERRITT

is still writing, just not with the speed and constancy of years past. She and hubby are living in southern Nevada again, falling back on old habits of loving the long, warm or slightly cool winters and trying almost desperately to head north for the months of July and August, when the fiery sun bakes people and cacti alike.

Was Maddie so desperate that she'd start thinking Noah Martin was interesting?

Good grief, she thought in abject self-disgust. She could have men by the droves, if she wasn't always so picky. She insolently lifted her chin and narrowed her eyes right back at Noah. "Thanks for the wrap, Doc. But it looked to me as though you enjoyed opening my robe just a little too much."

Noah was thunderstruck. Jumping up, he gathered his things and strode angrily over to his medical bag.

Maddie's heart sank. She'd gone too far. "I...I..." she stammered.

Noah swung around, his face furious and his eyes glowing like live embers. "I won't demean myself by even attempting to deny your charge."

Maddie, who rarely cried, suddenly felt tears drizzling down her cheeks. "I...feel like I've lost touch with everything that has been real and good in my life."

Noah walked over to Maddie. He cradled her head in his hands and tenderly pressed his lips to hers. He felt her startled reaction, but in the next instant she was kissing him back....

Prologue

Dr. Noah Martin, internal specialist and surgeon extraordinaire, pulled his dark-green SUV to a stop directly in front of Mark Kincaid's home. Instead of immediately getting out of his vehicle, Noah left the engine and heater running—the outside temperature on this early-February day was hovering in the low twenties. He frowned uneasily at the house, as though the attractive structure—blue-gray siding, red brick trim—contained something ominous. In truth, the only thing it contained—beyond furnishings and personal possessions belonging to Mark and his bride, Darcy—was a young woman named Maddie who happened to be Mark's sister.

Noah's promise to look in on Maddie while Mark and Darcy were on their honeymoon weighed about ten thousand pounds, and at the moment Noah would give almost anything to have stumbled upon some reason for *not* doing this favor for Mark. It would have to be something feasible, of course. Noah didn't have a trainload of friends, mostly due to his loner personality and disdain for the human race in general, but he and Mark had hit it off from their first meeting, unusual for Noah.

Truth was, Mark Kincaid was the closest thing Noah had to a real friend in this little backwater town of White-horn, Montana, to which he'd moved to escape the ghosts of a love gone sour. He had learned, of course, that changing one's residence did not eradicate memory—a painful lesson in the implacability of human emotion. There were moments when the image of beautiful, sophisticated Felicia, his former fiancée and the love of his life, was so real in his mind that it seemed as though he could reach out a hand and touch her. The utter foolishness of that sort of mind game never failed to anger him, and there were many, many days when he did his job without smiling even once.

Not that he would take Felicia back if she suddenly appeared in Whitehorn and pleaded with him to mend their broken relationship. She'd left him flat, announcing with her regal chin high in the air in a symbolic effort to look down on him—ridiculous when she was five foot five and he was six feet tall—that she was tired of playing second fiddle to his medical career. It was over for her, and nothing he'd said had altered her decision.

The whole thing—giving a woman everything he had to give, rushing to comply with her slightest whim, worrying that he loved her far more than she loved him, and on and on ad infinitum until the breakup—had created a brand-new Noah Martin. As a snake sheds its skin, Noah shed all ties to the past—or so he'd believed when he traded San Francisco for a small town in Montana.

He'd found out differently, and while he did his best to combat bitterness, it was an undeniable part of his personality. He angered easily, resented trivial slights that he wouldn't even have noticed before meeting Felicia and ultimately falling under her spell. And perhaps most unfortunate of all, his former commendable bedside manner had vanished, and other than the medical side of his relationship with patients, he really didn't like them.

Now, on this raw February afternoon, staring broodingly at the front of Mark's house he again regretted a promise he couldn't get out of keeping. It didn't alleviate Noah's bad mood to realize that the main reason he'd agreed to this annoying interruption in his regular routine was Mark's worried comments about Maddie having had some kind of accident during a rodeo. The details had slid through Noah's mind, but the gist of the conversation had been that he and Darcy could not leave on their scheduled honeymoon without someone dependable keeping an eye on Maddie.

"I'll tell you now," Mark had said, "Maddie's a handful. But I think you just might be the one person around who can handle her."

Noah narrowed his eyes and wondered exactly what "handling Maddie Kincaid" would entail. He sure as hell didn't need another woman enforcing her will over his. In fact, since the charade with Felicia, he'd made it a point to stay completely away from the opposite sex. Except in a professional setting, of course.

Thinking that Mark was going to owe him big-time for this, Noah turned off the ignition and got out. The outside cold, made more penetrating by a gusting north wind, turned his breath to freezing fog. There was a thin layer of snow on the ground—frozen into tiny ice pellets, Noah was certain—and every step he took made a uniquely wintry crunching sound. He walked to the front door and rang the bell. No one came to the door, nor could Noah hear any movement from inside.

Frowning, he left the small front porch and walked around the house to the side door. From there he could see a long white trailer and a strikingly handsome white one-ton pickup truck residing in the extra parking space Mark had behind his garage. The truck sparked Noah's interest. It had chrome running boards and tail pipes, chrome rooftop lights, and probably every other conceivable add-on, Noah decided. It was an obviously costly vehicle, and when he gave the trailer another look, he thought the same about it. Apparently Mark's sister was not here because of a lack of funds, but then no one had said she was. She was here to recuperate from an accident. A rodeo accident, Noah thought, puzzling about something that he probably should already know, given Mark's concern for his baby sister.

Certain that he'd get the lowdown from Maddie Kincaid herself, he knocked. After a few seconds he knocked again, and then again. Muttering several choice curse words under his breath about "some women's lack of consideration for a man's time," he impatiently yanked off his glove and dug through his pockets for the key Mark had given him.

Unlocking the door, he stepped into the house—more precisely, into the messiest kitchen he'd ever seen. "Good Lord," he mumbled. Mark and Darcy had only been gone one day and Maddie had done this much damage? How injured could she be? There were pans covered with dregs of food on the stove and counters, dirty dishes and cutlery in the sink and on the counters, and empty soup cans spilling out of a full trash container.

One thing *wasn't* in the kitchen—Maddie Kincaid. Shaking his head disgustedly at the unwashed dishes scattered around the room, Noah went looking for her. He spotted a lump under a big soft comforter on the sofa in the living room and decided that he'd found her.

Maddie had awakened just enough to know that someone was in the house. Groggy from the pain pills she'd been taking as prescribed, she nonetheless felt suddenly frightened. Mark and Darcy had left for their honeymoon. Had that happened this morning? Yesterday morning? Well, whatever morning it had been, they weren't back already. And the doors were locked! Mark had locked everything up nice and tight before his and Darcy's departure, and Maddie had had no cause to unlock anything.

With her heart pounding hard enough to hear, Maddie moved the comforter a fraction so she could at least get a glimpse of the intruder. She'd been sleeping with the soft down-filled blanket over her head, because she hadn't been really warm since she'd arrived, even with the gas furnace going full blast. She'd actually forgotten how cold February could get in Montana, which was odd when she'd grown up with blustery north winds and temperatures that could bring tears to the eyes of the most stalwart—and warmly dressed—outdoorsman. But apparently she'd spent too many winters in the southern states to expect instant acclimation.

Peering through the tiny gap she'd created within the folds of the comforter encapsulating her, Maddie saw a man. A tall man with broad shoulders in winter garb, who appeared to be looking in her direction, although she couldn't be sure that he realized the bulky comforter contained a person. If she didn't move again—maybe he hadn't seen her cautiously create the viewing gap she was looking through—would he eventually go away without harming her?

Dear God, why had he broken into this particular house? Did he know that Mark and Darcy had gone away and was planning to take everything they owned in their absence? Even if he wasn't aware that she was staying there and, in fact, lying on the sofa and watching him this very second, could she do nothing and let him steal Mark and Darcy blind? What she should do was to leap up, grab a poker from the stand by the fireplace and whack him over his thieving head.

She could see herself doing it, maybe even knocking him silly without the poker. She could leap up, whirl around and kick him in the chin, do another whirl and give him a good one in the chest with her heel. Another kick to the groin should just about finish him off.

It was pure fantasy. She was in no condition to do a super-heroine leap off the sofa, let alone any dramatic whirls and high kicks. As for using the poker for a weapon, it was too far away. This villainous cretin certainly wasn't going to stand still and wait for her to limp over to the fireplace, for Pete's sake.

Moving just her eyes, Maddie searched for something closer with which to defend her honor—and possibly her life—along with her brother's possessions. The paperweight on the end table would have to do, she decided, and sucking in a big breath for courage, she threw back the comforter, stumbled to her feet and lunged for the paperweight.

Noah could hardly believe his eyes. A tiny little woman wearing what looked to be a set of her brother's two-piece long johns and huge woolen stockings was assuming an attack position, with her weapon being a paperweight! Her short, light-brown hair was spiky, totally disarrayed, and the right side of her face was every color of the rainbow, obviously in varying stages of the healing process. A soft cast was on her right hand and halfway up her forearm, and besides all of that, the paperweight she was threatening him with in her left hand was one with artificial snow in it. The "snow" kept swirling within the globe because Maddie—she *must* be Maddie—was so unsteady on her feet that her hand couldn't stop her weapon from wavering.

Maddie Kincaid was truly the most hilarious sight Noah had ever seen, and he started laughing. He laughed until tears rolled down his cheeks. He laughed so hard that he could just barely stand erect and so he fell into an overstuffed chair. He laughed until his sides ached, and all the while Maddie stood there weaving back and forth trying very hard to look vicious and dangerous, which kept feeding Noah's laughter.

Finally Maddie merely looked disgusted, which was exactly how she felt. What kind of lunatic moron was this guy? Breaking into a house and then laughing himself sick because there was someone home to defend it and he'd believed it to be vacant had to indicate some sort of mental problem. He probably belonged in a padded cell! Somehow she needed to get to one of the phones in the house and call the police, but...but...to Maddie's chagrin, she started blacking out.

She looked suddenly pale, Noah saw and, recognizing the signs of an impending faint, he stopped laughing and made a dive for this oddball little woman. The paperweight dropped from her lifeless hand and thudded on the carpet. Noah got to her before she ended up next to the little globe and swung her up into his arms to lay her back on the sofa.

She couldn't weigh much more than a hundred pounds, he decided while tucking the comforter around her shoulders. Then he gently shook her and said, "Maddie? Come on, wake up. You only fainted."

Her eyelids fluttered open, and she found herself looking into the dark blue eyes of...of... She couldn't give him a label, though heaven knew she was scared to death of the many horrible things he might be. Actually he didn't look like an ax murderer or even a burglar—he was very *good*-looking, in fact—but then how many truly sinister people had she met in her twenty-three years?

Then something clicked in her brain and she asked nervously, "Did you, uh, say my name?"

"Yes. You're Maddie, Mark Kincaid's kid sister. I'm Noah Martin. Mark asked me to keep an eye on you while he and Darcy honeymoon in Europe."

"You're a baby-sitter? *My* baby-sitter? No way, buster! And get your butt off of this sofa! In fact, get your butt out of this house!"

Noah stood up. He understood now why Mark had described his sister as a "handful." What he didn't quite comprehend was why Mark thought *he* was the one person in Whitehorn who could deal with her!

Chapter One

Ten Days Earlier

Maddie Kincaid loved the rodeo atmosphere. Sitting her horse, Fanchon, because they would be performing in the barrel racing event in a few minutes, Maddie basked in the noise from the stands, the sounds of the horses and bulls in the holding pens and the mixture of odors, from hot popcorn to the sweat of nervous animals. Even Fanchon, or Fanny, as the mare was more commonly called, evidenced excitement.

With her gloved hand Maddie stroked Fanny's neck and murmured, "Hold on, girl. We're up next. Stay calm."

Her touch always soothed the beautiful gray quarter horse mare, and Maddie let her gaze drift around to the men and women in jeans, boots and big hats awaiting their events. She could hear snatches of conversations and recognized the same thrill of competition in their voices that she felt in the pit of her stomach.

A roar went up in the stands, and Maddie heard over the loudspeaker that Janie Weston had knocked over a barrel during her race, which meant that if Maddie made a good ride, she would again win the trophy and the purse. Barrel racing was Maddie's specialty, and she could fill a small room with trophies, if she had a room. But her home was a long trailer that she pulled with a one-ton pickup truck. And so whenever she was in Austin, Texas, as she was now, she would go to her rented storage space and unload the trophies that she'd picked up since her last visit.

Maddie never let herself get overly confident, nor did she ever even think *hallelujah* when her toughest competitor knocked herself out of the race. It could happen so easily, and it had happened to Maddie a time or two. Besides, rodeo contestants were, for the most part, good sports and great people. Maddie knew a lot of them by name, especially those that followed the rodeo circuit, as she did.

Janie rode from the arena with a downcast expression, but when Maddie's name was announced as the next contestant, she sent Maddie a thumbs-up.

Maddie acknowledged Janie's courtesy with a smile and a nod and urged Fanny forward. At the starting post, she again touched Fanny and spoke quietly. In seconds the blare of the starting horn put both Fanchon and Maddie into action. At lightning speed Fanny circled the first barrel and then the second. Every movement made by Fanny and Maddie was smooth and necessary. Maddie's mind was totally focused on her race against the clock, and she barely heard the crowd now.

Then something happened. Fanchon took a sudden nose dive and Maddie went flying. She landed hard on her right side and blacked out.

The crowd fell silent, and the announcer didn't have to shout to be heard. ''Folks, Miss Maddie Kincaid ran into a bit of trouble. As you can see, the medics are putting her on a stretcher. They'll see to it that Maddie is well cared for. I'll keep y'all posted."

The rodeo continued, but Maddie knew nothing for a good ten minutes. When she came to she was in an ambulance with a wailing siren, lying on her back with an IV needle in her arm and an attendant watching her vital signs.

"Fanchon," she said weakly.

"Your horse? She's fine. Not even a scratch."

"Are you sure?"

"Very sure."

Maddie closed her eyes. She couldn't find a spot on her body that didn't hurt and finally whispered, "Pain."

"Yes, I know," the attendant said. "There's a mild sedative in your IV drip, but we can't give you anything stronger until you're checked for concussion. Try to relax."

The rest of Maddie's trip to the hospital was spent in "trying to relax." But her body hurt like hell and her mind was clouded just enough to make sudden, clear thoughts jump out at her—especially any thought pertaining to Fanny. After all, when the man in the white suit didn't know if she had a concussion or not, would he tell her the truth if Fanny had been seriously injured in their fall?

Being transported from ambulance to emergency room was fast and little more than a blur for Maddie. Then began the tests—a battery of them—and finally a pain shot that did some good. She went out like a light and woke up hours later in a hospital gown and bed. Her brain was fuzzy, and she was thirsty enough to drink water from a horse trough—right along with the animals.

It seemed like a simple matter to get the tall glass of water she could see on the stand next to the bed, but when she tried to raise her right arm, it refused to cooperate. She finally lifted it high enough to see the thick blue fabric encasing her hand and lower arm. She knew what it was—a soft cast. She'd broken something. Not her wrist, because that would be in a hard cast. She'd seen many casts and bandages during her rodeo career. Banged-up cowboys and cowgirls were not a rarity, but this was Maddie's first accident that had put her in a hospital bed.

She rang for the nurse, and in a minute or so one came in. "You're awake. Good. What do you need, hon?"

"Some water, which I can't seem to reach for myself, and maybe a rundown on what else is broken besides my arm."

The nurse held the glass so Maddie could suck water through the straw. "Your arm's not broken, hon, it's a couple of little bones in your hand. You have no other fractures, but your entire right side is badly bruised."

"I feel…awful," Maddie said in a whispery unsteady voice.

The nurse checked her watch. "You're due for another pain shot. I'll get it." She hurried out and returned almost at once with a syringe. "You have to turn a bit so I can reach your hip."

Turning even a "bit" was unbelievably painful for Maddie. In comparison, the sting of the needle was nothing.

"Your doctor will be in to see you sometime this evening," she said before leaving.

Maddie was already drifting off again, only alert enough to be glad about the doctor. She had questions, or she'd *had* questions when the nurse had talked so briefly about her injuries. Maybe she would remember them when the doctor appeared this evening. She hoped so.

As it turned out, the doctor showed up around four-thirty that afternoon. "I'm Dr. Upton," he said while reading the notations on what Maddie supposed was her chart. Finished with that he sat on the one chair near her bed. "How're you feeling?"

"I hurt," she said bluntly, if with very little force behind the two words. Along with varying degrees of pain

from her head to her legs, she felt horribly weak, but had
to find out everything she could about her injuries.

Dr. Upton nodded. "I don't doubt it. You took quite a
spill, young woman. It's somewhat of a miracle that all
you broke were two small bones in one hand. It's the hand
you landed on, of course. Your abrasions were caused
from being dragged through the dirt."

"Dragged? By what?"

"By your horse."

"Fanchon is a gentle mare and would never drag me!"

The doctor smiled indulgently. "Sorry, Maddie," he
said gently, "but that's exactly what happened."

"Then she was afraid."

"Possibly. Undoubtedly," he added. "She was falling,
as well. Fear is only natural in that instance."

"Where is she? Do you know?"

"I knew that would be your first question once you
were lucid, so I made some phone calls to find out. Fanchon is stabled at the rodeo grounds. She's fine and so
will you be in time."

"In time?" Maddie repeated suspiciously. "How much
time?" She should be on the road right now, heading for
Abilene and the next major rodeo on the circuit calendar.

"I'd say at least a month." Dr. Upton got to his feet
and began writing on the chart. "Even small bones take
time to knit, Maddie, and I believe you'll require some
physical therapy on that hand once the healing process
reaches a certain stage. Now, I'd like you to stay here
through tomorrow night, so we can keep an eye out for
infection. If all goes well, I'll release you the following
morning."

"Infection? In my hand?"

"Maddie, your right side is one huge abrasion from
your forehead to midcalf. We had to pick minute pieces
of gravel out of your skin with medical tweezers. There
are antibiotics in your IV and antibiotic salve under the
dressings on the worst of your injuries. You've also been

given a rabies shot because of incurring open wounds around horses. Infection is a very real threat and...'' He saw the horror in Maddie's eyes. "You haven't looked in a mirror yet? You've been up.''

"I have?''

"Twice, according to the nurses' notes on the chart. To use the bathroom, Maddie. You don't remember?''

"No.''

"Well, your pain medication is quite powerful. I'm going to keep you on it tonight and then change it to a less potent drug in the morning. A nurse will be in later to check your dressings. I'll see you in the morning.''

Maddie was in shock. She could handle a broken hand, but abrasions from her forehead to the middle of her calf? That, of course, was where her leg started being protected by her sturdy riding boot. "My God,'' she whispered. Was she going to be disfigured?

Maddie clenched her good fist and told herself differently. Dr. Upton hadn't even hinted at disfigurement, and she was not going to lie in this bed and imagine the worst.

But she was going to be laid up and useless for a month. "No!'' she whispered. A whole month of doing nothing? She'd go nuts!

A dinner tray was brought in then, and Maddie looked at the cup of bouillon, the small bowl of green gelatin and another cup containing hot water for tea with very little interest. In the first place she wasn't hungry, and if she were, it wouldn't be for bouillon.

If she were a weepy type of woman, she'd lie there and bawl.

But she *wasn't* a crybaby, she was a doer, and she was *not* going to be an invalid for four miserable weeks, she simply wasn't!

The few times Maddie woke up in the night, she worried about her horse. When she came wide awake at six, she figured out that her pain medication must have been reduced during the night, because her head was clearer than it had been since the accident. Instantly, although in severe physical discomfort, she again worried about Fanny. Was a responsible person feeding her? Making sure she had fresh water? Taking her outside for exercise?

Barrel racing demanded total unity between horse and rider, and Maddie had no doubt that Fanchon was the deciding factor in her success in the arena. Without Fanny, Maddie knew she would be just another rodeo hopeful. Along with loving Fanny with all her heart, the quarter horse was extremely valuable monetarily, and what if someone should steal her from the rodeo grounds?

Maddie shuddered. She had to get out of this hospital today. Dr. Upton had said that if all went well he would release her tomorrow morning. That wasn't good enough for Maddie. She was not going to lie here all day and worry.

And so, when breakfast was delivered—solid food this morning—Maddie forced every bite of a bowl of sticky oatmeal down her throat and drank her glass of orange juice like a good little girl. When a nurse asked how she was feeling—it had been a long time since her last pain shot—Maddie lied and said, "Much, much better, thank you."

The nurse unhooked her IV and then brought in some pills. Maddie asked what they were and the nurse replied, "The blue one is an antibiotic, the white one is for pain."

"I'm only going to take the antibiotic," Maddie said with a hopeful little smile. "Is that all right? If I was in pain...but I'm not...and..."

The nurse frowned. "No pain at all?"

"Very mild discomfort. Not nearly enough to knock myself out with pain medication, and even if the pill isn't that strong, I really detest that fuzzy-headed feeling I get from sedatives."

"Well...all right, but you are to ring at once if you start hurting."

"Oh, I will."

The charade was more difficult when bath time rolled around. "I can do it myself, really," Maddie told the young woman who came in to give her a bed bath. The woman finally believed her and left, and Maddie soon learned how inept she was with her left hand. She hurt so badly that she nearly rang for that pill a dozen times. Gritting her teeth throughout the ordeal, she bathed herself and struggled into a fresh nightgown. Exhausted and not daring to show it, she waited for the young nurse to return and check her abrasions.

This time Maddie asked for a mirror, which was brought to her. "Oh, my God," she whispered when she saw the right side of her face.

"It looks worse than it is because it was painted with red antiseptic," the young nurse told her. "It's all up and down your right side. See?"

Maggie saw all right, and her heart felt heavy as lead. "Will...it wear off?"

"Of course it will. When you're strong enough to take showers, it will disappear in a few days. You're healing nicely, Maddie. My orders for this morning are to apply antibiotic cream to your abrasions but to leave them uncovered."

"There's no sign of infection, then?"

"None at all." The young nurse was finishing up. "Dr. Upton will be in to see you, probably within the hour." She left the room.

Maddie closed her eyes. Weepy type of woman or not, she truly felt like bawling. She looked like a character in a horror movie!

Even terribly uncomfortable she dozed. She opened her eyes when Dr. Upton said, "No pain medication today, Maddie?"

"Hello," she said with as much normalcy as she could muster. "Should I take a drug I don't need?"

"No, you shouldn't, but I have to question *why* you

don't need it." He checked her chart for another minute or so, then set it down on the foot of the bed and bent over her. "Look at the far corner of the room," he instructed and then beamed light into her eyes with what appeared to Maddie as a slender little flashlight.

"What's that for?" she asked.

"Just a precaution. I'm glad to see that there's still no sign of concussion. You were very fortunate, young woman."

He'd said that before, Maddie thought somewhat resentfully. Would he think himself fortunate if it were he lying in this bed with more bruises than a map had roads, hurting something awful and not daring to show it because he had to convince a doctor that he was well enough to get out of here today, instead of tomorrow?

He was writing on the chart, and she knew it was a forerunner to his leaving. Panic assailed her, but before she could ask for an early release, he said, "You're doing remarkably well. Keep this up and you'll be going home in the morning."

She cleared her throat. "Dr. Upton, I'd like to go home today."

He looked at her sharply from under a dubiously arched eyebrow. "I would say that's pushing it, Maddie."

"I feel fine, and I have responsibilities."

"We all do, but an accident such as yours really puts everything else on hold. Or, it should. You haven't had a lot of visitors. Don't you have family or friends living in the vicinity?"

"I'm from Montana, and my friends go where the rodeos take them. Doctor, I've been completely self-sufficient for years, and I'm perfectly capable of applying antibiotic creams or salves to my scrapes and bruises, and taking pills on a timed schedule. I can't just lie here and wish for a miracle. I want to go home today. Right now, in fact, or as soon as I can be checked out. Please release me, Dr. Upton. Please."

The doctor studied her chart. "Well, your vitals have been stable for more than twenty-four hours," he murmured, and appeared to be thinking for several moments. Then his gaze lifted. "How would you get home? Is there someone you could call to come and pick you up? I don't want you driving today, Maddie."

Her pulse quickened because he hadn't immediately refused her request. "I would call a taxi," she said honestly. "I don't have a vehicle here if I wanted to drive home, which I don't."

"Okay, tell you what. Let me see you get out of bed and walk around. I'll release you today if I see that you are truly mobile."

Maddie gulped, but she forced herself to sit up, shove her sheet aside and then cautiously slide off the bed to put her feet on the floor. There were hospital slippers down there somewhere, but she was afraid that if she bent over to look for them she might pass out. So she held the back of her gown shut with her left hand and took a barefoot stroll around the room, fighting nausea and dizziness every step of the way.

"Okay, you've convinced me," Dr. Upton declared. "It will take about two hours to check you out. You'll be taking prescriptions for antibiotics and painkillers with you. Get them filled right here in the hospital pharmacy or on your way home, whichever you prefer. I'd like to see you in my office in a week. Call for an appointment and tell the receptionist to fit you in. I'll try to remember to tell her your name and to expect your call."

"Thank you," Maddie said with her very last ounce of strength. She was so glad that Dr. Upton left right away that she could have cheered. Instead, she stumbled to the bed and groaned under her breath while struggling to get herself back on it. Finally prone and covered with the sheet again, with her heart beating overly fast from the exertion, she shut her eyes and suffered in silence.

But the pain didn't matter. She was going to be free to

check on Fanny in a matter of hours. For that privilege she could stand anything.

Maddie had managed to relax some when a nurse came in and stated cheerfully, "So, you're leaving us already." The woman took Maddie's wrist and checked her pulse.

"Yes, I'll be leaving as soon as..." It hit her suddenly and hard enough to make her groan.

"You're in pain again?" the nurse asked with a concerned expression.

"No, I just realized that I have nothing here...no money, no credit cards, not my insurance card. How can I check out without my insurance information?"

"Aren't those things in your purse?"

"That's exactly where they are, but my purse is in my trailer." Maddie really did feel like bawling then. This brick wall she didn't need!

"Maddie, your purse is in the closet with your clothes. Don't you remember? A very nice young woman brought your purse...she said that you'd probably need it...and it was put with your other things."

Maddie's head swam in a concerted effort to figure out who the "nice young woman" was. For one thing, her purse was—or had been—in her locked trailer and she was the only one with a key. She took nothing with her to a contest, which was fairly common practice amongst rodeo contestants. Even loose change in a pocket could cause injury during a fall, so everyone pretty much did his or her thing with empty pockets.

Given the circumstances she could only conclude that what had been delivered by visitors she had absolutely no recollection of seeing was something other than her purse.

But she was curious about it, all the same. "Would you mind getting it for me?"

"Wouldn't mind at all." The nurse went to the closet and returned with...Maddie's purse!

"How...who...for goodness sake," she sputtered. "It

is my purse, but how did someone go into my trailer to get it?''

"Wouldn't know, honey. See you later." The nurse departed.

Maddie opened her purse and saw, with relief, her wallet. She also saw a rosy pink piece of paper, which she knew for a fact hadn't been in there the last time she'd looked. She took it out and unfolded it. It was a handwritten note and Maddie quickly read it.

Maddie,
I'm terribly sorry about your accident. Most of us in rodeo are not happy to win by default, which is what happened today. This is one trophy for which I feel no pride. At any rate, after they took you away in the ambulance I got to worrying about you being so alone in Austin. It also occurred to me that you didn't have anything important with you, such as your wallet. So here it is.

I'm sure you're wondering by now how I got into your trailer to get your purse. Don't worry, I didn't break in. It was only logical that you would have a door key hidden on or near the trailer, so I went hunting for it. Obviously I found it or you wouldn't be reading this note but it took me a while.

I'm off to Abilene and then Laredo—you have the schedule—and since I feel certain that you'll hit the circuit as soon as you're able, we'll be seeing each other again. I hope it will be very soon.

Janie Weston

Maddie almost couldn't believe what she'd just read. It was so nice of Janie to go out of her way like this that Maddie was truly stunned. While she and Janie were friendly to each other, they'd never really been buddies. Frowning slightly, Maddie couldn't elude the fact that she had very few close friends. In fact, she was hard-pressed to come up with even one. It was the lifestyle, the endless traveling, the moving on to one rodeo while a person who might have become a good friend went in another direction to the rodeo of her or his choice. For that same reason and the fact that followers of rodeo usually hung out in groups, it had been ages since Maddie had done more than drink a beer or have a dance with a man.

Sighing heavily, Maddie took out her wallet and flipped it open. The very first thing she saw was the snapshot of her brother. "Mark," she whispered, and studied the handsome features of her older brother. With their parents gone, Mark was all she had. Oh, there were plenty of Kincaids living in the Whitehorn, Montana, area, but none of them meant to her what Mark did.

Loneliness suddenly beset her. She needed to talk to Mark. Maybe she needed to hear him say something sympathetic, something kind and loving that would bring tears to her eyes and joy to her heart.

No, she didn't want sympathy, not even from Mark. But she really would like to talk to him, and years ago he'd made her promise that if she was ever ill or injured she would let him know. He didn't entirely approve of her unsettled lifestyle, and no doubt she'd get a brotherly lecture on the dangers inherent in her chosen career. But he'd be sweet, too, once she told him about the accident.

There was a telephone on the bedstand, and she tried not to jostle her sore and aching body while reaching for it. She needed a pain pill badly and knew that she should have taken the one offered by the nurse this morning, even though her own sheer bravado had convinced everyone that she was ready to go home. Truth was, if she knew for a fact that Fanny was being properly cared for, she would gladly stay in this bed for another night.

After dialing Mark's home and getting no answer, Maddie looked up his work number in the little address book she carried in her purse. Mark was a detective for the

Whitehorn police department, and Maddie doubted that he'd be sitting at a desk hoping the phone would ring. To her surprise—which was accompanied by a sudden attack of nerves—the man who answered her call asked for her name and then told her to hang on a minute. Raising his voice, he said, "Hey, Mark, your sister's on line three."

Almost at once Mark's voice was in Maddie's ear. "Hey, this is a nice surprise. Where're you calling from?"

"Austin, Texas. How are you?"

"Couldn't be better."

"Marriage agrees with you then." Mark could still measure his marriage to Darcy Montague in weeks, and Maddie was extremely happy that he'd fallen head over heels for a woman who seemed so perfect for him.

"More than I ever thought possible. So, what's up with you?"

"Uh, I had a little accident," Maddie stammered, suddenly very uncertain about the wisdom of this call. "In the arena."

The tenor of Mark's voice instantly changed, from that of a glad-you-called-just-to-say-hi brother to that of the protector he'd been to his baby sister all her life. Mark was thirty, seven years older than Maddie, and from the day of her birth he'd watched over her. That protective side of him was undoubtedly the reason he didn't like her driving her truck all over the country, pulling her trailer and happily heading for the next rodeo.

"How little is 'little'?" he asked suspiciously.

"Um…no major bone breaks…just a couple of tiny bones in my right hand."

"And that's all?"

"No," she said weakly. "I'm pretty badly bruised. The doctor wants me to take it easy and to stay away from rodeo for a month, which is rather extreme, I believe, and—"

"And nothing! Maddie, you do exactly as that doctor says, do you hear me? In fact, if you have to take it easy for a whole month, I want you to come home and do your recuperating in Darcy's and my guest room."

"Well, of course," Maddie drawled. "That's exactly what newlyweds need, to share their little love nest with the groom's sister. Mark—"

"Stop right there! You're at least fifteen hundred miles away and alone. Damn it, Maddie, if it were the other way around and it was me laid up and alone, you'd be here so fast my head would spin. Hey, I just thought of something. Are you calling on your cell phone from your trailer? We've got a really clear connection, which doesn't usually happen when you call on your cell."

Maddie rolled her eyes. Mark was a natural born detective. She should have known he'd recognize the difference between her cellular calls and this one. She'd had no intention of telling him everything, but now she had no choice.

"I'm not using my cellular phone," she said quietly. "I'm…calling from the hospital."

"You're in the hospital! Maddie, you said a 'little' accident. What really happened?"

After a heavy sigh, Maddie related the fall she and Fanny had taken. "I have no idea what caused it, but there it is. Apparently Fanny wasn't injured, but the medics took me to the hospital. I can't be too bad off because I'm being discharged sometime today. That's the whole truth."

"Except for what the doctor told you to do."

"Mark, I can't do nothing for a whole month!"

"You could if you were under my roof. Look, why don't you put Fanny in a good stable, leave your truck and trailer in a safe place—I'm sure a city the size of Austin has rental spaces available for RVs and such—and fly home? I hate the thought of you limping around that little trailer you live in and trying to fix yourself something to eat. With one hand yet. And surely you're not thinking of taking care of Fanny yourself. Maddie, it's just not sensible for you to stay in Texas.''

He was making sense, and Maddie's resolve to take care of herself was weakening. But fly to Montana and leave Fanny in Texas? No way, Maddie thought, and avoided that topic entirely by asking, ''Mark, are you sure Darcy wouldn't mind? You have to think of her first now, you know.''

''I *know* Darcy wouldn't mind. She's a very special lady, Maddie. So, have I convinced you? Are you coming home?''

''I...guess so.''

''Great! Phone me with your flight schedule.''

''It'll probably be a few days before you hear from me. It will take, uh, some time to do everything here that will need, uh, doing before I can leave.'' She wasn't exactly lying to the brother she adored, she told herself. She simply wasn't telling him everything she was thinking and planning.

''That's fine. Just call when you know something.''

''Bye, Mark.''

''Bye, Maddie. Take care.''

Maddie hung up and, completely done in, she closed her eyes and wished with all her heart that she would fall asleep in spite of the pain racking her body.

She really shouldn't have phoned Mark, she thought hazily, because now she had to go home to Montana, and she was *not* going by herself. She wouldn't leave Fanny behind for all the oil in Texas, which Mark would have thought of if he hadn't immediately started worrying about Maddie's condition instead of looking at the whole picture.

''The hits just keep on coming,'' Maddie whispered while wondering how on earth she was going to manage to drive fifteen hundred miles when she could just barely move without pain medication, which she certainly couldn't take and then do any driving.

Chapter Two

Checking out of the hospital took hours, most of that time spent in waiting. Maddie waited for someone from administration to do the paperwork, then waited for her prescriptions to be filled by the hospital pharmacy. Her final wait was for a nurse to come to her room to instruct her on home care of her abrasions.

By then Maddie was hurting so much that when a runner delivered her prescriptions in the middle of the nurse's instructions, Maddie immediately tried to get a pain pill from its container. She couldn't use her right hand, of course, and she simply wasn't adept with her left, especially when it was trembling from the burning, stinging pain raging all along her right side.

The nurse took the bottle from her, opened it and shook out one pill into Maddie's outstretched hand. "Let me tell you something about pain," the woman said while Maddie swallowed the pill with a drink of water.

"You refused pain medication much too soon and you

are suffering unnecessarily. I know many people do not like some of the side effects of painkillers, but believe me, Maddie, it's far better for you to rest and recover than to spend your time gritting your teeth in a futile attempt to will yourself well. Take these as prescribed, properly tend to your scrapes and abrasions, drink at least eight glasses of water a day to keep your system flushed and, while you must do some walking to keep your muscles toned and supple, you also should rest as much as possible. Finally, of course, be sure to make that appointment with Dr. Upton.''

"Yes, ma'am," Maddie said softly. She was only going to follow *some* of this pleasant woman's advice, and she truly hated deceiving her. But she had no choice. It wasn't as though she was going home to a family that would cook her food and pamper her, after all; *she* was all she had in Texas. When she got hungry, she'd have to order in or cook. Thank God for cell phones, she thought, because it would be her one connection with the world beyond her trailer, once she got there.

In truth, she couldn't even pamper herself when she got home. At least, she couldn't until she checked on Fanny. Maddie didn't dare let herself wonder if she could manage to do what needed doing because there simply was no one to do it for her. She *had* to take care of Fanny, and she had to take care of herself. Last but far from least, she had to drive fifteen hundred miles.

Thinking of that long, long drive caused Maddie's breath to stop in her throat, but only for a second. The pain pill was beginning to work its magic, and along with the sharp edges of her physical anguish floating away, she felt light-headed and much less stressed. She listened to the nurse repeat instructions about applying antibiotic ointment to her abrasions—apparently a crucial step in the healing process—and then talk about tub baths versus showers, and how Maddie mustn't let her soft cast get wet whichever way she bathed.

By the time the woman left, Maddie was pain-free and woozy. She closed her eyes and dozed off thinking of Montana and home. It was where she truly wanted to be, and it would happen. She would *make* it happen, the same way she had made everything else that was good and productive in her life happen since she'd been old enough to understand that a teenage marriage, babies and tying herself to Whitehorn, Montana, would, at the very least, stifle the best part of her. At fifteen she'd won her first rodeo-queen crown and barrel-racing trophy. It had been a small local event, but it had been big for her, big enough that she'd felt refreshingly reborn, and the new Maddie Kincaid was determined to make a splash in the world of rodeo. Shortly after that contest she had acquired Fanny, and all of her spare time had gone into working with the young mare. Now, years later and drifting off with loving thoughts of Fanny, Maddie decided, without too much concern, that Mark might yell at her for driving home instead of flying, but Fanny went where she did, and in the end he would be glad to see her.

She was sleeping soundly when a cheerful young male aide with a wheelchair sailed into the room and said, "Wake up, princess. It's time to move out."

Maddie opened her eyes. "Wha-what?"

The young man grinned. "Don't you want to go home?"

"Yes…yes, of course. But my clothes…I haven't gotten dressed."

"You are one of the privileged few who get to go home in a hospital gown, robe and slippers." The young man sobered some. "Your clothes were pretty much ruined in the accident, Maddie, but even if they weren't, you couldn't be pulling close-fitting garments over your—" he grinned again and said "—ouchies."

Maddie appreciated his sense of humor and smiled. "You're right. My ouchies would scream bloody murder if I put on something tight."

The aide went to the closet and took out a bag. "Everything you had on is in this bag."

"Great. I'm sure my boots are still all right."

"Probably are." A nurse came in and helped Maddie into the robe and slippers she would wear home. Together then, they assisted Maddie from the bed to the wheelchair. The aide carried two bags while he pushed the chair, the one with Maddie's clothes and another containing her prescriptions, and she held her purse on her lap with her uninjured left hand.

The upbeat young man told jokes and talked incessantly during the trip from Maddie's room to the hospital's front door. A taxi was waiting, and in about one minute Maddie found herself on the back seat of the cab with her baggage beside her and saying "Thanks" and "Goodbye" to the aide.

"Where to, miss?" the driver asked.

Maddie told him the rodeo grounds, which was where both her trailer and truck were parked, although in different locations. "One more problem to deal with," she said under her breath, which was the God's truth. Certainly she couldn't have the taxi driver drop her off at the site of her truck, because she could just barely focus her eyes and didn't dare attempt to drive it anywhere.

Then there was Fanny, who Maddie absolutely had to see with her own eyes the minute she got to the rodeo grounds. The stables were about a mile from where her trailer was parked—another problem. She tried to work it out systematically, attempting to picture the triangle of trailer, truck and stables in her brain, which seemed to be stuffed with cotton candy and thus wasn't working very well.

She was lucid enough, however, when they arrived at the rodeo grounds, to realize that she couldn't wander around in a nightgown and bathrobe. Not with hundreds of vehicles parked in the lot and the huge reader board above the whole affair stating in bold letters that there was a meet of the Young Equestrians of Texas going on.

Another hit, damn it! "My trailer is way over there to the right," she said to the driver. "It's over thirty feet long and white. Do you see it?"

"Yeah, I see it," he told her, and turned the cab in that direction.

Then, quite unexpectedly, a surge of relief relaxed Maddie's tension, because even with her stuffy brain she suddenly knew how to proceed. When the cab stopped next to her trailer, she laid out her plan for the driver. He agreed, and she got out—moving slower than molasses, she thought, feeling impatience with her own infirmities— unlocked the door of her trailer and managed to climb the two steps to get inside.

It was far from a mansion, but it felt good to Maddie to be in her own special little place, and she wished that all she had to do right now were to crawl into her familiar and comfortable bed. Instead she entered the tiny bedroom, shed her hospital clothes as fast as she could manage and then stood before her closet and wondered what to put on. A dozen pair of jeans hung neatly on hangers, her favored apparel, but she also had some slacks and skirts.

"Something loose," Maddie mumbled, and reached for a long, flowered skirt. But then she spied something better— a cream-colored cotton dress that flowed softly from shoulder seams to hem line.

Getting dressed wasn't easy, but she finally was ready to leave again. Taking only her purse, she carefully exited her trailer and got back into the cab.

"Thanks," she said to the driver. "My truck is parked near the stadium, the second row, middle section, I believe. I'll direct you."

They found her truck amongst the many parked vehicles without too much trouble, but Maddie made no attempt to get out. All she'd wanted was to make sure it was still there, and it was. She was satisfied.

"You've got some things on the windshield," the cab driver told her. "Held down by the windshield wiper. Want me to get 'em."

"Would you please?"

The driver returned with two pieces of paper, one warning her to remove her vehicle at once and the other threatening a fine and impoundment if she didn't comply with the first notice.

She sighed heavily and told the driver where to find the stables. Once there, he asked if she'd like him to help her find her horse.

"You're a kind man," she replied. "Yes, I would appreciate your help very much. Thank you."

As they slowly walked to the stables, with her hanging on to his arm, he asked how she'd gotten so banged up.

"My horse and I took a fall in the arena. I have no idea how it happened, but I hit the ground pretty hard. I'm just thankful that my horse wasn't injured."

"I have a couple of daughters about your age…and three other kids…and we're all riders. I think every one of us has taken a spill at one time or another, but none of us was ever hurt as bad as you."

"It could've been worse," Maddie said with a little smile at the cabby. "A lot worse."

"You're taking it well."

"I'm not one to sit around and mope over something I can't do anything about."

"Looks that way, all right. You've got spunk, little lady."

"Yes," she agreed. "I do have spunk, but probably no more than most of us who are so drawn and loyal to rodeo. You don't last very long in this field without spunk."

"I'm sure you're right."

They were finally inside one of the long stock barns.

Maddie's strength had been fading during the walk, and she knew she was on the verge of collapsing. "There's a bench. Let me sit for just a minute."

"You sit right there and let me find your horse. What's its name."

"Fanny. Fanchon, actually, but I call her Fanny. What's your name? I truly appreciate your help."

"I'm Joe. Now, you stay here and rest. I'm sure I won't be long."

Maddie leaned her spinning head back against the wood wall and closed her eyes. She needed to be in bed, and she would be, just as soon as she made sure Fanny was all right.

Joe, the dear man, was back in minutes. "Okay, Fanny is in the next barn, stall twenty-two. Can you make it that far?"

"I have to make it. There's no way I can really rest until I see her." Maddie got to her feet and gladly took Joe's arm again. Not everything is a "hit," she thought, realizing that her taxi driver could have been some grump who wouldn't help another person to save his soul.

The second they entered the other barn Maddie heard Fanny whinny. "She knows I'm here," Maddie told her companion. And then, at long last, she was hugging Fanny's neck and wishing she'd brought some apples or carrots with her. The mare was visibly happy to see her mistress. Maddie believed it, anyway, whether it was true or not, and she told Fanny in quiet words that she was relieved to find her in good shape and that she would be back tomorrow.

"Okay, we can leave now," she said to Joe.

They returned to the cab, and Joe took her back to her trailer. Maddie paid the fare, tipped him very well and expressed her heartfelt thanks. He did one last thing for her. He assisted her from the cab to the door of her trailer.

Again Maddie climbed the two stairs that had never been a problem and now seemed to be a mile high, and went inside. Taking off her clothes, she donned the hospital gown again, as it was handy and she really didn't care what she wore to bed, as long as it wasn't tight. After checking the timing of her prescribed doses for each of her medications, she swallowed another pain pill, pulled back the blankets on her bed and crawled in.

It felt like pure heaven to her aching body, and she went out like a light.

Sometime in the night she began dreaming about her childhood, about her brother, Mark, the parents she remembered to this day with an ache in her heart and Aunt June. Dear, sweet Aunt June, who had really been a great-aunt and had been the person who had insisted that thirteen-year-old Maddie come and live with her when her parents had been killed in a car crash. Mark had been twenty, and he'd stayed in his parents' home to sell it, along with other things they'd left their children. When everything had been accomplished about a year later, he had half of all proceeds put into the Whitehorn bank in Maddie's name.

Aunt June had been on Maddie's mother's side of the family, and some of the Kincaids, her father's family, had offered their homes to Maddie at the time of the tragic accident. But Aunt June Howard hadn't merely offered. She'd talked long and hard to Mark about letting Maddie come and live with her because the child would be alone far too much if she remained in the family home with Mark, who, after all, was a man with a job and a life of his own. When he finally agreed—albeit reluctantly—that it would be best for Maddie to live with Aunt June, she had packed Maddie's things and taken her home with her.

Aunt June had been a plump, short lady, with graying hair and green eyes, the same color eyes that both Mark and Maddie had been blessed with, and she had loved her niece and nephew as though they'd been her own offspring. Widowed young, June Howard had not had kids of her own. She had never remarried and had explained to Maddie when she'd asked why not one time that there just wasn't another man on the planet who could replace the one true love of her life.

"And remember this, my sweet girl, if you truly fall in love, and I'm speaking of the real thing here, the kind of love that brings two people so closely together that they start thinking as one, don't let go of it. You'll know if and when it happens. You'll feel it in here." Aunt June had gently tapped Maddie's chest. "In your heart, darlin', in your heart," she'd added when Maddie had looked rather perplexed.

Mark had visited his baby sister—and Aunt June, of course—often, and one evening when he dropped by he had quietly and a little sadly told Maddie that he was leaving Whitehorn. "I'm not making enough money to even buy a decent car, Maddie. Someday you'll understand why I have to go."

She had answered, "I understand now, Mark."

He'd studied her gamine face with its smattering of freckles and her big solemn green eyes, and then pulled her into a big bear hug. "You really do, don't you?" he'd said emotionally.

It was true. She had always adored her big brother. Mark was handsome and bright and deserved better than he had in Whitehorn. And when she grew up, she was going to do something else, too. That feeling was in her bones, a deeply embedded part of herself, and it surfaced in all of its glory when, at age fifteen, she won that first rodeo contest using a borrowed horse.

Once she bought Fanny and dedicated herself to training her very own horse, Maddie couldn't be stopped. Aunt June didn't quite approve of a young woman being so involved with rodeo, but Maddie's happiness came first for June Howard, and besides, she hadn't been feeling well for some time and had become quite involved with doctors and medical tests. Her diagnosis, finally, had been congenital heart failure with severe complications, which, she'd been told, would gradually take its toll.

She deteriorated more rapidly after age sixty-three, and Maddie had taken over more and more of the household duties as time passed. To Maddie's intense sorrow, dear Aunt June passed away at age sixty-five. Maddie was eighteen and had just recently graduated from high school. Mark came for the funeral, stayed with Maddie for a few days and then returned to New York City and his job as a detective with the NYC police department. He'd wanted Maddie to go with him, but she hadn't even been able to imagine herself living in the East. She was Western through and through, a country girl at heart, and while she would greatly miss her beloved aunt, Maddie wasn't even slightly afraid to face the future by herself.

That had been the real beginning of her rodeo career, which through the years had only grown more and more exciting. Of course, she'd never been injured before.

Trying almost desperately to keep the sweetly soothing dream from escaping her awakening mind, Maddie finally opened her eyes. In amazement, she realized that she felt wonderful. Obviously she'd slept through the night—a fabulous night of sound sleep and lovely, heartwarming dreams—because bright morning sunshine was streaming through the tiny openings of her window blinds.

That "wonderful" feeling, however, lasted only until Maddie tried to get up. Falling back to her pillow, Maddie groaned. Every ache and pain was firmly in place; no way was she going to recover this quickly.

But even while feeling despondent over her present physical limitations, something important occurred to her. The pain medication must have completely worn off during the night because her mind was clear and rational. She would be able to drive now!

And so a plan to transport herself and Fanny from Texas to Montana took shape. She would use over-the-counter pain medication during the day, which would certainly help enough to enable her to get around. She would drive until she grew tired—maybe only a few hours a day, maybe much more—then when she went to bed at night she would take a prescription pain pill.

Satisfied with her idea, which seemed sane and sensible, Maddie cautiously got out of bed and began the day.

The trip was long and hard and at times seemed never ending. Maddie phoned Mark twice in the first few days of the journey and, to her relief, got his voice mail each time. She left brief messages about seeing him soon, but never mentioned that she was driving instead of flying. She had flown to Montana only recently to attend Mark and Darcy's wedding, so it wasn't as though Fanny hadn't ever been left behind. But this was a completely different situation. Maddie felt pretty certain that she would be in Montana for a month, and she knew that she wouldn't relax for a second if Fanny was so far away from her for so long a time.

So each morning she got out of her warm and comfortable bed, bathed, tended her wounds as instructed, ate breakfast, took her antibiotic pill along with an over-the-counter pain medication, and then limped outside to feed and water Fanny before leading her back into the trailer for that day's drive.

Maddie's trailer was a marvelous unit for people like her. The back one-third was your basic horse trailer, but the front two-thirds was like a tiny apartment, cozy and convenient. It was long and heavy and required a powerful truck to pull it, which accounted for the big costly truck Maddie drove—and loved.

At any rate, she had all the comforts of home wherever she went. And so did Fanny.

Since she was heading north in February, though, Maddie ran into some really foul weather. There was no way to avoid it and still end up in Montana, and so she took the shortest route, which at least cut down on her mileage.

Every day seemed a little colder than the one before, and Maddie had a hard time finding things in her closet that were both warm and loosely fitted. Finally she stopped in a town in Colorado and bought some lined pants and jackets in a large size. Since she wore a size six, her new suits hung on her. But they were warm and didn't cling to her sore right side.

The biggest inconvenience was her useless right hand, even though she was getting better at using her left. Also, she had started noticing something that struck her as strange. Her left knee had developed a throbbing ache, which made no sense to Maddie when all of her injuries had been to the right side of her body. She would, of course, see a doctor in Whitehorn as soon as was feasible after arriving there.

She felt like weeping with relief when she finally crossed the Wyoming-Montana border and knew that tomorrow she would make it to Whitehorn. The trip had been a terrible ordeal, far worse than she'd thought it would be. She looked and felt like hell, and if Mark got mad when he realized that she'd driven all those miles in her condition, she wouldn't dare get sassy. If the shoe were on the other foot and it was he nearly killing himself as she was doing, she'd be mad, too.

As it turned out, Maddie overslept the next morning from sheer exhaustion and didn't arrive in Whitehorn until after dark that evening, the very first time she'd driven after nightfall on this trip. But she had to get there today, even if it was late in the day. She honestly didn't think that she could go on past today, not when she hurt so badly that she could hardly sit behind the wheel. Mark would take care of her, and God knew that she needed someone's care.

Traversing the familiar streets of Whitehorn, Maddie felt tears in her eyes. She had made it; she was home.

She pulled her truck and trailer to a stop in front of Mark's house, turned off the ignition and opened her door.

She slowly—the same way she did everything these days—got out and then limped to the front door and rang the bell. From inside came the sound of her brother's voice calling out, "I'll get it, honey," and Darcy responding, "Okay."

The front porch light came on and the door opened. Maddie tried to smile, but the shocked expression on Mark's face would not be erased by a sheepish, feeble smile from her.

"Maddie! Good God, you look half-dead!" he cried.

She felt three-quarters dead, to be honest, and now that she could quit gritting her teeth and forcing herself to keep going, her knees buckled. Mark grabbed her before she went all the way down, then swung her up into his arms and carried her inside.

Darcy gaped wide-eyed at her sister-in-law. "Mark, my goodness, what happened?"

"She drove that damn truck all the way from Texas, pulling her trailer no less," Mark said grimly.

Darcy ran ahead of him to the guest bedroom and yanked back the blankets on the bed. Mark laid Maddie down, and Darcy pulled off Maddie's shoes. Then they covered her up, clothes and all, and Maddie said weakly, "I'm sorry, guys."

Mark glared at her. "Have you lost your ever-loving mind?"

Darcy intervened. "Mark, please. Maddie, what can we do? Are you hungry? Do you want to get undressed?"

"Fanny's in the trailer," she said in a shaky little voice. "It's terribly cold here, and she needs shelter, food and water."

"You're more worried about a horse than yourself," Mark said disgustedly. "Do you know what you look like? Darcy, I think we should take her to the emergency room at the hospital."

"No...please...I'm just done in. Darcy, if I could have

a bowl of hot soup and a few crackers, then I could take a pain pill.''

"You've got it," Darcy said, and took her husband's arm to lead him from the bedroom to the hall. "Take care of her horse, darling, and I'll make her comfortable. She's totally exhausted, poor little thing."

"She *should* be turned over my knee," Mark said.

"You know you don't mean that."

"I know. Darcy, she's all beat to hell. She didn't tell me how bad that fall really was."

"Because she loves you and didn't want you worrying." Darcy kissed her husband's cheek. "I'm going to heat her some soup, then I'll do whatever she wants done after that."

"You're an angel."

Maddie had heard nearly every word said by Mark and Darcy; he was angry, which Maddie had expected, and Darcy truly was an angel, which was a wonderful thing to have discovered about her still very new sister-in-law. Mark was a lucky man to have fallen in love with the right woman, Maddie thought, recalling Aunt June's sincerely well-meant words about the wonders of true love.

Darcy came in with a tray bearing a large cup of soup, some soda crackers and a small pot of herbal tea. She helped Maddie sit up to eat, and when she was finished Darcy brought a glass of water so Maddie could take a pain pill from the bottle in the pocket of her jacket.

"If I take one of these without eating something first, my stomach rebels," Maddie told her.

"I understand. Maddie, your pants and jacket are huge. You don't want to sleep in them, do you?"

Maddie lay back and explained everything, including her reasons for driving instead of flying and her oversize clothing. After a while she managed a genuine if small smile. "The pill is starting to work. Darcy, I packed a little overnight bag with things like my toothbrush and nightgown, because I was pretty sure that I'd be staying in the house. The bag is on the bed in my trailer. I should have asked Mark to bring it in before he went out in the cold, but I simply didn't think of it.''

"He'll get it, Maddie."

"It's so great finally being here," Maddie murmured drowsily. "I really needed to come home, Darcy. I hope you don't mind."

"You're Mark's only sister, and you will always be welcome, Maddie, under any circumstances. You're going to fall asleep. Let's get you undressed and into one of my flannel nightgowns. You can brush your teeth in the morning.''

"Yes…okay," Maddie mumbled thickly.

It was later, after Darcy had helped her into a warm nightgown and then tucked her back into bed, and Maddie lay with her eyes closed, soaking up warmth and comfort that was really twofold, both physical and emotional, that she heard Mark ask, "How is she, honey?"

"Sleeping. Oh, Mark, you should see her undressed. Well, you saw her face, and that's enough for you to imagine the rest. But nearly every inch of her right side is discolored from being scraped and bruised. How in heaven's name did she drive all the way from Texas and take care of her horse and even herself with her right hand in a cast and the inevitable distress from such extensive bruises?''

"Darcy, when Maddie makes up her mind to something, she gets it done. She's always been that way. You know, I think this is the first time she's had to admit to needing someone's help since Aunt June died.''

"Mark, we can't leave her here alone while we honeymoon. It just wouldn't be right.''

"I know," Mark agreed, sounding deeply concerned. After a minute he added, "We won't get a refund from the travel agent, you know. And all our plans are set, the flight and hotel reservations, everything.''

"I realize that," Darcy agreed softly. "But we just can't go off as though Maddie wasn't here, darling."

In the dreamlike twilight zone in which Maddie was floating, the voices seemed like soft warm breezes passing through the semidarkness of her room, sounding harmonious, lyrical and totally unattached to anything of substance. Nothing being said made much sense to her, and she finally fell into a benumbed sleep without pain, worry or discomfort of any kind.

In the morning, however, she remembered it all, every word, and whispered, "They haven't taken their honeymoon yet. They have plans, wonderful plans, and my coming here in this condition ruined everything."

Maddie pursed her lips. She was *not* going to be the cause of something so awful. She didn't care if she herself ever had a honeymoon, but it was obviously very important to Mark and Darcy.

Well, she'd done it once before—in the hospital—and she could pretend to be much better off than she really was one more time. Her good acting had convinced Dr. Upton to release her a day early, and it was going to convince Mark and Darcy that she could get along just fine on her own. They were going on their honeymoon, as planned, *whatever* she had to do to prove that she did not need a caretaker!

Throwing back the blankets, Maddie got out of bed, pasted a bright, cheery smile on her face and left the bedroom to begin her charade.

Chapter Three

And thus, ten days after her accident Maddie found herself on her brother's sofa in Whitehorn, Montana, hugging a comforter to herself and staring up at a man who didn't look like a baby-sitter any more than he did a burglar. She tried to sensibly assimilate the situation. Had Mark really asked this...this weird stranger to keep an eye on her? And if so, had Mark told her that he'd arranged for someone to drop in on her from time to time and the information had slipped through the cracks of her less-than-alert brain?

She narrowed her eyes on Noah. "How did you get in?"

"Through a door. Isn't that how *you* enter someone's home?"

"An unlocked door?" she asked, concerned that Mark might have inadvertently missed locking one of the doors and she hadn't been safe from intruders at all, which she, within the foggy reaches of her mind, had been counting on.

"Nope." Noah produced the key. "With this."

The sight of that key panicked her. "You have a key? You mean you can just walk into this house anytime you take the notion?"

Noah stood there looking down at her. She was probably cute as a cuddly little doll when she wasn't black-and-blue, but it was hard for him—with his medical training and experience—to get past the blotchy bruises on her face. Even so, he still felt remnants of that incredible fit of laughter he'd enjoyed—yes, *enjoyed*—only minutes ago. He couldn't remember when he'd let go and laughed so uninhibitedly, and it certainly was the last thing he might have expected from today's begrudged duty. In a way he couldn't quite define but still knew to be true, those moments of uncontrollable laughter had created a bond between him and Maddie Kincaid; she might not feel it, but he did, and some rusty, rather tarnished part of him cherished the sensation.

"I rang the front doorbell and knocked on the side door before using the key," he said. "I promised Mark that I'd take care of you while he's away, and that's exactly what I'm going to do." In his own mind Noah realized how he had just expanded his promise to keep an eye on Maddie into *taking care of Maddie,* which gave him a start.

But someone should be caring for her. She certainly didn't appear strong enough to be doing everything for herself. Her weakened condition explained the messy kitchen, of course. What Noah could not comprehend was how Mark could have gone off and left his frail little sister alone in the house. Didn't he realize how badly off Maddie really was?

Noah shed his winter scarf and jacket and laid them on the back of a chair, aware that Maddie Kincaid's eyes had grown wary and suspicious.

"Don't get paranoid just because I took off my jacket,"

he told her. "It happens to be hot as Hades in here. What temperature do you have the furnace set on?" He looked around. "Where's the thermostat?"

"It's in the kitchen, but don't you dare lower that dial!"

"Maddie, you can't be cold. You're dressed in thermal underwear…" He couldn't help coughing out another laugh over the image that comment conjured up but he managed to stifle it before it got out of hand. After clearing his throat, he continued, "And you're wrapped in a goose down comforter."

"So?"

Noah frowned as the physician in him took over. "You really are cold? Are you having chills?"

"If I am it's none of your affair," Maddie retorted, hoping she sounded in keen command of her senses and authoritative. After all, what could she really do to defend herself against *anything* this guy might do? Regardless of her physical ineptitude, though, her mouth and don't-tread-on-my-space attitude were working just fine, and she demanded haughtily, "What do you think you are, a doctor?"

"As a matter of fact, yes." He approached the sofa and sat on the sturdy wood coffee table, which had been in the way when he'd carried Maddie back to her bed but was handy as all get-out now. "Let me take your pulse."

Maddie was gawking at him with her mouth open. He was a doctor? *Yeah, right.* "Oh, like I should believe you?"

Noah reached into the back pocket of his jeans for his wallet, which he flipped open right in front of Maddie's face so she could see his medical ID card. "What does that say?" he asked a bit smugly.

She studied the photo on the card and then Noah's face and realized with a sinking sensation that he was almost unbelievably handsome. He was, in fact, the kind of man that idiot women the world over—of which she was *not* one, thank you very much—chased after like a dog on the scent of a bone. This guy had thick black hair, eyebrows and lashes, vivid blue eyes, a sensual, kissable mouth if she'd ever seen one, and a strong masculine chin that announced a massive stubborn streak. With his height and build, he was one drop-dead package, which was unnerving for a woman whose few romantic relationships had been with your everyday, average-looking men.

But his stunning good looks and normally noble profession didn't make him trustworthy, and she *didn't* trust him. Why would she? Doctor or not, he had walked into this house without an invitation from her, which, in her estimation, was an invasion of privacy, whatever he might call it. Well, he was going to find out that she was no pansy, however he made his living. Instead of giving him the satisfaction of a straightforward answer to his irritating question about his ID, she drew her left hand from under the comforter and held it out. "So, go ahead and take my pulse, if that's what turns you on."

"Turns me on?" Noah chuckled. "You're quite the little comic, aren't you?" He took her wrist and counted pulse beats while looking at his watch.

"Apparently *you* think so," she said with heavy sarcasm. "You got positively hysterical when you first saw me."

Noah tucked her hand and wrist back under the comforter. Her pulse was a little too fast; he needed a temperature and blood pressure check.

"You'd have gotten hysterical, too, if you could have seen yourself. What did you think you were going to do with that paperweight? Wait, I know, you thought you'd laugh me to death."

"You're so corny you should be ashamed to open your mouth and say one word."

"Yep, that's me, old cornball himself." Noah stood up. "I want to take you to the hospital."

Maddie scoffed. "Just try it and you'll think you got

hold of a wildcat, buster. Oh, excuse me, that's *Dr.* Buster.''

"Maddie, I need to run some tests. You could have an infection.''

"Read my lips. I am *not* going to the hospital. Besides, I'm taking antibiotics so I do not have an infection.''

"Where are they? I want to see what it is that you're taking.''

Maddie had to think a minute. "They're probably on the kitchen table.''

Noah found them and returned. "Okay, these aren't too bad, but you might need something stronger. Maddie, do you have a doctor in Whitehorn?''

"No...not yet.'' She closed her eyes because she was getting very tired again. Being brave and courageous with very little strength as she'd been doing since "Dr. Buster'' had intruded upon her rest was rapidly depleting her already low energy level.

"Go away,'' she mumbled. "I need to sleep.''

Noah did go away; he headed for Mark's bathrooms. Searching the medicine cabinets, he finally found what he was looking for—a thermometer. Dousing it in alcohol, which was also in the same cabinet, he hurried back to Maddie.

"Open your mouth,'' he told her. "I'm going to take your temperature.''

"No, leave me alone,'' she mumbled thickly.

"Maddie, open your mouth!'' Noah worked the tip of the thermometer between her lips, and she finally stopped fighting him. In a couple of minutes he had his answer. Her temp was 101.6 degrees, not dangerously high but too high to ignore. He could force her to go to the hospital by calling an ambulance and giving her a knockout shot, but that seemed pretty drastic at this point. But to do anything at all for her, he needed his medical bag, some supplies and a different antibiotic.

"Maddie, listen to me. I'm going to leave for a few

minutes. I won't be long. You stay covered up and rest, all right?'' He didn't wait for a reply. Grabbing his jacket, he put it on as he strode through the house to the kitchen door and went outside. Using Mark's key, he turned the inside dead bolt, giving Maddie the security she'd obviously thought she'd had all along. One of two things had happened, Noah reasoned: Mark hadn't locked the door before leaving, which Noah couldn't quite believe, as Mark Kincaid was a very dependable sort, or Maddie, for some reason, had unlocked it and then forgot to *re*lock it. In her present state, she could do almost anything and then forget it. How in God's name had Mark not noticed?

During the cross-town drive to the hospital, Noah thought about Maddie's medications. Besides the antibiotic pills, she also had a bottle of painkillers, and Noah had to wonder exactly how much pain she was in. From the soft cast on her hand, her accident hadn't caused too much damage as far as injured bones went, but then there were the discolored bruises and healing abrasions on her face to consider. Even so, were a few scrapes that were well on the way to full recovery causing enough pain for Maddie to be taking strong pain-blocking medication? He didn't like her slurred words and the hard time she seemed to have focusing her eyes.

There was one other possibility, though. She could have further bruising—possibly quite severe—under her clothes. He would have to check that out when he got back to the house.

And then, just before reaching the physician's parking area at the hospital, Noah finally let his thoughts go to that tingle deep in his belly that any man in his right mind would recognize. He hadn't felt it in a very long time, and why he should feel it now because of a little bit of a woman with the attitude of a guard dog was a total mystery. In the first place Maddie Kincaid was not the type of female he'd ever been attracted to. When he'd been in the market for *affaires d'amour* he'd liked his women tall, long-legged and sophisticated. Maddie hardly fit the bill.

And yet that tingle was unmistakably present. Not that he would ever do anything about it. Along with his possessing a distinct distaste for the complications of a romantic liaison, Maddie was Mark's sister. A man with any self-respect and dignity did not lure a friend's sister into bed just to satisfy a ridiculous tingling in his system.

Besides, Maddie needed medical attention far more than she needed anything personal from him, or any other man.

Still puzzling over Mark and Darcy leaving Maddie alone as they'd done, Noah walked into the hospital. He was ready to leave again in about twenty minutes, this time with his medical bag. It was packed full of items he thought he might need in caring for Maddie, and he *was* going to care for her. He suspected she'd yell—or try to yell—and that her objections to his even being in the house might make a very long list, but he was not going to let her chase him off. Not only because he'd given his word to Mark to keep an eye on her, but because in his professional opinion Maddie needed more than just a casual now-and-again glance.

Even before actually leaving the hospital, Noah saw the falling snow through some windows. Setting down his bag, he took the gloves from his jacket pocket, pulled them on and then continued his trek to the outside door nearest the physician's parking area. Outdoors it seemed to be a little warmer than it had earlier and the snow was not yet a heavy downfall. The flakes, which were small and feathery, fluttered to the earth from a pale-gray sky that appeared smooth and almost satiny.

Noah frowned over that upward view. He'd seen that deceptively innocent sky once before since moving to Montana, and it had buried the town in two- to five-foot snowdrifts before blowing itself out. He usually listened to morning radio while showering and dressing, and the snowstorm that had been predicted for several days now had obviously arrived.

Before he reached his vehicle, a powerful gust of wind blew snow in his face, which was one more sign that the encroaching storm might be a true blizzard. Once settled in his SUV with the engine running, Noah checked his bag to make sure he had his cell phone with him. It was a safety precaution that probably wasn't necessary; electricity and telephone service weren't *always* disrupted during a storm.

But he drove away from the hospital feeling better knowing that if the storm got really bad and he happened to get stuck or stranded somewhere he could always call for assistance.

By the time Noah got back to Mark's house—a ten-minute drive in good weather, about twenty minutes this trip—he was positive that the storm had already turned meaner. If that was really the case, this storm could be one for the books, he thought as he pulled into Mark's driveway. Carrying his medical bag, he kept his head down and quick-stepped to the house.

Inside he felt as though he'd just stepped into an oven. Setting his bag on a chair, he shed his outdoor gear and found the wall thermostat, which he turned down. Then he hurried to the living room to check on Maddie.

The small lump in the comforter looked as though it hadn't budged at all in his absence, so Noah cautiously pulled back the top of the blanket to see Maddie's face. She appeared to be in a deep sleep, but he had to make sure that a nurturing sleep was all that was happening with her. Gently touching her neck just below her jaw with the tips of his fingers, he felt her pulse and took note of the temperature and moisture of her skin. She wasn't sweating, nor was her skin hot and feverish to the touch. He would let her sleep for the time being.

Carefully returning the blanket to its former position, Noah returned to the kitchen, rolling up the long sleeves of his shirt as he went. He knew he was a neat freak, but he couldn't help despising dirty dishes. Of course, Maddie had an excuse, he reminded himself while stacking the dishwasher and then wiping down flat surfaces with a clean, slightly soapy dishcloth.

When the kitchen was cleaned and tidy, Noah took his bag and returned to the living room. This time he approached Maddie *without* caution. Taking out his blood pressure gauge and stethoscope, he sat on the coffee table again, pulled back the comforter and wrapped the pressure cuff around Maddie's left arm.

Her eyes fluttered opened. "Wha-what's going on? Oh, it's you. What are you up to now?"

"I'm taking your blood pressure."

"I would think a doctor would know enough to let a tired person sleep."

"You can sleep all you want to after I check you out."

"You're not my doctor."

"I am now. Stay silent for a minute, okay? I can't hear myself think, let alone what's going on in that puny little body of yours."

"My body is not puny! God, talk about a revolting bedside manner."

"Just shut the hell up!"

Maddie clamped her lips together. Good-looking or not, this guy—what had he said his name was?—was a total jerk, certainly not the kind of man she would *ever* give a second glance.

Noah removed the blood pressure cuff from her arm, then placed the little round sound receiver segment of the stethoscope on her chest.

"Hey!" Maddie slapped away the instrument. "Just stop it!"

Noah was fast losing patience, something that he wasn't overloaded with, in any case. He gave his friend Mark's mouthy little sister a look that was colder than the outside temperature and then asked with equal frostiness, "How many doctors do you know in Whitehorn who would make a house call? Either you let me examine you properly or I swear I'll call an ambulance and put your butt in the hospital. It's up to you. Take your pick.''

Maddie tried to scoff away her immediate misgivings with a snappy comeback but it came off pretty weak. ''You wouldn't dare,'' she said, and actually felt a chill go up her spine from the icy expression in his eyes.

''Just try me.'' He focused the icy glare onto her eyes.

She absolutely, positively would not look away first. ''I'm not afraid of you, you know,'' she said, realizing at the same time that she was getting angry. *She* knew that anger without the physical strength to back it up wasn't very formidable, but common sense wasn't controlling her at the moment. What ticked her off so much was that this…this cretin doctor thought *he* was.

Noah was in no mood for foolish bickering, and he spoke flatly, without a dram of warmth. ''There's no reason you should be afraid of me.'' Then he added, sounding angry himself, ''Good Lord, woman, don't you know when someone's trying to help you? What kind of doctors have you been seeing? What kind of people have you been associating with?''

''*My* friends and doctors are at least recognizable. I haven't the foggiest notion of what or who you are.'' Maddie was literally gritting her teeth. No one told her what to do, *no one,* and this…this pompous know-it-all wasn't going to get away with it, either.

''You most certainly do know. I told you my name before and showed you my medical ID, as well.'' He could see confusion in her eyes and added, ''My name is Noah Martin…Dr. Noah Martin…and I'm Mark's friend.''

''All right, you're a doctor, but why should I believe you're Mark's friend?''

''Maybe because I have a key to his house?''

He was boxing her in, which only made Maddie angrier. "There's no way you could put me in the hospital without my permission," she said daringly.

"Oh, but there is. If a person is mentally unbalanced because of fever or other symptoms of illness, I have every right to hospitalize her…or him."

Maddie's jaw dropped. "I am *not* mentally unbalanced, you…you retard!"

Noah glared right back at her. "You want me to think you're a tough little nut, don't you? Well, you're not, and I don't, and what's more, you *are* going to get a medical exam today. Now, are you going to let me do what's necessary or should I phone for an ambulance?"

She was livid, or as livid as she could be under the circumstances. Looking horrible and feeling almost as horrible all but destroyed her normal ability to hold her own in just about any situation. Maddie never looked for a fight—or even a mild disagreement—with anyone, but she'd been a self-sufficient grownup for too long to take orders that went against her grain. It really galled her when Noah Martin folded his arms across his chest and then sat there waiting for her to give in.

"I really hate you," she said, meaning it heart and soul.

"No, you don't. You just hate being told what to do." Maddie couldn't help being startled, and her wide-eyed expression made Noah grin. "You'll get over it."

"Don't hold your breath," she snapped. "And don't you dare laugh at me one more time!"

Noah's grin vanished. "Fine, I won't laugh or even smile for the rest of this perfectly delightful day. So, what's your decision about that examination?"

Maddie hadn't missed the sarcasm in his voice when he'd called the day "perfectly delightful." Oddly, the fact that he wasn't enjoying this fiasco any more than she was made her feel a little less like throttling him, if she had the strength to throttle anything, that is.

"What kind of examination are you talking about?" she asked.

"Let me ask you a question before I answer that. Besides the injuries to your hand and face, were you hurt in any other way? Any other area of your body?"

"If you think for one minute that I'm undressing for you, think again! Now I'm on to your game, buster!"

"Oh, good Lord," Noah muttered. "I don't know what kind of accident caused all of this, but to have such screwy ideas you must have landed on your head. Listen to me. I couldn't care less about seeing you undressed. I'm a doctor, and, speaking professionally, the human body, clothed or unclothed, does not affect me. What I know about your condition so far is just enough to warrant further examination. You're taking painkillers and running a low-grade temperature. It's possible that your blood pressure is elevated, but without prior records I can't be positive of that. At any rate, I need to know...and see...the extent of your injuries, and if that means undressing, then you will undress. I brought a gown from the hospital to make an exam easier for both of us."

Noah reached into his medical bag for the gown and laid it on the comforter. "Can you get up and change into this by yourself?"

Maddie had become stiff with fury. "This is not a doctor's office! This is a house, my brother's house!"

"It's here or the hospital, Maddie. Take your pick." Noah spoke quietly, impersonally, firmly. Even though patience had all but vanished from his system—not a new experience for him—he managed to convey professional concern to his patient, which he considered Maddie Kincaid to be at this point. Yes, that ludicrous tingle was still nudging his libido, but he'd go down in flames before doing anything about it.

She crooked her good left arm over her eyes so he wouldn't see how degraded and defeated she felt.

"Maddie?"

He *would* phone for an ambulance, the wretch. She

knew it as surely as she knew anything, and she was going to have to look him in the eye and *admit* defeat.

"I'm not getting up with you watching. Wait in the kitchen. I'll change in the bathroom," she said dully.

"You do have more injuries than what I can see on your face and hand, don't you?" he asked quietly.

"Yes, damn you!"

Noah got to his feet. "I'll wait in the kitchen." He started to walk away, then stopped for one more thing. "I'd like you to be lying down for the exam. A bed would be better than this sofa."

"I'm *sure* it would be much better," she retorted with a venomous glare.

"Don't get any silly ideas. This is strictly impersonal for me."

"Are you married?"

"Uh, no. Why?"

"Because I'd feel better about this…this fiasco if you were!"

Noah was getting very close to giving up on Maddie Kincaid. Not that he'd drive off and just forget about her, but he could probably find another doctor among his peers that would take her case.

He considered doing exactly that, but only for a few moments. No way was Maddie Kincaid going to best him in this. Who was the doctor here, anyhow, certainly not her! Besides, it wasn't merely an examination of *all* of her injuries that mattered to him. She mattered, and he could question why she did until doomsday and maybe never know the answer. But he wasn't leaving her alone in a blizzard that he could hear growling and snarling outside, getting fiercer by the minute. He couldn't see the storm, however, because the drapes and blinds on every window in the room were tightly closed, which suddenly annoyed the ever-loving hell out of him.

Going to a window he yanked open the drapes. The density of the blowing, swirling snow outside actually shocked him. He couldn't see across the street. He couldn't even see the big trees in Mark's front yard! Craning his neck he tried to spot his SUV in the driveway and failed. All there was beyond the window glass was an angrily moving sea of white. This was the worst storm he'd ever seen, and it was scary, damned scary.

Cursing under his breath, Noah shut the drapes again and left the room, telling Maddie over his shoulder to get up and into that gown. He'd find whichever room she was waiting in, he told her, and added that he'd give her ten minutes before leaving the kitchen. "And put on the gown so that it opens in front."

Maddie wanted to bawl. Better yet she'd like to scream Noah Martin's ears off! "Big man," she sneered, despising him for backing her into a corner the way he had. People rarely got around her deeply ingrained sense of self, and she had always taken pride in her strength and independence. Well, she wasn't strong now, was she? Or independent?

Admitting weakness in the face of adversity nearly killed her, but there was little question that Dr. Noah Martin, first-class jerk and hometown yokel, was holding all the cards. When exactly had he descended upon poor unsuspecting Whitehorn? The town's citizenry, as Maddie remembered it, was accustomed to kindly doctors, such as old Dr. Slater, who'd taken such good care of Aunt June.

Memories of June's last years, especially her final months, gave Maddie a chill. For the first time ever she admitted possessing a fear of invalidism, of having to rely on others for the simplest task. She had taken very good care of Aunt June and had never resented a moment of the responsibility she'd undertaken, but by the same token she couldn't bear the thought of herself being in Aunt June's shoes.

And wasn't she there right now, far sooner and at a much younger age than even her dread of the possibility had ever placed her? Noah Martin was treating her as though she was his responsibility, and she wasn't, damn it, she wasn't! Maddie gritted her teeth. Dr. Noah Martin was *not* going to examine her, and that was final! She'd playacted her way out of the hospital in Austin a day early and then convinced her brother and sister-in-law that she was doing just fine when she could just barely move without gasping out loud. But Mark and Darcy would not have gone on their honeymoon if she *hadn't* convinced them, and she'd suffered in silence until they had finally walked out the door with their suitcases. How could she possibly have guessed that Mark would bring a strange doctor into the picture? One who'd gotten all concerned and determined to heal, damn his hide!

Obviously, she was going to have to endure another game of pretense, Maddie thought with a sigh of premeditated distress. What's more, time was rushing by and she probably only had another few minutes before that nosy-Nellie friend of Mark's came looking for her, expecting her to be in that awful gown and lying on a bed awaiting his examination.

"That'll be the day," Maddie mumbled, and pushed away the comforter. Gritting her teeth again because it hurt like hell to move, even though groggy from pain-killers, she swung her feet to the floor, forced herself up and then hobbled her way to her bedroom. Shutting the door behind her, she immediately began undressing. Mark…or someone…she wasn't clear on that point…had brought a lot of her clothes in from her trailer. She pulled on a long skirt and her biggest, baggiest sweater.

Her next stop was the bathroom, and she washed her face, applied moisturizer and makeup and then brushed her hair until it looked almost respectable. For good measure she gave herself a small squirt of cologne, then wasted no time in exiting the bathroom and heading for the kitchen.

Noah jumped a foot when she walked in. "What in

God's name are you doing?'' he asked, sounding a lot like a bear with a thorn in its paw.

''Grump and complain all you wish,'' she said in a saccharine tone that didn't sound remotely genuine. ''But I'm not getting into that gown, and you are not going to examine even one small part of me. Oh, I guess I wouldn't mind if you checked my cast. Would that satisfy your craving to play doctor today?''

''You little idiot,'' Noah said. His lips were thin and disapproving, and he looked as though he really did think of her as an idiot.

She frankly didn't care what he thought. ''Whether you like it or not, you are *not* going to be my doctor. I'll check the phone book and make an appointment with one without your help.'' Maddie suddenly saw the storm through the window above the sink. ''Oh, my God!'' she cried. ''When did that start?''

''About an hour ago. It's a serious storm, which isn't nearly as crucial as your seeing a doctor today. So, if it's not going to be me, I'm going to phone for that ambulance.''

Maddie turned toward him with blazing eyes. ''You go right ahead and do that, and the second you're off the phone, I'll call the police department and file a complaint against you for home invasion and…and—'' she lifted her chin in a defiant gesture ''—and I might even include sexual harassment in that charge.''

''Which would be a damn lie,'' Noah snarled. ''Is that what you are, a liar?''

''Not usually, but your pushy attitude just might drive me to do a lot of things I wouldn't ordinarily do. Now, let's get to the bottom line, all right? I believe you've accomplished quite enough in this house for one day. Your uncooperative patient is out of bed and dressed. As any fool could see, if there were more than one in this kitchen with me, I'm fine and functioning under my own steam. In other words, I don't want you hanging around any longer. Are you getting the message?''

Noah was just about to growl an appropriately nasty comeback when Maddie suddenly shrieked, ''Fanny! My God, where's Fanny?''

He thought she'd lost the last of her marbles, which he'd been suspecting were already dangerously low in quantity, especially when she hung over the sink to get her face closer to the icy window to see outside. ''She'll die in this,'' Maddie moaned. ''What did Mark do with her? Fanny, Fanny, where are you?''

Chapter Four

Something akin to panic assaulted Noah's senses. Who or what was "Fanny"? A pet? A child? And was Fanny outside in that raging blizzard?

He went to Maddie's side and tried to see out the same window. There was nothing outside but the density of whites that only a winter storm of this magnitude could produce. Noah glanced at Maddie, who had her good hand curled around the inside edge of the sink and seemed to be holding on for dear life. Her face was deathly pale, and what she was really doing up and dressed struck him like a ten-ton truck.

"You little fake," he muttered, and moved closer to her, just enough to place his hands on her upper arms. "You'd walk through fire to avoid a trip to the hospital or an exam from me, wouldn't you?" His intention was to support and steer her to a chair, because she looked ready to fall down. The second he touched her she cried

out, sounding so much like a wounded animal that he
instantly released her and jumped back.

She bent from the waist and laid her forehead on her
hand clutching the edge of the sink. Noah couldn't see if
she was crying, but she made a pathetic picture all huddled over as she was, and her being so small and desperately in need of help, even if she wouldn't admit it.

He felt an unfamiliar confusion. He couldn't leave her
and she wouldn't let him help her.

What should he do?

Anger began gathering in his gut, and with it came a
clearing of his mind. Somehow Maddie had tricked Mark
and Darcy into believing she was well enough to be left
alone. Noah knew that now, because she'd just tried to
pull the same stunt with him. Only she'd seen the storm
and remembered Fanny, whatever or whomever Fanny
was, and Maddie's personal plight had taken a back seat
to *that* concern.

Noah was almost afraid to ask about Fanny, but he'd
seen that long sleek trailer parked behind Mark's garage,
and what if there was a pet in it? A little dog or cat that
Maddie had decided would be better off in its own home
than in a strange house. That concept really didn't make
sense for Noah, but he couldn't let himself think that
Fanny might be a person.

He was on to Maddie's dangerous game of pretense
now, and it infuriated him as a physician that she would
let modesty, resentment and stubborn pride stop her from
accepting treatment from him. Yes, Mark should have told
her that he'd be dropping by, but...

That point was suddenly clear to Noah, as well. Mark
had told Maddie. She just didn't remember it! Those
damn pain pills! How many had she taken today? A person alone could so easily get off schedule with painkillers
and take more of them than had been prescribed. Plus,
some people were overly sensitive to pain medication, and
a perfectly acceptable dose for one patient could knock

another for a loop. That would explain Maddie's slurring of words, her desire to be left alone so she could sleep and even her physical weakness when she was on her feet.

Noah was pretty certain that he'd figured everything out—except for Fanny's identity. He drew a long breath and felt a tightening in his gut, but he had to ask.

"Maddie?" She slowly straightened her back but didn't look at him. "Maddie," he repeated from his position behind her, "who's Fanny?"

"My horse," she said dully.

Noah experienced such enormous relief that his knees got weak. But just for a second, because both he and Maddie couldn't be weak in this crazy situation.

"And you're thinking your horse is where?" he asked calmly, hoping his gentle demeanor would inspire calm in her.

"I...don't know. Wait...I...I think I went outside this morning, and...and..."

That explained the unlocked door, Noah thought. "And what?" he prompted.

"I couldn't...find her."

"So she's not in Mark's garage or staked out in the yard someplace?"

"No...she's not. There's something..." Maddie let go of the sink and raised her hand to her temple. "I can't seem to think very well, but...I...I have a foggy glimpse of memory about Mark saying something about boarding Fanny."

"Then you have nothing to worry about. I'm sure if Mark said he was going to board Fanny so you wouldn't have to care for her while he and Darcy were away, then that's what he did."

Maddie finally turned around, wincing visibly as she did it, apparently forgetting, Noah observed, that she'd gotten dressed to convince him that she was perfectly all right.

"Boarded where?" she asked with a note of panic in her voice.

"Probably a nearby ranch. There are several not too far from town that board horses. Maddie, you have got to lie down again. You look terrible."

"What every girl wants to hear from a man. But I...I do feel sort of..." Once again she started folding up, and once again Noah rushed forward and caught her before she reached the floor.

"You little fool," he muttered, picking her up and carrying her from the kitchen. Ignoring the sofa this time, he brought her to a bedroom and laid her on the bed. Rushing around, he got smelling salts from his medical bag and a wet washcloth from the nearest bathroom. Returning, he laid the cloth on her forehead and was just about to wave the vial of ammonium carbonate under her nose when he got a better idea.

Very cautiously he raised the hem of her blouse, saw the bruising on her right side, then did the same with her skirt and scrutinized the continuing bruising all down her hip and thigh. She had darned good reason to wince every time she moved, he thought with loads of sympathy, and then decided that he'd better check for infection while he had the chance. He saw nothing in that regard and he quickly straightened her clothing and then held the vial under her nose.

She came to with a gasp and a cough, and then slapped at his hand. Once she got her breath she demanded to know why she was on her bed and then stated emphatically, "You are not getting me out of my clothes for an examination!"

"That's fine with me." Noah sat on the edge of the bed right next to her and spoke plainly. "Here's my diagnosis. You ingested at least one too many pain pills today. Do you remember how many you took since waking up this morning?"

She frowned and looked perplexed. "Uh, no."

"That's what I thought. Okay, you will not have access to your medication from this moment on. I brought with me what I feel is a better antibiotic for your injuries, and I will administer that along with your pain pills."

"You most certainly will not! You're not moving in here, you know."

"You're dead wrong about that, and don't waste your energy arguing. When did you last eat?" He saw the stricken look on her face. "Don't strain your brain. I can see clearly that you're not remembering much of anything. That's all right, that mushy sensation in your head will pretty much wear off by tonight. In the meantime I'm going to fix you something to eat. From the look of the kitchen trash can that greeted me when I first walked in today, I'd hazard a guess that soup is a favorite of yours, so that's what I'll fix for now. You stay here. I'll bring in your comforter, and when the soup's hot I'll bring that in, as well. Rest and try not to worry." Noah rose and started for the door.

Maddie made no reply, but even with that "mushy sensation" fogging her brain, she knew she would not *stop* worrying until she knew where Mark had taken Fanny.

Darn it, why couldn't she remember anything in its entirety? Surely Mark had told her *where* he was boarding Fanny!

Several hours later Noah paced between kitchen and living room. He had opened curtains, drapes and blinds to bare the windows so he could see the storm, which hadn't let up an iota since reaching its peak of ferocity around noon. It worried Noah, and he had phoned the hospital to let personnel know where he could be reached, in case an emergency situation arose and he was needed.

Maddie had eaten a bowl of soup, drunk some herbal tea and then, almost immediately, had fallen into a deep sleep. She worried Noah as much as the storm, possibly more. She would recover, of course. Her injuries, though undoubtedly painful, were not life threatening. Rather, they didn't *appear* to be, he thought wryly, wishing he had access to whatever notes and X rays the attending physician had generated at the time of her accident.

At any rate, it was Noah's professional opinion that Maddie should not be left alone, and his third worry was that the hospital would call and he'd *have* to leave her alone. When that concern became dominant, he phoned the hospital again and talked to the head nurse, explained the situation and asked if she knew of an off-duty nurse— either registered or practical—who would come to the house and tend Maddie Kincaid for a few days.

She'd been polite and respectful, but Whitehorn was a small town and there never had been a surplus of nurses just biding their time and hoping for work. "I'm sorry, Dr. Martin, but everyone I know works a very tight schedule. Also, we have the storm to deal with. I've already called in my off-duty nursing staff."

"Vehicular accidents?" Noah asked.

"And frostbite and some broken bones from slipping on ice. I understand the state patrol has issued a warning for everyone to stay at home. Everyone won't, of course. Folks around here aren't afraid of bad weather, and so the accidents will keep the E.R. busy throughout the blizzard. Sorry I can't help you, Doctor."

After that conversation, Noah racked his brain for the name of someone—a friend, a neighbor, almost anyone would do—he might phone and ask to come to the house. He didn't miss the irony of the situation. Since moving to Whitehorn he'd avoided casual friendships. Hell, he'd avoided any kind of friendship, preferring to suffer the pain of Felicia's desertion all by himself. Mark Kincaid was an exception, but Noah knew that even though he liked Mark they would never be close enough to confide their innermost thoughts and feelings to each other.

They'd gotten acquainted at the gym, where they both worked out or, on occasion, played basketball. The thing that Noah liked best about Mark was that he didn't pry. In fact, Mark seemed to sense that Noah didn't want to talk about "life before Whitehorn," thus never asked.

And so their relationship was one of mutual respect for each other's privacy. Standing at a window and looking out with a serious frown on his face, Noah thought about Mark's wedding. If he'd attended the affair instead of merely sending a gift to the bride with a note of regret because he couldn't be there, would he have met Maddie?

Damn, he knew so little about her! Where she lived, for instance. Obviously, she didn't make her home in Whitehorn, but why didn't she? And why on earth would she be driving a huge truck and pulling a trailer...? *Wait a minute!* That trailer was how she transported Fanny. But transported Fanny from where? Where, precisely, were Maddie's roots? Her home? Okay, so she got hurt at a rodeo, but where was the rodeo, and what caused the accident?

Recalling how upset Maddie had become when she realized that she didn't know at which ranch Mark had boarded Fanny, Noah went to the kitchen phone again. This time he searched the phone book for ranches that boarded horses. There were three listings fairly close to town, and operating under the assumption that Mark wouldn't put too much distance between Maddie and her horse, he wrote those names, numbers and addresses on the pad of paper next to the phone.

A crashing gust of wind actually shook the house, and Noah jumped up from his chair and hurried to the nearest window. He'd thought the storm had already peaked, but it looked even worse outside than it had only minutes ago.

Shaking his head he returned to the phone and picked it up with the intention of calling ranches until he found the one that had taken in Fanny. Instead of a dial tone, however, all Noah heard was an ominous silence. The phone was dead. His stomach sank some, but all he could really do was hope that the electricity didn't go off, too.

After getting his cell phone from his bag, he began making those calls. Because of the storm there was a great deal of static to contend with, but Noah's second call proved fruitful. Fanny, or Fanchon, as Mark had signed the horse in as, was being boarded at the Braddock ranch—the Braddock Reserve, as the family who'd been buying up land around Whitehorn and beyond for some time now, called its horse and cattle ranch. Noah hadn't personally met any of the Braddocks, but he'd heard the name mentioned many times. Immense wealth was always fodder for gossip in a small town, and apparently, from all reports, the Braddocks were loaded.

Noah wrote "seven miles west of town, county road 34" on the pad, then underlined that, the Braddock name and phone number several times. When Maddie woke up, he would relay Fanny's whereabouts. The information, he figured, would cheer her considerably.

He sat there then, doodled on another sheet of paper and thought about how he'd taken Maddie Kincaid under his wing, so to speak. As a physician he helped people every day, but this was different. What he was doing for Maddie—in spite of the fact that she'd rather be left alone—went far beyond anything he'd done for another human being for a very long time, if ever.

Actually he couldn't remember another circumstance where he'd given so much of himself, so it was entirely possible that he never had. With that in mind, he had to question if he was doing this for Mark or for Maddie.

It was a disruptive, unnerving question, because his friendship with Mark could hardly be described as lifelong or heartfelt, and, by the same token, he couldn't let himself think that he'd let another woman penetrate his guard and slither into his psyche. Besides, why on earth would he be feeling anything for a woman of Maddie's disagreeable nature? Other than a precautionary strategy to protect himself from her ungrateful wrath, he should be symbolically keeping her at arm's length and viewing her as impersonally as he did all of his patients.

A glance toward a window abruptly ended Noah's self-analysis. If he was going to stay in this house to keep watch on Maddie, which appeared to be the case—at least for tonight—then he had better risk a drive to his own home to pick up a few things. Noah got up and checked the refrigerator and cabinets for food. Maddie might subsist just fine on canned food, but he didn't. He was a vegetable addict, and he liked them cooked or raw, as long as they were fresh.

Okay, he thought, there was meat in the freezer and the essentials in the refrigerator. Along with his toothbrush, shaving gear and a change of clothes, he'd bring back from his house his supply of fresh vegetables and make Maddie—and himself—a truly nourishing dinner.

He put on his jacket to brave the storm, when he decided that a note was in order, just in case Maddie woke up. He wrote a quick message about being gone for about an hour, then brought it to the bedroom Maddie was occupying and propped it up against the base of the lamp on the bed stand. Thinking that she could hardly miss seeing it, he took a moment to make sure she wasn't feverish or sweating, then he left.

He wasn't gone twenty minutes when Maddie stirred and opened her eyes. The fierce sounds of the blizzard were frightening, but only because Maddie's first thoughts were about Fanny. Where had Mark taken her? Was Fanny in a barn or some other type of shelter, or was she standing in knee-deep snow with her head down and her hind quarters toward the wind?

"No...no," Maddie moaned, shaken to her soul by that horrifying image. She had to do something, she *had* to! Where was that...that person...that Noah?

She yelled his name and got no response, and so she pushed back the comforter and slid off the bed. Come hell, high water or a record blizzard, she was going to find

Fanny! Not until she saw with her own eyes that Fanny was warm and dry would she stop worrying.

But to do anything outside she had to dress warmly. Her mind was much clearer than it had been, and she knew that warm clothing was a must. Discarding her skirt and blouse, she checked her abrasions and applied more antibiotic ointment to them. They were healing nicely, although she still had more aches and pains in her joints and muscles than she could count. But she couldn't take another pain pill and do any driving, and finding the ranch where Mark had boarded Fanny wasn't going to be accomplished without some driving.

She donned Mark's thermal long johns again, then pulled on a pair of his ski pants. Her own things were just too fitted to be comfortable, and while she swam in Mark's huge clothes, at least they didn't chafe her bruises.

Bundled in a jacket, scarf, lined boots and gloves, Maddie left the bedroom wing of the house and lumbered to the kitchen. Eyeing the telephone she wondered about trying to locate Fanny that way, rather than driving around the countryside in a blizzard without an actual destination. It made sense, she decided, and picked up the phone, only to hear the same deadly silence that Noah had.

Frowning, Maddie wondered again where he was. Since he wasn't in the house it appeared that he'd deserted her, but she was glad that he had as he was too darned bossy for her taste. She set down the phone and only then noticed the pieces of paper that someone—it could only have been nosy Noah—had doodled and written on.

The underlined words stood out, and she read aloud, "Fanchon. Braddock ranch, seven miles west on county road 34." Maddie knew exactly where county road 34 was. It was an old road that led to the Meadows, an area of ponds and springs that had been a favorite hangout on hot summer days during her teen years. Was there a ranch out there now? Must be, she thought, looking at the words "Braddock ranch" again.

Well, she could certainly drive seven miles, and if Fanny wasn't under cover she would lead her into the trailer and bring her back here. If nothing else, she could tether Fanny in Mark's garage, which had little space to spare but would still be better for Fanny than being outside in the storm.

Moving cautiously in spite of so much determination to get this done, Maddie opened the kitchen door and was nearly driven back inside by the force of the wind. She lowered her head and pushed into the fray, making sure the door was locked behind her.

Wading through drifts, she huddled deeper into her oversize clothing and finally reached her truck. The trailer was still hooked onto it, which gladdened her, and she climbed up into the driver's seat of the truck and inserted the key into the ignition. The engine was cold and took its sweet time in starting. But finally it was running smoothly, and even the heater began throwing warm air.

Pushing the floor lever she put the truck in four-wheel drive, then the transmission in drive and stepped on the gas. The truck began rolling, grinding its way through the snow. The wipers kept the windshield relatively clear and the defrosters and heater were beginning to melt what snow still clung to the front window.

Maddie was on her way, leaving Mark's backyard, towing the trailer behind the truck and finally entering the street, which, to her dismay, wasn't plowed!

"Thank God for four-wheel drive." She spoke passionately, feeling gratefully positive that she'd have no trouble in reaching her destination with such a powerful truck.

At his own house Noah got a small suitcase from his closet. After packing the things that he felt were necessary for an overnight stay away from home, he carried the case to the kitchen and set it down. Raiding the refrigerator, he filled a sack with fresh vegetables and fruit. Moving purposefully, he checked his telephone and found it to be dead, also.

Carrying his things then, he left the comfort, warmth and familiarity of the very pleasant ranch-style house he'd purchased only last summer, and braved the freezing cold and blowing snow to reach his SUV. He got in fast and after laying his suitcase and sack on the passenger seat, he wiped melting snow from his face and started the engine.

Driving back to Mark's house, he was relieved to see so little traffic. People were staying in, which was only wise during such a fierce blizzard. He'd be inside for the rest of the day and tonight, and maybe by morning the storm would have abated. It might even be over by then. Hell, it could be over by the time he parked in Mark's driveway.

He drove slowly and with due precaution. Beneath the drifts, and the blowing snow that was all but eliminating visibility, the roads were slippery and treacherous. For about the tenth time that winter he thanked heaven that he'd bought a rig with four-wheel drive. Two-wheel drive just didn't cut it in snow and mud, and sometimes mud was a problem on back roads during and after a hard rainfall.

He realized that today's storm—or last month's mud—wasn't the primary crisis on his mind. Maddie Kincaid was a royal pain, but she was in a heck of a situation and he couldn't turn his back on her. To be perfectly honest he would like to, he thought grimly, noticing that the streetlights were beginning to come on. They were barely visible and really provided only one thing: a demarcation of streets for the few people who *were* out and about.

For idiots like me, Noah thought in total self-castigation. He hadn't had to promise Mark anything. At the very least he should have swamped Mark with questions. What's your sister's attitude toward strangers? How did she get hurt? Are you certain about the extent of her injuries? Will she listen to and heed my advice?

But no, he'd asked nothing, Mark had given him a house key and that had been that. You damn fool, you deserve Maddie Kincaid!

But then, for some unknown reason, Noah started thinking about laughing himself weak when Maddie threatened him with that paperweight. God, that had been funny. Had he ever seen anything funnier in all of his life? For that matter, had he ever met a spunkier woman? Okay, so she was exactly the handful that Mark had said she was, but wasn't the incredibly good laugh she'd provided him practically priceless?

But there was something else drawing him to Maddie, and while he didn't like thinking the words *sex appeal,* what else caused a man's blood to stir in that one special way? Besides, sexual attraction was nothing more than hormonal chemistry and he shouldn't get all tensed up over a physiological phenomenon he could do nothing about. Self-control was in the intellect, *not* in a man's groin! All he had to do was disallow any emotional involvement with Maddie, which, considering the state of her health, shouldn't be all that difficult.

Finally reaching Mark's home, Noah steered his SUV through the snow that was all but concealing the driveway and parked. He hoped the nerve-racking journey to his house and back had been his final foray of the day, as he was more than ready to go inside and *stay* inside. Taking his suitcase and bag of fruit and vegetables in one hand, he pushed open the driver's door and then got the house key from his jacket pocket.

He slogged through the snow to the house and unlocked the door. Daylight was growing weaker; the storm was causing a premature nightfall, and Noah felt a strong and rather discomfiting sense of isolation. Probably everyone within the perimeter of the blizzard's ferocious appetite felt it, he thought as he flipped the wall switch to turn on the kitchen's ceiling lights.

The kitchen that he himself had tidied earlier looked cozy and welcoming. Warm air blew from the furnace vents. Noah set his sack on a counter and his suitcase on the floor, then shed his cold-weather gear. The laundry room was just off the kitchen, and Noah hung his things on some handy hooks near the dryer.

Returning to the kitchen he picked up his suitcase and strode toward the bedroom area. Since the house contained only two bedrooms, he would have to sleep in Mark and Darcy's bed. He couldn't imagine them minding, not when he told them about Maddie's trickery and that she'd been ten times worse off than she'd made them believe. She had a story in her, none of which he'd heard yet, but he would.

Determined to take hold of the upper hand the second he saw the deceitful Miss Kincaid, Noah passed the open door of her room. He glanced in and stopped dead in his tracks. Maddie wasn't on the bed sleeping, as she'd been when he left, and so far he'd neither seen nor heard anything that would lead him to believe she or anyone else was in the house. So, where was she?

The bathroom door was ajar and Noah, feeling wary and highly suspicious of the silence that now seemed to cause pressure in his ears, rapped on it and called, "Maddie?"

The continuing silence didn't surprise Noah, but it did cause him the start of a tension headache. Leaving his suitcase on the hall carpet, he began going from room to room and calling her name. He couldn't imagine a grown woman playing a foolish game of hide-and-seek with him, but she had to be somewhere in the house.

He looked everywhere, even moving clothes aside in closets and checking under beds. Muttering curses, getting angrier by the second, he wound up back in Maddie's bedroom. Only then did he spot the blouse and skirt she'd been wearing earlier on the foot of the bed, lying in a heap.

His gaze next went to the note he'd left on the bedstand, still propped up exactly as he'd arranged it. Hadn't she seen it? Read it? Where in God's name had she gone? Why had she gone *anywhere* on a day like this?

Suddenly deeply shaken, Noah rushed back to the kitchen. There, by the telephone, was the pad he'd used to keep track of his calls to find Maddie's horse. *She saw this, and she's out looking for her damned horse! My God, my God, she could die in this storm.*

Noah was positive she was not running around in this record-breaking blizzard because of having ingested too much pain medication. He'd seen to that quite effectively, and had even gone so far before he'd left the house to secrete his medical bag on a high shelf in one of the laundry room cabinets. Not that he could let himself actually believe that Mark's sister would go through his medical bag looking for drugs, but it was always better to be safe than sorry.

Following that credo and hoping ardently that the bag hadn't been touched, he got it down from its perch and looked through it carefully. Nothing had been disturbed; everything was in its place. He breathed a sigh of relief and regretted his slight but still unmistakable suspicion that Maddie Kincaid would do such a thing.

Grim desperation was his next emotion. Placing the medical bag on the kitchen table, he once again put on his outside gear. Where he would start looking for her, he didn't know, but he couldn't just stay in this nice warm house and ignore the fact that she might be wandering around outside—maybe just in her brother's yard, if she was truly disoriented—and could freeze to death in a very short time. For one thing, how was she dressed? What had she put on in place of the skirt and blouse?

Worried, furious and sick at heart, Noah went outside. It was darker than when he'd gone in, and soon it would be *very* dark. The falling snow was so dense that visibility was practically nil. A streetlight was merely a distant and all-but-useless ball of diffused light.

Wading through the deepening snow to his vehicle, Noah took out his flashlight and turned it on. After taking a few steps from his SUV, he shouted, "Maddie!" and heard the howling wind and heavy snowfall muffle his voice to a disturbing degree.

He kept going, shining the beam of his flashlight around Mark's yard only because he didn't know where else to look. His mind raced with possibilities. For one, maybe a friend had dropped in and Maddie had gone with her or him. But that hope was so lame. People weren't out visiting friends today; people were staying home today!

Abruptly Noah decided to call the police for assistance, and he slapped his jacket pockets in search of his cell phone. He didn't have it! Where had he left it? When had he last used it?

He had reached the area behind Mark's garage and was so overloaded with fear and dread that he could not, for the life of him, remember what he'd done with his cell phone. Panic beset him, for the house phones were dead and now he was totally without communication of any kind.

"Maddie! Maddie!" he yelled as loudly as he could. The wind took his words and carried them away. In the very next heartbeat Noah stared, wiped snow from his face and eyes and stared again. He shone the flashlight around, zipping it one way then another, and told himself that he wasn't seeing clearly.

But he was. Maddie's white truck and trailer were gone!

Chapter Five

The wind was brutal, lifting and hurling ground snow as well as what was still falling, creating a surreal world that was at the same time precariously authentic. This was no irrational dream, and Noah fully understood the dangers of Maddie driving her heavy truck and trailer in this harsh, unmerciful storm with only one hand. His other concern—more like intense worry—was her state of mind. Was she even seeing clearly, let alone thinking that way?

It took only minutes for Noah to follow the ruts Maddie's rig had cut in the snow to the road and another few moments to ponder and then fully grasp what it was that she'd really done. She's actually out there driving! My Lord, she isn't just risking her own neck but also the life of everyone who *has* to be on the roads tonight!

Anger hit Noah then, striking him with more force than the wind ever could. This was an internal blast, fueled by resentment, fear and despair. He'd accepted responsibility for Maddie Kincaid's well-being, and how would he face

Mark or anyone else in Whitehorn, for that matter, if she met with some awful end because of his negligence? He should never have left her alone today, certainly not for such a lame excuse as needing his own razor and toothbrush.

He ran—if one could call slogging through deep snow running—to his vehicle and got in. He started the engine, then muttered a vile word and got out again. Hurrying to the house, he went inside, grabbed his medical bag and rushed out again.

Driving through that heavy, wind-tossed snowfall was as close to driving blind as a man could get, and to think that Maddie, with all of her physical injuries and half-baked grasp on reality, was also out there daring the elements made Noah a little bit crazy.

He wanted to speed in the worst way, to press the accelerator to the floor and fly, but he knew that even with four-wheel drive he'd end up in a snowbank if he did anything so rash, so he played it safe and kept it under thirty. Less than that in many places. His SUV was powerful, but it wasn't a snowplow, and there were drifts across the road, swept smooth as a white tablecloth by the treacherous wind, that brought his speed down to a mere crawl.

He finally reached the turn onto county road 34 and stopped for oncoming traffic. There wasn't any, not a car, a pickup or anything else. What's more, there were no streetlights that far out of town, and from that point on his headlights would be his only guide.

Remembering his missing cell phone, Noah switched on the overhead light and looked all around the front seat for it. If he'd ever needed a cellular telephone, it was now. But it was nowhere to be found, and with a grim set to his lips and a discomfiting knot in his gut that contained a dozen opposing emotions he put his SUV in motion again.

He drove even slower on country road 34, because he

felt that he should check both sides of the road for ruts or other evidence that someone may have skidded into snow too deep to get through, or into a ditch. Noah recalled that a substantial segment of this road had a man-made drainage ditch on its left side, but it was impossible for him to pinpoint the exact area, so he had to stay alert all the way.

He was also keeping an eye on the odometer, because the stable housing Fanny was located on that portion of the Braddock ranch that connected with this road, seven miles from town, he'd been told. Two miles passed, then three, and he saw that he was nearing the four-mile point when he thought he saw a light on the right. He stopped the car and peered through the passenger window, then reached over and rolled it down because if there was a light out there he'd lost sight of it. He debated taking a closer look on foot or driving on.

Scowling and furious that Maddie would cause both him and herself such unnecessary misery, he got out, braving the ferocious elements one more time. He trudged through the snow toward what he thought was a spot of light. He sensed more than saw the trees all around him. In fact, something black suddenly loomed right in front of him, and he halted his stride just in time to prevent a collision with a big pine. It irritated the devil out of him that he'd been so totally focused on Maddie and her shenanigans that he'd left his flashlight in the car. He almost went back for it, but the urge to do so was quickly dispersed by a surge of common sense that told him to get this done fast. He forged on.

Shortly thereafter Noah spotted the light again. It hadn't been his imagination after all! Relieved, he noted how the light appeared and disappeared with the fluctuations of wind and snow, and that it looked to be shining through a small square. Was there a cabin out there? A house?

He nearly ran into the back end of Maddie's trailer. It was as white as the snow and damned near invisible in the storm. And to realize that she'd driven a white truck and pulled a white trailer in this deadly blizzard just about did Noah in.

Well, she hadn't made it to the Braddock ranch, had she? It almost made him happy that she hadn't, because she obviously was a selfish nitwit who did what she wanted regardless of the trouble she might cause someone else.

But how had she gotten so far off the road? Maddie Kincaid was a menace to herself and everyone else in the area, and she shouldn't be allowed to even possess a driver's license!

Scowling, Noah walked around the trailer and located the entrance door. He pounded on it and yelled, "Maddie!"

To his surprise *she* opened it, pushing it outward and missing his head by no more than an inch. Noah jumped back and growled, "I know you'd like to be rid of me, but there must be a simpler way than murder by door!"

"Oh, for Pete's sake. What're *you* doing here?" Maddie left him standing there and walked away.

"Hey, it's more like, what are *you* doing here?" Noah grabbed hold of the assistance handle next to the door and pulled himself up and into the trailer. The steps—probably electrically powered—weren't out for usage, and he wondered how Maddie had managed to haul herself inside.

"Would you please close the door?" she said with a look of utter exasperation. "You're letting all the heat escape."

"What heat?" The second he spoke Noah felt the warmth of the trailer's interior and noticed that Maddie wasn't wearing a jacket. Huge ski pants ballooned on her lower half, but on top she was again clad only in her brother's thermal underwear. He quickly pulled the door shut because the outside storm was trying desperately to huff and puff its way inside.

It was then that he saw the difference in Maddie. Her

eyes were no longer glassy, nor was she looking pale and dazed. Standing, the top of her head was on a level with the middle of his chest. She was a pretty little thing, even with that taut, resentful expression on her face, and it amazed Noah that he would care *how* she looked, or that he would even notice her unusually green eyes, small nose and beautifully shaped lips. Pretty women weren't uncommon anywhere a man chose to live his life, Noah had discovered. But his attitude toward the opposite sex—toward people in general, for that matter—was uncommon enough in a small town to have stirred up plenty of speculative gossip among those citizens of Whitehorn who enjoyed dissecting everyone else's personality, habits and lifestyle.

Noah apologized to no one for his usually unsmiling and unfriendly countenance, however. He frankly didn't care what people said about him. It was his life and he'd live it his way. In fact, today's ludicrous events reinforced his preference for strictly peripheral involvement with the community and its occupants. Maddie Kincaid had run him ragged during what would likely turn out to be the worst storm of the year, and the resentful expression on her face wasn't even close to the degree of resentment *he* felt.

"Would you please stop staring at me and explain why you've dogged my footsteps all day long?" she said coldly.

"For one reason and *only* one reason, you little ingrate, which I already told you."

"Mark thought I was just fine when he and Darcy left! Why would he ask you to intrude on my privacy?"

"Probably because he knows what a lying little sneak you are."

Maddie's jaw dropped. "How dare you? And you're supposedly Mark's friend? Hah! Just wait until he gets back and I tell him the horrible things you said to me. He won't be your friend after that, Mr. Bigshot-Pain-in-the-Neck!''

Noah felt a sudden wave of helplessness. Not that he was concerned about losing Mark's friendship over this miserable fiasco of a day—which wasn't yet over, he unhappily reminded himself. But he'd never met anyone quite like Maddie Kincaid. She looked sweet and softly feminine and wasn't even close. With her fierce independence and tendency to yell first and ask questions later, she could probably blister paint when she got really worked up. Hard to handle? She was *impossible* to handle, and while she might have some stories to tell her brother after his honeymoon, so did Noah.

He knew one thing for certain. He would keep his promise to look after Maddie, regardless of her objections, but once Mark was back home, she was *his* problem. It was relieving to envision the day when he would never have to set eyes on Maddie Kincaid again, let alone be the target of her sassy mouth. In the meantime he was through exchanging insults with her, for what would that sort of childish behavior accomplish?

''What happened? Did you skid off the road?'' he asked.

She was surprised and then suspicious. He'd sounded like any other normal person making normal conversation, and she didn't trust him. Warily she replied, ''No, I didn't skid. I missed a curve in the road and drove a straight line into the trees.'' The gleam in her eyes dared him to laugh, as he'd done when he'd first seen her, which raised her ire every time she thought of it.

''There's hardly any visibility out there,'' Noah said. ''So I can see how that could happen. But what about now? Is your truck stuck?''

''It's high-centered. Probably on a log under the snow.'' Why was he being nice? Or *pretending* to be nice? If he could pretend so easily, couldn't she do the same? After all, her situation required *someone's* assistance.

She tried very hard to speak calmly. "Maybe when you get back to town you wouldn't mind calling a tow truck and letting the driver know how stuck I am. I always carry a cell phone with me, but I haven't been able to find it. I mean, I thought it was here in the trailer, and it's not, so I don't know if Mark brought it into the house with my other things, or what."

"I lost mine, too. I have the feeling that it's somewhere at the bottom of a snowdrift, either at my house or at Mark's. Look, I really don't think you or I or anyone else is going to get a tow truck to go anywhere tonight unless it's a life-and-death situation, which this isn't. I know what you think of my opinions, but I really feel that you should ride back to town with me. I'm sure the plows are out working as we speak, and once this road is cleared, anyone with a tow truck would willingly come to the rescue."

His logic irritated her. "And I should just walk off and leave my truck and trailer out here?"

Her *lack* of logic irritated Noah. "Well, it's hardly going anyplace!"

"What about vandals?"

"In this weather?" He cocked a cynical eyebrow at her.

She flushed slightly and glared at him. "You get a big kick out of being rude, don't you?"

Noah glared right back at her, but he wasn't going to let her draw him into another battle. "I left my car running on the road. Are you coming with me or not?"

Maddie again had that frustrating boxed-in feeling. She'd met bossy, egotistical men who had to have everything their way before, but none to compare with Noah Martin. Of course she had to go with him, but why had fate sent *him* out here? Why not someone else, some nice person who didn't grate her nerves raw and constantly regard her with that superior, better-than-thou look in his eyes? Boy, was she ever going to lambaste Mark when he got home!

Noah had unbuttoned his jacket and taken off his gloves when he first came in. Now he reversed the process and said, "Call me impatient, but I'm leaving."

Maddie sent him a murderous look and went for her jacket. Noah looked around and realized that there was more than one room to this cozy little setup. Obviously, he was standing in the living room-kitchen area. It had a stove, refrigerator, dining booth, small couch, recliner chair and a built-in television, all done in shades of blue with attractive wood trim.

"I thought this was a horse trailer," he called out.

Maddie returned from her bedroom with her jacket. She didn't like giving in and making small talk with this over-bearing person, but while *he* relished rudeness as a way of life, she normally did not.

"It is a horse trailer. This is my space, and the back third of it is Fanny's quarters. As long as we're becoming such pals," she drawled, "would you mind helping me into this jacket?"

"That supporter on your hand and arm gets in the way, doesn't it?" Noah asked, ignoring the sarcasm he'd heard in her voice, and took the jacket from her. "Maddie, may I look at your injured hand?"

"Must you?" she asked coldly. She did not want him for her doctor.

"No, we'll both keep right on keepin' on if I never see it, but I can't help being curious. Is it painful?"

She didn't want to answer questions. She would never think of him as anything but one of those people who barged in where they weren't wanted and then trampled over everyone else's wishes and rights.

"It's only aching a little," Maddie said, speaking with a reluctance Noah didn't miss.

"Your hand was X-rayed, of course."

"I suspect that's standard procedure in hospitals in any state."

"And the accident occurred in what state?"

"In Texas."

"Is that where you live?"

"I live wherever my truck and trailer take me. What are you doing?" He had laid her jacket on the dining booth, removed his gloves and gently taken hold of her cast.

"Removing this apparatus so I can see your hand," he replied in a no-nonsense tone. "Stay still, and I promise this won't hurt." She was too startled to voice an objection, and his professional all-business demeanor was rather daunting, although she kept a wary eye on every move he made.

Noah wasn't even aware of her "wary" eye. He was far more interested in seeing what was under the deep-blue fabric encasing her hand, which was more of a sturdy wrap than a cast. He wasn't a bone specialist, but he'd seen this type of support before and he'd always linked it more with pulled tendons or muscles than with fractures.

"Do you see this strap?" he asked her. "I'm going to undo it so I can bare your hand." Without waiting for a reaction from Maddie, he began working the strap loose. "Where in Texas?"

"Where what in Texas?"

"Where did the accident happen?"

"Oh. In Austin."

"Mark said you were at a rodeo."

"Not at. In. That's my profession…or career…or whatever you'd like to call it." She'd dropped her wary eye to her own arm, and the gentle way he was removing what she'd considered to be totally *un*removable until her hand healed. "Are you sure you should be doing this? I was told to be careful about even getting it wet."

"Let's leave the rodeoing to you and the doctoring to

me, all right? I find your choice of profession intriguing. How'd you get started in that?''

"It's a long story that I'd rather not get into tonight.'' With the cast removed, he gently unwound a gauze bandage and bared her hand. Maddie's eyes widened. "The skin on my hand looks all shriveled!''

"Your skin is fine.'' He held her hand in his and peered at it from several angles. "I wish I had those X-rays, but from the small amount of swelling in this area—'' he pointed "—it appears that you injured several of the metacarpal bones.''

"That's Greek to me, Doc,'' Maddie said dryly.

"No one explained your injuries before?'' Maddie shook her head. "All right, here's a condensed anatomy lesson on the bones of the human hand. Up here, just below the bones of the forearm, the radius and ulna, are eight small bones called carpals. Four of those wrist bones articulate with the radius and ulna, and the rest are connected to the five bones of the palm, the metacarpals. Next come the phalanges, or in layman's language, your fingers.''

His explanation incited Maddie's interest, and she forgot how much she resented his intrusiveness. "So, do you think my metacarpals are healing properly?''

Noah almost laughed, which shocked him to an almost sour-faced sobriety. Laughing at a patient's question simply wasn't done, and besides, Maddie hadn't said anything funny. It was just that she tickled his funny bone like few people ever had. He didn't know why she did, but there was something about her that made him want to gather her up into a huge bear hug and laugh and be happy.

It was such a stunning departure from his normal behavior that his facial expression became even more tense and sour, and he even spoke stiffly. "Are your other injuries causing you pain? I know the medication you took this morning has worn off by now.''

"Yes, and I should have brought it with me.''

"You couldn't have. I destroyed it."

"You *what?*" Maddie's eyes flashed angrily.

"Don't get your dander up. I have something better for you to take. It will ease your physical discomfort without messing with your mind. It's in my bag, which is in my car, which, I hope, is still sitting out on the road with the motor running. Let's get this thing back on your hand for now, but I have a better idea for this, too." Noah began wrapping her hand.

"My, you're just full of better ideas, and what I'd like to know is who put a nickel in your slot and made you king of the prom."

Noah looked up from her hand and into her deep-green eyes. Laughter bubbled within him; her mixed metaphors seemed truly hilarious. But he was also enjoying the sensation of simply looking into her eyes.

Maddie suddenly felt breathless. This was one of those moments that made the permanent list in a woman's book of memories. And it was happening with Noah Martin? She gulped and held out as long as she could but finally had to suck in a big breath.

A bolt of lightning could not have affected Noah more than Maddie's revealing gasp for air. His blood pressure rose with his increased pulse rate, and all of his normal physical reactions to a sexual stimulant culminated in the pit of his stomach. Something quite powerful was developing between him and Maddie Kincaid—threatening to run wild, in fact—and he couldn't permit it!

Tearing his gaze from hers, he quickly finished up with her hand, then held her jacket up so she could slip into it. Feeling emotionally jarred and confused, Maddie got into her jacket and was almost positive that she felt his hands linger on her shoulders for just a second—a completely unnecessary contact. Frowning, she wound a woolen scarf around her head, another around her injured hand and then fished a ring of keys out of her jacket pocket.

She held them out. "Maybe you would lock up when we're outside? It's a big stretch for me to reach the door lock with the trailer so out of level."

Noah plucked the keys from her hand. "Which key do I use?"

"That gold one with the spot of red fingernail polish on it. Do you see it?"

He saw that every key bore a spot of a different color. It was a smart and rather adorable way of keeping track of which key was which, and he again felt the urge to hug her.

Disgusted with urges he wasn't at all accustomed to feeling, he asked gruffly, "Are we finally ready to leave?"

Maddie shot him a dirty look and answered in the same nasty-voiced way. "Open the door and get going, for pity's sake! I'll be right behind you. I have to turn off the lights or they will drain my batteries dry."

Noah realized that there was a lot about trailers he didn't know, but he certainly wasn't going to start seeking information on that subject tonight. He reached out to open the door and heard Maddie say, "Be careful. It's a long way to the ground."

"I noticed when I climbed in," he answered sharply, as though she thought him too dense to recall something that had occurred only minutes ago. "In fact," he added, "I wondered how *you* managed to get yourself inside."

"Don't let my size influence your opinion of my capabilities. I usually manage to do whatever I decide to do," Maddie said coldly.

Now *that* was a topic he would like to pursue, Noah thought darkly while translating her egotistical declaration to mean, "I do what I want when I want, and if you or anyone else doesn't like it, tough!"

But he was ready to get out of there. Ready to return to his nice warm car and brave the hazards of driving through the blizzard from hell until he reached a safe ha-

ven, in this case, Mark Kincaid's house. Without Maddie
on his hands, he would, of course, drive to his *own* home.

But he had only himself to blame for having Maddie
Kincaid on his hands. He should have said a decisive,
"No, sorry, but I'm just too busy," when Mark asked
him to check on his sister. Well, it would be a cold day
in hell before he committed himself to another favor for
anyone.

Hitching up his jacket collar around his ears, he turned
his back on Maddie and opened the door of her trailer.
Wind and snow hit him hard, but he forged on and took
that long step to the snow-covered ground.

The lights went out inside the trailer, and Maddie became a shadowy figure in the doorway. "Here, you'd better let me help you," he said brusquely, and held up his
gloved hand toward her.

She ignored him completely and neatly swung herself
down by hanging on to the assistance bar next to the door
with her good hand.

"You had to prove it, didn't you?" Noah said disgustedly.

"Prove what?" The wind was louder than their voices,
but she made herself heard, just as Noah had.

"How independent you are! Come on, let's get the hell
away from here!" Without asking for or waiting for permission, he took her arm and said, "That's just so we
don't get separated, and don't think it couldn't happen."

Maddie knew that as well as he did, but arguing about
anything in this killer storm was just too ludicrous and
she said nothing.

They began trudging through the ever-deepening drifts,
battling the fierce wind and blowing, billowing snow.
Noah led her through the trees, and for a time she worried
about actually reaching the road. He could be taking them
in the wrong direction, after all. The density of the storm
disoriented her, so why wouldn't it do the same to him?

But then she saw it, something dark up ahead with

barely discernible globes of diffused light. It had to be Noah's car. "Thank God," she murmured. At this range she could admit to the weakness causing her body to tremble. And she hurt badly—her hand, almost her entire right side and her left knee. That was a new point of pain, and it concerned her. What had she done to make her left knee ache? That climb into the trailer? Just the drive from the house? The bumpy ride over ground and in between trees that had told her she was no longer on the road? The abrupt stop when she'd high-centered the truck on a log?

Suddenly despondent—she'd only wanted to make sure that Fanny was all right, and instead she'd caused a big fat mess—Maddie's eyes got teary. It could have been from the bitter cold, and God knew she could make that claim should Noah catch on to her emotional upheaval, but he couldn't possibly give a whit if she laughed or cried at this point. Obviously, he disapproved of everything she said and did, and why wouldn't he? He'd never seen any evidence of her usually dominant sane and sensible side, and Maddie's hunch was that he didn't give people too many chances. If ever a man lived with anger as a constant companion, she thought, it was Dr. Noah Martin.

Upon reaching the SUV, Noah quickly opened the passenger door and helped Maddie to get in. Giving the door a push to close it, he hurried around the front of the vehicle and got in himself. They both hooked their seat belts. The heater was throwing hot air, and the snow on Noah's face immediately began melting. He yanked off his gloves and wiped his eyes. He could see that Maddie was doing the same.

"Are you feeling all right?" he asked.

"Yes." What else *could* she say? Getting back home was their biggest problem at the moment, not how she felt. Anyhow, her guilt over being the cause of this fiasco was worse than all of her aches and pains combined. She could tell that he thought of her as completely brainless.

She really didn't like anyone thinking of her that way, but there was precious little she could do tonight to alter his opinion.

Noah turned on the windshield wipers and cleared away some of the snow that was totally covering the glass. He'd left the defrosters off so he wouldn't have windshield ice to contend with, but now he switched them on. He got the SUV moving—very slowly, Maddie noted—and in a minute or so he turned it around and they were headed back to town.

"Apparently you know how to drive in snow," she said.

He sent her a somewhat withering glance. "If you're going to live in this area, you'd better know how to drive in snow."

His resentful expression and tone of voice spoke volumes for Maddie. It said clearly that he would rather not be drawn into any small talk. Maddie put her head back and shut her eyes. He was a good driver and would get them home safely. That didn't concern her, but there were other facets to her life besides the bad weather to give her pause. For instance, his confession about having destroyed her pain pills. That really was too damned nervy. Had she so much as hinted that she would like him to be her doctor in Whitehorn? Even Mark hadn't suggested that, for heaven's sake. All he'd done—according to Noah himself—was to ask Noah to drop in occasionally and check on her. So yes, Dr. Noah Martin was nervy beyond belief. And once she was home, she was going to tell him exactly what she thought of such outrageous tactics.

Noah was trying to remain relaxed behind the wheel. Gripping the wheel too tightly or overdriving was dangerous business in weather like this. The road was icy under snow that was several feet deep in drifted areas. He paid very little attention to Maddie, because all of his attention was focused on the road or rather on making sure they *stayed* on the road. He understood how Maddie

could have driven a straight line into those trees as there
were stretches of nothing but white when he couldn't
make out the road at all. Obviously, she hadn't taken the
curve she'd missed because she simply hadn't seen it.

But she shouldn't have been out at all! he thought with
a resurgence of resentment. She had risked her life for
what? To visit a horse. Good Lord. Noah's lips thinned
from the massive disapproval gripping his vitals, disapproval that was wholly aimed at Maddie Kincaid. He
didn't like thinking that she might be a little light in the
upper story, but what woman in her right mind would put
a horse before her own safety, especially when she wasn't
physically sound to begin with?

He heaved a long, drawn-out, put-upon sigh. It was
loud enough that Maddie heard it, and she raised her head
and gave Noah Martin a blistering look. *She* was the one
who should be doing the melodramatic sighing!

"What a jerk," she mumbled under her breath, and
when she saw his head snap around so he could see her,
she added in a louder voice, "What made you think I
needed rescuing?"

Noah gaped at her incredulously for a second before
returning his gaze to the road. "Are you telling me you
didn't need rescuing?"

"I was perfectly all right," she said icily.

"You were stuck in a snowbank!" he shouted.

"I most certainly was not! My truck got high-
centered!"

"And that's even worse than being stuck, you...you
pain in the butt!"

"I'm a pain? *I'm* a pain? You're worse than a pain!
You're a...a damned gnat that keeps flitting around a person's head until they're driven crazy!"

"It was a short drive with you, sweetheart!"

"Meaning I was already crazy? Oh, how I pity your
patients. *If* you actually have any, that is. It wouldn't surprise me if poor, sick people saw you once and never

returned. With your cold-fish personality, you could evacuate an entire hospital in five minutes flat!''

''Just shut the hell up. I'm trying to keep my mind on the road, and it's not easy with you shrieking in my ears.''

''I wasn't shrieking! Believe me, if and when I ever do shriek, you'll know it!'' Maddie turned her face toward the side window and blinked back tears.

Finally, on the outskirts of town, Noah breathed a quiet sigh of relief. He maneuvered the empty roads of Whitehorn—spotting several plows at work as he drove—and at long last pulled into Mark's driveway. It was over. He'd rescued Mark's nitwit sister—however loudly she denied needing rescue—and he would stay the night in Mark's house.

But come tomorrow he was going to find someone else to take care of Maddie Kincaid if he had to haul a stranger in from off the street.

He had had his fill of her.

Chapter Six

The house was warm and welcoming. They were both glad to be back, and especially glad to be out of the storm, though neither said so. In fact, they said nothing at all to each other upon entering Mark's home. Each bore his or her own brand of resentment toward the other, even though neither was actually dwelling on it at the time. They had other things to think about and to do, and they frankly ignored each other once in the house.

Noah walked over to the kitchen phone to check for a dial tone, and Maddie immediately went to her bedroom and started undressing. She felt almost too done in to move, but her need for a hot shower was greater than the exhaustion urging her to just crawl into bed and forget this hapless day.

Because Noah had so easily removed the cast from her hand, Maddie undid the straps and took her first shower without it since the accident. It was while she was standing under the deliciously hot spray that she wondered why she found Dr. Noah Martin so irritating. True, he could hardly be labeled Mr. Personality, but he *was* a doctor and she'd known since leaving the hospital in Austin that she would have to establish a medical relationship with someone in Montana. Why not Noah? Considering the ghastly weather, she should probably take advantage of having medical care under her very own roof. Could anything be more convenient?

That progression of thoughts aroused Maddie's ire. Noah, the big jerk, had destroyed her pain pills, and she hadn't done one single thing to make him think that she was his patient! He had no right to play lord and master with her, certainly not with the medication prescribed by another physician, and neither did he have the right to stick his nose into where she might have gone today. Rescue, indeed! He was probably preening, gloating and patting himself on the back for saving that witless Maddie Kincaid's life!

That image was too much for Maddie to accept without retribution of some sort. She had to show Noah Martin that he and his overbearing methods didn't faze Maddie Kincaid in the least. She'd dealt with much tougher hombres than Dr. Know-It-All Martin, and she had discovered years ago that the best way to put a man in his place was to beat him in his own arena. She'd been on her own for a long time, and a woman alone needed to know how to take care of herself. Noah wanted to play doctor with her? She'd *let* him play doctor.

Turning off the shower spray, Maddie got out and, being careful not to bump her bad hand, she dried off—gently touching the towel to the fading abrasions dotting the right side of her body—and then put on peach silk panties and her peach velour robe. After brushing the wet hair out of her eyes, she moisturized her face and bit her lips for color. Leaning closer to the mirror she inspected the bruises on the right side of her face, which were still visible but not nearly as bad as they'd been. Actually she was healing quite rapidly, she thought, and in a few weeks she should be able to leave Montana and once again join the rodeo circuit.

"Hmm," she murmured in a perplexed way when she didn't feel the elation or anticipatory excitement that thought usually brought her. It was odd, but after the day she'd just put in, why wouldn't her emotions be all messed up?

Actually, her left knee was causing her more discomfort than any other part of her body, she realized. Again she wondered why that knee, which the medical people she'd dealt with in Austin hadn't diagnosed as injured in her fall, should start acting up at this late date.

Looking into her own eyes in the mirror, Maddie said, "That's a good question for Dr. Intrude-Where-You're-Not-Wanted, I would say." Then she took her tube of antibiotic ointment and her blue cast and left the room.

The house seemed quiet—maybe only in comparison to the raging snarls of the blizzard outside—but it was possible that Noah had left her alone again, and she stopped in the hall to listen. It gave her a peculiar feeling to think he might have deserted her for good this time. She'd harangued him on and off all day because of his intrusiveness, but now she wasn't all that comfortable with the idea of being alone.

No, he was still here, she realized with relief flooding her system when she heard sounds from the kitchen. Should she analyze that unmistakable sense of relief? she wondered uneasily. She certainly didn't like the man, and yet she was less tense because of his presence in the house.

There was just no understanding some things, she decided with a slight tossing of her head. The only thing she could possibly want from Noah Martin was medical attention. Anything else was unthinkable!

Reaching the kitchen doorway, Maddie stopped and surveyed the surprising scene before her. Noah, wearing house slippers and a white dishtowel for an apron, was cooking! Glancing around, she spied his boots parked next to the outside door. It was understandable that he didn't like wearing heavy outside boots in the house, but wasn't it rather forward of him to help himself to a pair of Mark's slippers?

Everything about that man is forward, Maddie thought with a fresh supply of resentment. In truth, even though she'd suffered that strange pang of anxiety when thinking that Noah had gone and left her alone, was she comfortable with the idea of his staying the night? He was certainly making himself at home, cooking and using Mark's things as though he had a right to do anything he pleased.

She cleared her throat to get his notice, and he turned partly so he could see her. He blinked twice, then stared, because she was a vision in that very pretty, very feminine robe.

"Uh…are you, uh, feeling all right?" he asked, surprised that he would mangle simple words over a pretty peach bathrobe.

She couldn't be nice, she just couldn't be, and *that* surprised her. But out of her mouth came an icy comment. "I don't see a sign on your forehead giving you the right to destroy other people's medications. *Prescribed* medications, I might add."

Noah shook his head in disgust and turned back to the stove. "If you've come in here looking for a fight, just trot your nasty little self back to whichever room you prefer pouting in. I happen to be making some dinner, which you're welcome to share. But I will not put up with your bad humor while we eat it, do you understand?"

Maddie felt stabbed, wounded, even bleeding. No one talked that way to her and got away with it, no one!

"I didn't come in here looking for a fight, you quack! But I need some pain medicine and I don't have any!"

"What you were taking was too damned strong!" Noah turned off the burner and pushed the pan he was using to the back of the stove. Then he walked over to Maddie and glared right into her eyes. "How much pain are you in right now? On a scale of one to ten."

She glared as coldly as he was doing. "I'm not writhing in agony, as you can well see," she snapped. "But I'm far from…"

"Give me a number."

"Oh, for Pete's sake! Fine. I'm probably a four or a five. Does that satisfy your perverse need for numerical precision?"

His face grew harder, colder. "If ten is the worst pain one could endure, a five is pretty severe. Are you sure you're feeling that bad?"

"How would I know what number I am? I've never heard of anything so dumb! Call me a two if it makes you happy. I'm not in agony and I've never taken anything in my life that wasn't prescribed by a doctor. What do you think I'm hoping to do here, convince you to give me drugs I don't need? And stop scowling at me! You're not my doctor and you're sure as hell not my boss!"

Noah gaped then. "You've removed the supporter from your hand. You shouldn't have done that."

"Why not? You did it. Look, I wanted a shower without it. Is that such a terrible crime?"

"Give it to me and sit over there."

She wanted to tell him to go to hell, that she wasn't taking orders from him under any circumstances. But as grating as it was, she needed his help, and she moved to the chair he'd indicated and sat.

Noah went into his medical bag and brought out an array of items that he placed on the table. After getting a glass of water from the kitchen sink, he moved a chair close to Maddie's and sat down.

"I'm going to wrap your hand with an elasticized bandage and support it with a sling," he said sternly. "You'll be a lot more comfortable. Probably more mobile, as well. That type of stiff supporter you've been wearing is very constricting. But before I see to your hand, take one of these.'' He picked up a small packet, shook out a pill in her hand and gave her the glass of water.

"What is this?" Maddie asked with her eyebrow cocked at a suspicious angle.

"It will take the edge off your pain without raising hell with your mind. You'll start feeling very relaxed in about fifteen minutes."

"Is this a muscle relaxant?"

"It's primarily a painkiller. Take it.'' Noah picked up another packet. "These are the antibiotics I want you to take. Two each day, one after breakfast, one after dinner. There are enough tablets in here for two days, which, from what I've seen of your abrasions, are all you need.''

"You haven't seen everything, you know." Maddie swallowed the pain pill.

"Yes, I have."

"How? When?"

"When you fainted."

Maddie's mouth dropped open. "You examined me without my knowledge? That's a breach of medical ethics!''

"Don't you ever get tired of being on the attack? Good God, you're enough to make a doctor tear up his license to practice and look for another profession.''

"Try cowboying," she retorted dryly. "I'd love to see you thrown from the back of a bucking bronc.''

"As you were?"

"I wasn't thrown! Fanny tripped…or something. I fell, but I wasn't thrown! For your information, I've *never* been thrown.''

"In that case you must've been riding sawhorses," Noah drawled. "For *your* information, I'm a good rider and have no intention of getting thrown for your amusement. Now, shut up, sit still and let me wrap your hand.''

Maddie fumed over his orders—over the superior way in which he issued orders was more like it—and she had all she could do to stop herself from belting him a good one. Not that she went around socking men, but had she ever before met one that made the prospect of slapping him silly actually seem fair and just? And deserved. Oh, yes, if anyone deserved a clout to the jaw, it was Noah Martin. Could he possibly be as rude and overbearing with his regular patients as he was with her?

Maddie kept a close and wary eye on him while he once again inspected her injured hand, and when he turned it over for a look at her palm, she winced.

Noah caught her reaction, lifted his gaze to meet hers and said, "Turning your hand is so painful?"

Maddie took a breath and nodded without breaking eye contact. He had the bluest eyes she'd ever seen, and along with their glorious color, his eyes were bright with intelligence and something she could only describe as supreme masculinity.

Noah, who was again admiring the deep-green color of Maddie Kincaid's eyes, was having similar thoughts about her femaleness. He told himself that he wasn't thrilled with the electricity suddenly dancing around the two of them, and yet there was that tingle deep in his body that was clearly a thrill of some sort. Something flashed in his brain, then, a huge red neon sign repeated the word Danger... Danger, as though every heartbreak he'd suffered over Felicia was poised and panting to attack him again.

He tore his gaze free of Maddie's and reached for the roll of bandage he'd placed on the table. Unaware that his lips had become tense and his facial expression hard as rock, he set to work wrapping her hand.

Maddie blinked as though she'd just stepped out of a trance. She felt hot and cold and prickly and on edge, one very weird combination of feelings and emotions, and in a dazed sort of way she questioned what had just occurred. Noah had been looking at her not as a doctor but as a man! And what had she done in return? She'd sat there like some mindless ninny who simpered whenever *any* attractive man looked her way! She didn't simper, dammit, she didn't, so what really had just taken place? What force had kept their gazes locked for…for how long? A second? An eternity?

Noah's head was bent over her hand, only inches from her chin, actually, and it was almost impossible to avoid looking at his hair. It was thick and shiny and smelled wonderfully clean. At the same time that she was breathing in the scent that was uniquely Noah Martin's, Maddie realized how gentle was his touch as he wrapped her hand. He might talk and act like a grump, and even put on a grump's face while speaking with a patient—or, at least, with her—but he couldn't disguise his naturally gentle touch in tending an injury. He was, obviously, a physician through and through, although the fact that he'd said that he liked riding horses was rather interesting.

Face it, she told herself, *he's* interesting! All of him, his looks, his profession and yes, even his forbidding personality. And don't forget that he has a sense of humor even if the only proof you've seen of it was when he laughed at you. Actually, you've never met a more challenging man, and maybe a challenge matters. It mattered in your career choice, so why wouldn't it matter in a personal relationship?

A personal relationship with Noah Martin, the man who could hands down take the intruder-of-the-year award, if there was such a thing? Maddie nearly choked on that totally nonsensical idea. The man didn't like her, for God's sake. So what if he'd looked into her eyes? He'd probably been seeking signs of fever or fatigue or whatever doctors thought might be lurking in the depths of a patient's eyes.

"There, all done," Noah said after applying the last clip to secure the bandage. "How does it feel?"

Maddie looked down at her hand. "It feels fine. Better than it did in that…that *thing*."

Noah couldn't help smiling a bit, although he was still

somewhat stunned over the impact of their extended eye contact. *Intimacy* was a word with a hundred subtitles, and an interlocked gaze definitely made the top ten on the list. Talk about giving a man something to think about! Even when he didn't *want* something to think about. For sure he didn't want erotic images cluttering his mind, but they were there, a wild assortment of them, already seemingly permanently imbedded! Now, just what was he supposed to do about that?

He cleared his throat and mumbled, ''Now for the sling.'' He slipped a loop of corded fabric around her neck and then laid her wrapped hand within its confines. ''Try not to move your hand. The bandage can be removed for bathing and I'll replace it while I'm here, but you should learn how to put it on yourself.''

''How long do you think I'll have to keep it wrapped?''

''Another week, at the very least. If this storm ever passes, I'd like you to see a bone specialist. We have one in Whitehorn and he's a good man.''

''Fine. Maybe he can tell me what's wrong with my left knee.''

Noah frowned. ''I didn't know you were having trouble with that knee.''

''I wasn't…until very recently.''

''Let me see it.'' Noah didn't wait for approval, he simply opened the lower portion of her robe and began examining her left knee. ''You have some swelling under the patella…the kneecap. You noticed nothing before this?''

''I can't say for sure, but I'm pretty certain this was not caused by my fall. So, what else would cause swelling under the kneecap?''

''Any number of things. Twisting it in an unnatural position could do it, or—'' he narrowed his eyes on Maddie because in spite of that ''intimate'' moment of eye contact between them, he was still ticked off at her foolhardy behavior today ''—maybe driving a truck around in a blizzard and then if that wasn't enough, driving completely off the road and into a field of snow that obviously concealed little things like downed trees.''

Maddie gaped wide-eyed at him. Was she a woman so desperate for a man that she would start thinking a jerk like Noah Martin was interesting? And challenging? Good grief, she thought in abject self-disgust. She could have men by the droves, if she wasn't always so picky. But her dream—her completely *private* dream—had been shaped by Aunt June's stories of love and romance, and Maddie had been contented to wait for that one perfect mate. He was out there somewhere and someday they would meet. They would know at once...at once...

Her adolescent fantasies were showing, she told herself.

She insolently lifted her chin and narrowed her own eyes right back at Noah. ''Thanks for the wrap, Doc. As for your advice about my knee, I'll have another doctor treat that. It looked to me as though you enjoyed opening my robe just a little too much...opening it without my permission, I should add...and then groping my leg like a...a...pervert.''

Noah was thunderstruck. ''Like a *what?* Are you deranged?'' Jumping up, he gathered the few things he hadn't used in treating Maddie and strode angrily over to his medical bag to stuff them into it.

Maddie's heart sank. She'd gone too far. My Lord, how can I undo something so horrible?

''I...I...'' she stammered.

Noah swung around, his face furious and his eyes glowing like live embers. ''I won't demean myself by even attempting to deny your charge.''

''It wasn't a charge! I mean, I...spoke without...without thinking! You hurt me by insinuating that I was stupid for driving around today, and maybe I was, but all I wanted to do was to make sure that Fanny was all right. So I guess I wanted to hurt you back, and that…that awful word just came out of my mouth without conscious intent.''

Maddie, who rarely cried about anything, suddenly felt tears drizzling down her cheeks. ''And it was all for nothing,'' she said hoarsely. ''Because I still don't know if Fanny's warm and dry, and now my truck and trailer are stuck miles from town, and I…I feel like I've lost touch with everything that's been real and good in my life.''

Noah studied her in silent reproach for a long moment, then sighed and relented. ''Your horse is fine. I talked to the woman running the stables at the Braddock ranch, and Fanny is inside and being very well cared for. Now stop crying. Things might look bleak to you right now, but everyone in western Montana is probably feeling the same depressing effects of such a severe storm. I know I am.'' With a wry, ironic twist to his lips, Noah walked over to the stove. ''Some hot food might make both of us feel better.''

To Maddie's chagrin, her tears got worse instead of better. Fanny was fine and Maddie knew she should be feeling incredibly relieved, and instead she sat there bawling and trying to keep it quiet. Praying that Noah wouldn't turn around and look at her, she kept wiping away tears that were immediately replaced by more tears. Finally a huge sob escaped her throat, and Noah heard it and *did* turn around.

''You're still crying?'' he asked. ''Why?'' Grabbing a handful of tissues from a box on a counter, he walked over to Maddie and put them in her hand. She held them to her eyes and cried even harder. ''Hey,'' Noah said. ''What's going on?''

Maddie was so embarrassed that she wished she could evaporate. ''I…never…cry,'' she gasped between sobs, her voice muffled by the mass of tissues held to her face by her good hand.

''Uh, sorry, but I think you do,'' Noah said dryly.

She kept right on blubbering and humiliating herself,

thinking within the despair gripping her mind that she would never be able to look Noah Martin in the eyes again.

"Okay, let's take a look here." Kneeling just in front of her knees, Noah took hold of her hand and pulled it away from her face. "It's a flood, all right," he said while removing the damp tissues from her hand. "Just as I suspected."

"Give me those." Maddie snatched back the tissues and used them on her wet cheeks.

"Why don't you tell me what's so bad that it rates this degree of emotional turmoil?"

"Why don't you tell me what isn't that bad?" she retorted, looking down at the ball of damp tissues in her hand.

"Maddie, no matter how bad things get, life is still worth living."

She did what she was positive she would never be able to do again: she looked into his eyes. "Now you're a psychologist?"

"I'm speaking from personal experience, not from training."

"Oh? You've been where I am?"

"Yeah, I have been. Still am at times." He couldn't help it, he felt damned sorry for her, probably because he'd had such painful reasons to feel sorry for himself since Felicia's crushing desertion. Gently he pushed some wet strands of hair back from her forehead and temples. "This will pass, Maddie. The emotional pain, I mean. We carry memories forever, but time dulls the pain. I swear it."

Still on his knees, he cradled her head in his hands and tenderly pressed his lips to hers. He felt her startled reaction, but in the next instant her lips had parted and she was kissing him back.

His heartbeat went wild, and he tried desperately to keep the kiss sane and minus the desire suddenly running rampant in his body, but Maddie's response was making that impossible. His only salvation was to break this up *now,* and he did it by getting to his feet and leaving her dazed and staring while he returned to the stove and turned on the burner.

Maddie was no longer crying. Instead, she was bewildered and questioning. Had he really kissed her? Had she really kissed him? My God, how does something like that happen between two people who've done nothing but irritate each other from the second they met?

"I...I think I'll go to bed now," she said in a weak, whispery little voice.

"Stay put," Noah said gruffly. "You need some hot food."

"But I'm not hungry." Maddie got up and realized that her legs were shaky and unsteady. He'd done that to her, she thought. Noah Martin's kiss had turned her into a helpless female who would probably start simpering any second. Maybe she would even bat her eyelashes the next time he looked at her, a flirtatious practice she'd seen other women do and which had never failed to nauseate her.

"No, you will eat dinner and *then* go to bed." Turning only slightly, Noah saw that she was standing. "Sit down!"

Hanging on to the table with her good hand, Maddie snapped, "I don't have to take orders from you!"

"Yes, you do. Either sit down on your own, or I'll put you in that chair. You *are* going to eat some dinner, and then the rest of the night is yours to do with as you please. I promise not to bother you for any reason."

"The rest of the night? You're staying here tonight?"

"Don't worry, your virtue will not be under siege."

"Don't *you* worry! Believe me, I know how to take care of myself."

"Yeah, you've proved that all day!" Noah turned back

to the stove and gave his pan of chicken and vegetables a stir.

Maddie felt like crying again. She couldn't get the last word with Noah no matter what the topic, and she should have slapped his surly face instead of kissing him back when he'd dared to make that pass!

Swallowing hard, she lowered herself to the chair again. She would eat—but only because she was hungry, not because Noah had demanded it—and then she would retire for the night, and if she was lucky he would rise early, leave and get completely out of her life before she woke up in the morning.

Not a word was spoken while Noah finished cooking his stir-fry and washed down the table very thoroughly, Maddie noted. He then set the table, took two small bowls of salad from the refrigerator, placed one at Maddie's setting and one at his own, poured two glasses of milk and finally dished up the chicken and vegetables straight from the pan to their plates. She didn't tell him thank you or object to the much-too-large portion he spooned onto her plate. Noah sat down and they began eating.

The silence in the room was not a pleasant, peaceful quiet but rather it felt heavy and burdensome. It felt, Maddie thought, as though the air she was breathing was thick and weighted with something terribly gloomy. Along with the blizzard from hell raging outside that showed no signs of slowing down, let alone of stopping, the entire atmosphere felt stifling.

After a few bites of her very tasty dinner Maddie was surprised that Noah could cook so well. She stole a quick glance across the table and saw him eating, with his eyes on his plate and an expression on his face that she'd come to know quite well—it was one of pure granite.

The phrase *heartless vermin* entered her mind, and it sort of fitted Noah, but it would have fitted much better if he weren't a doctor. Maddie realized then that she had a special respect for men and women who worked in the field of medicine. It wasn't anything she'd thought about before, and she wasn't positive she could apply that seemingly ingrained respect to Dr. Noah Martin. The doctors and nurses she'd dealt with so far in her life had been much nicer people than Noah, after all. Oh, some of them had been all business and even a bit stern, but it seemed to Maddie that Noah went miles out of his way to avoid being nice.

She took another bite and chewed slowly, thinking about their kiss. She would bet anything that he was being eaten alive by regret for giving in to that impulse. That's all it had been, of course, a stupid impulse, and of course he was regretting it. Her big regret was that she'd sat in this very chair and *let* him kiss her. No, worse than that, she'd kissed him back! What on earth had possessed her?

"How is your hand feeling?" Noah asked.

His voice startled Maddie so much that she dropped her fork. It clattered on the floor, and Noah got up from his chair, walked around the table to pick it up and take it to the sink. He returned with a clean fork, which he placed in her hand.

"Sorry," she mumbled. "And…thanks."

Seated again, he said, "I only asked how your wrapped hand was feeling. I didn't expect you to jump out of your skin over a simple question."

"Well, I didn't *expect* your simple question!"

"Obviously," Noah said dryly. "So, how is it?"

"It feels fine. Better than before. I suppose I should thank you, so…thanks."

"You're welcome. You're not eating very much. Don't you like it?"

"It's very good, and I *am* eating. I just eat more slowly than you do."

"Yes, I know I eat too fast. Comes from eating on the run too often, I guess."

"During training?"

"Actually, it happens a lot right here in Whitehorn,

which I didn't expect from a small town. A waiting room full of patients, an emergency situation at the hospital and zap, there goes a decent lunch or dinner break.''

Maddie marveled that he was actually talking to her like a grown-up, but she didn't trust it to last. He'd made it much too plain today that he considered her to be a pain in the neck, an annoyance he didn't need, and that his promise to Mark was the only thing binding him to a troublesome situation he would never have gotten close to on his own.

But could she blame him? The day had been a night-mare for her—a rather vague nightmare at times, to be sure—so what must it have been for Noah? Since she'd done such a good job of convincing Mark and Darcy that she was well enough for them to be left alone, Noah couldn't possibly have anticipated the kind of mess he would run into when he dropped in to keep his promise.

''Your face,'' Noah said then.

Maddie blinked. ''What about it?''

''What are you using on those bruises?''

''Oh, I forgot.'' Maddie fished her tube of antibiotic ointment from the pocket of her robe. ''This is what I've been using.'' She held it across the table and Noah took it.

He read the label, then nodded. ''This is fine. But when did you last use it?''

''This morning...I think. This morning is pretty...uh, chopped up in my mind.''

Noah again got up and this time came around the table. ''I'm going to put some of this on your facial bruises, and you tell me if that's how you've been using it.'' He laid the tube on the table.

Maddie frowned as he went to the sink and very thor-oughly washed his hands. Drying them on a paper towel, he returned and picked up the tube. ''You must wash your hands...or your usable hand...before applying the oint-ment.''

She stared up at him and felt a most compelling urge to giggle. "Are you actually giving me a lesson in how to apply ointment to a boo-boo?"

"Are you trying to be funny?"

"No, but feel free to laugh at me again anytime the mood strikes you."

"If I offended you this morning by laughing, I apologize. Now, please sit still and let me do this." He tipped her chin and began gently rubbing ointment to the discolored blotches on the right side of her face. "How does that feel?" he asked.

"A little better than it should. Sort of like that kiss you laid on me, Doc."

Noah stepped back and scowled. "That shouldn't have happened."

"I agree with you ten thousand percent. It shouldn't have happened, and since you too know that so well, you've taken a different tack with me." She snatched the tube of ointment from his hand. "Believe me, I know how to use this stuff. I've been doing it for two weeks! If you want to touch me so badly, try smiling!"

"What do you think you are, an irresistible sexpot that even a physician can't keep his hands off of you? Think again, babe. Oh, and you might try remembering how you looked this morning when I laughed myself sick."

"I think *sick* sums up your character quite well. Thank you for the insight." Rising, Maddie walked out of the kitchen, wishing with heart, mind and soul that she had the strength and dignity to *sweep* from the room. Someday, when she felt good enough, she was damned well going to do something to put Dr. Noah Martin in his place! If there was any justice in this world, it would happen. It *had* to!

Chapter Seven

Whitehorn was under siege by the vicious blizzard, as were eastern Washington, northern Idaho and *all* of western Montana, Whitehorn's location. The plows made little headway in keeping the streets of the town clear, but they worked nonstop. Business in Whitehorn had come to a screeching halt. The only restaurant that remained open was the one at the truck stop, and it was packed with truckers who had parked their rigs in the huge lot to wait out the worst of the storm.

Retail shops in Whitehorn had closed early in the day, only hours after the blizzard hit. Every school had shut down and administration had sent the kids home, or delivered them if they were bus riders. The kids, of course, were ecstatic, and before night had fallen numerous snowmen had been constructed all over town. Many of the youngsters and teens exchanged their scooters and skateboards for snowboards and used the massive drifts as slopes. People throughout the storm belt left their jobs early and then got home any way they could. If their own vehicle got stuck, they hitched a ride with someone else. Law enforcement agencies were out in force, helping stranded motorists and making sure that everyone did get home safely. Telephone linemen were out working to repair the break in service, the problem being that the wind had snapped more than one line. People were surprised that they hadn't also lost electric service and were concerned that it could happen at any moment.

It was, TV and radio newscasters reported, a storm that the hardy souls living through it would long remember, and "It's not over yet, folks," one cheerful weatherman announced. "We have at least one more day of heavy snow and wind with gusts up to fifty miles an hour. High temperatures will remain in the low thirties. Our lows could get down to the zero mark, and below zero, so make sure your water pipes are wrapped and protected."

Noah watched television in the living room, tensely listening to all that good news, along with advice that was repeated over and over for everyone to stay at home and inside unless faced with an emergency situation. He kept the volume low so it wouldn't disturb Maddie, who had vanished into her bedroom. He assumed she was sleeping and he was damn glad to finally be rid of her.

At least that was what he kept telling himself. It was odd how *many* times he had to tell himself that simple premise, at the same time passionately defending his natural antipathy toward uncooperative and ungrateful people. His strong defense for harboring a clearly antisocial attitude toward Maddie Kincaid was that she could probably make any man a little bit crazy with her stubborn independence and quick-on-the-trigger, totally unnecessary retorts.

Okay, so you don't like her. But if you're so certain that's the bottom line, why did you kiss her?

Noah squirmed in his chair every time that question

slammed him, which it did a whole lot more than he wanted it to. He argued with himself about it.

Is she so gorgeous you simply can't resist her?

Good Lord, no!

Well, is she one of those women who exudes sex appeal in such massive quantities that any man who gets within sniffing distance also gets weak in the knees?

That question took a lot more thought than the one about Maddie's beauty. First of all, no one woman attracted *all* men. That wasn't just his theory, it was scientific fact. The type of woman who appealed to one man went completely unnoticed by another, and, of course, it worked the same way from the female point of view. It was the reason why Noah could look at a couple and see a bright, attractive young woman and a creepy looking guy and wonder how in hell they had ever gotten together. Sex appeal, the human race's potent connector, Noah thought cynically.

But that was quite beside the point, as far as Maddie Kincaid went, or rather, it proved his point. However irritating she was, Noah couldn't deny her sex appeal. He didn't like admitting it, he *hated* admitting it, but truth was truth and fact was fact. Maddie, with her short, unruly, rather lackluster light-brown hair and less than imposing stature exuded clouds of that mysterious element known to all of mankind as sex appeal. It wasn't something one could buy in designer bottles and then spray on certain men. You either had it or you didn't. Some men got hung up on it with a particular woman, others didn't. Maddie Kincaid, the most disruptive, irascible little woman he'd ever had the misfortune of running into, had it, and he, Dr. Noah Martin, was much too aware of it.

"Damn," Noah muttered as he turned any and all residue of anger left over from their dinner confrontation on himself. Just because that nasty little female suddenly seemed like God's gift to horny men the world over didn't mean that he had to succumb. He was above such adolescent behavior, for pity's sake. He had barely noticed that half of the population was female for far too long a time to ruin his record over a shrimp of a girl who lived in a pull-trailer with her horse and made a living in rodeo.

Of course, she did have the loveliest green eyes he'd ever seen.

That thought was a final straw for Noah. He wasn't going to sit there and debate Maddie's virtues, or lack thereof, and his ridiculous conduct where she was concerned a moment longer. Switching off the television set with the remote, he got up and began walking through the house extinguishing lights.

It was when he passed Maddie's door on his way to Mark and Darcy's bedroom that she heard him. She'd been only partially asleep, utterly relaxed and feeling better than she had since before her accident. That feeling of well-being included her wrapped hand—minus its sling—that rested easily and painlessly on her own tummy under the covers. Actually, Maddie had been listening to the fury of the storm outside and thanking the Almighty that she was inside, warm and safe.

And there were other things to think about, as well. As much as Maddie hated facing such an annoying truth, Noah Martin was probably the best doctor she'd ever seen for any reason. For one thing, his destroying her other pain pills, which had hotly fired her anger when he'd told her about it, had proved how smart Noah was. Since taking that one tiny pill he'd given her, she'd had absolutely no pain and her mind hadn't been affected an iota. It really did seem like some sort of minor miracle to Maddie that she could feel so horrible in the morning and so clearheaded and pain free that same night. Noah deserved high marks for that, if for nothing else, she decided.

But as physically comfortable as Maddie had been since retiring, she got a little nervous when the house became really quiet and she couldn't hear Noah moving around. Biting down on her lower lip she frowned and wondered if he'd left her alone again. Not that she really needed him in the house all night. Why on earth *would* she? But his presence had been...well, vexing, to be true, but hadn't it also added to her sense of safety and contentment? If the phones were working she'd feel just fine by herself, but the phones *weren't* working, and God only knew when the lines or whatever was wrong would be repaired. If only she hadn't misplaced her cell phone! She could have kept it charged and used it. It was odd, now that she thought about it, that Noah had also lost *his* cell phone.

He wouldn't have lied about that, would he? Maddie sighed. Was Noah Martin a puzzle she continually tried to solve simply because some perverse part of herself found him intriguing, or was it because she had nothing else to do in this house-bound situation?

She was still pondering that question when she heard Noah walk past her door. He was still there! And obviously going to sleep in Mark and Darcy's bed! Wasn't that rather presumptuous of him? What was wrong with the sofa?

Resenting him again, Maddie pursed her lips. But in a few moments she told herself to get over it and go to sleep. Noah Martin was going to do what he wanted, and nothing she said or did would ever alter his course. Admitting defeat once more, she settled down to fall asleep, but her eyes closed momentarily and opened again. The night-light plugged into a wall outlet cast a pleasant glow, and she found herself relaxing and again enjoying the sensations of warmth and safety.

But then her mind wandered again. Noah *is* intriguing, darn it! You've never met anyone quite like him before. Your love life certainly hasn't been anything to boast about, but you were perfectly happy with group dating and an occasional mild flirtation. Noah's personality runs dark and deep, and a virtual innocent like you are—a country girl at heart and proud of it—shouldn't even be

thinking of mixing it up with a too-good-looking guy with
an I'm-far-better-than-the-common-folk complex. Why
did he kiss me? Maybe he doesn't know why, the same
as I don't know why I kissed him back.

You're attracted to him!

I'm not! Well, maybe a little. But it doesn't mean anything.

To elude any more thoughts of Noah and that kiss,
Maddie concentrated on the happy day not too far in the
future when she could leave Whitehorn and return to rodeo. She would get the truck serviced and ready to go,
load Fanny in their trailer, say goodbye to Mark and
Darcy and then head south. This February blizzard
wouldn't last for long…a few days was usually the norm.
Then the sun would come out and the snow would melt
and Whitehorn would be back to normal.

But then she pictured her truck and trailer, where it was
and would have to stay until the storm passed, and she
groaned quietly. She should have known Mark wouldn't
board Fanny anywhere but at a place where the mare
would get the very best care. She just hadn't been thinking
clearly.

She was now, though. *Thank goodness for that!* Snug-
gling deeper into her comfy bed, Maddie settled down for
a good night's sleep. Her eyes were almost tightly shut
when everything went black.

With her heart suddenly in her throat, Maddie sat up.
The room was black as pitch. The night-light had gone
out!

She shoved the blankets back and turned in bed to feel
for the floor with her feet. Because of so much wrapping
on her hand and forearm, she had worn a sleeveless
T-shirt to bed. Her robe was in the closet, and besides,
she thought, she didn't need a robe to do a little checking
to find out if this was a power outage or just something
gone wrong with the house's electricity.

Rising, she hurried as much as she could in the smothering darkness and found the door. Her heart was racing and even though common sense told her there was nothing to fear—no monsters under the bed, none living in the closet just waiting for a night like this one to escape and grab any warm body within reach—she *felt* afraid. It was an unusual sensation for Maddie, because she had lived alone for many years and very, very little that occurred in life set off her fright sensors.

But they were ringing in her ears, flashing within her system, and it never once occurred to her to try the lamp next to the bed. She felt for and found the doorknob, warily opened the door, saw even worse darkness in the hall and nearly hyperventilated. Inhaling deeply in an effort to slow down the adrenaline spreading throughout her body with the speed of light, she took a step beyond the door and collided with human flesh! *Lots* of human flesh! Lots of *naked* human flesh!

"Oh, my God...my God...help! Help!" she shrieked.

"Maddie, for Pete's sake! The power went off, that's all that happened." Noah put his arms around her, and the shock of his total nudity caused Maddie to panic even more than their collision in the dark had.

"Let go of me!" she screeched.

Noah thought her terror was a disturbed-dream syndrome. She'd been sleeping, dreaming, been awakened suddenly by some sound—possibly when *he* got out of bed—and the inky blackness all around her had triggered a panic attack. He held her close just to keep her from running around half-cocked and playing bumper pool with the furniture in the pitch-black house. She wriggled and squirmed and kept on shrieking, calling for help at the top of her lungs. Didn't she realize that *he* was the only help around? Apparently not, because she seemed to think she was being confined within the arms of a terrorist!

"Dammit, Maddie, simmer down! You're going to hurt yourself," he growled, and then thought of one way of cutting off her piercing screams. Holding the back of her head steady—no small feat when she was much stronger than he'd thought and wiggly as a worm on a hook—he covered her mouth with his.

"Uh...uh..." She uttered odd noises deep in her throat for a few moments, then made one that sounded to Noah like a sigh of pure pleasure. It went through him like a hot knife through butter, and he deepened the kiss without conscious intent. She leaned into him and moved sensuously against him, which totally destroyed any ideas he might have had to keep this at a sensible level.

One kiss led to another, and then another, and when neither could breathe without gasping, Maddie whispered in a hoarse, fragmented way, "You...you're...not... wearing...anything."

"I sleep in the nude. Always have. Since I was a teen, anyhow." His hands slid down her back, cupped her buttocks and urged her lower body forward. At the same time he bent a little and lifted *her* a little so the crucial parts of their bodies could meet and meld. A groan of sweet ecstasy flowed from his throat when it happened. He felt as though electricity was passing between them, from her to him, from him to her, and he knew that she felt it, as well.

Maddie was dazed in the best sense of the word. She had never before gotten so marvelously dazed over a man, although she'd thought she had a couple of times. She wasn't a virgin, but neither of her two sexual experiences—each of them a very short-lived one-time affair—had scalded her blood the way standing in the dark and kissing a naked and hot-skinned Noah Martin did.

She felt more alive than she ever had, alive and wanton and womanly, with the most delicious sensation of falling deeper and deeper into a fairyland that promised abundant and never-ending joys. Dizzily she wondered if she was falling in love with Noah, and if it was even possible for a person to fall in love this fast.

Noah's thoughts were jumbled and easily as foolhardy

as Maddie's. He wanted her. His body wanted hers. His hands ached to touch every inch of her, and somewhere within the sexual fog clouding his brain he knew beyond a shadow of doubt that the most glorious gift in the universe would be to lie with her, to share her bed, to make love with her.

Neither of them was concerned with the blackout or the blizzard doing its best to blow the house into the next county. The inside temperature was already dropping because without electricity the furnace couldn't come on, but the heat generated by their hot kisses and caresses had each of their personal thermostats running on high.

In spite of his almost fierce passion, Noah was careful with Maddie's injuries. He could tell she had very little on—a sleeveless T-shirt and teensy-weensy panties—a far cry from the hilarious winter garb she'd been wearing at their first startling meeting.

He didn't ask for permission for what he did next, because Maddie's fervent response to his every kiss and caress was all the consent any man could possibly require. He bent and picked her up, lifting her without the slightest strain and holding her against his chest. Her arms, both of them, even her bandaged arm, went up around his neck, and she laughed. It was a husky, throaty sound that raised Noah's blood pressure another notch.

"Help to steer us," he said. "I don't want to run into anything and hurt you."

Maddie felt for the doorway to her bedroom and told him which way to walk. She felt weightless and so full of wonder and elation she marveled that she didn't fly into the room. But being carried by a very big, very strong man was better than flying, she decided dreamily. *How have I lived for twenty-three years and not experienced these incredible feelings at least once?*

Of course, if she *had* felt this way before she would probably be married or...or...something.

She was frowning slightly when Noah reached the bed

and gently laid her on it, only to immediately lie next to her and pull up the blankets over them. He touched her face then, and the frown disappeared completely, especially when the tenderness of his fingers on her face was instantly followed by a kiss of unabashed hunger.

Her mouth opened under his, and his tongue mated with hers. He slid his hand under the blankets and began exploring the beauty of her perfect little body. Her breasts were small with wonderfully firm nipples, her waist was a delightfully curved indentation and then he basked in the ripe femaleness of her hips.

Maddie did some exploring, too. She was mesmerized by his arousal. He was definitely big all over, she thought a bit impishly when she encircled his manhood with her hand. He was *beautiful* all over, from the top of his magnificent head of hair to...well, she hadn't actually seen his feet without shoes or socks, but she would bet anything they were beautiful, too.

Noah was mesmerized by Maddie's bold behavior in taking the initiative and caressing him intimately. It heightened his desire, and he was just about to make the final move when he remembered protection.

"Maddie," he whispered, "I've got to get up for a minute. Stay here. I won't be long."

"Wha— Why are you... I don't understand," she stammered, beset by confusion. She'd been so deeply involved, emotionally, mentally, physically, and Noah's abrupt change of pace truly took her by surprise.

Noah thought for a moment. He might know the facts of life in more anatomical detail than Maddie did, but his medical education shouldn't be the only factor making him knowledgeable about certain precautions during lovemaking. After all, neither of them was an inexperienced kid. At least, he wasn't, in spite of a rather long period of self-denial. He could only guess at Maddie's love life, but her feverish responses certainly didn't indicate sexual innocence or ignorance.

He spoke bluntly. "I need a condom, and you need me to use one. There are some in my medical bag. Do you understand now?"

"Yes...of course." Chastising herself for such stupidity, blaming her lack of experience and seeing it as a character flaw, she lay under the warm blankets and listened to Noah's quiet but easily discernible progress through the dark house.

And then, as her body and spirit cooled and began returning to normal, a question struck with awesome force: What in heaven's name was she doing? Or *almost* doing? She'd known Noah Martin one day. True, it seemed more like a year, given all that had happened, but the expansion of time in one's mind due to far too many events crammed into one short period didn't change a thing. She'd known Noah Martin for one day and she was going to bed with him?

"You can't, you just can't!" she mumbled thickly, truly shocked by her own unconventional behavior. This might be everyday stuff for Dr. Martin, but it wasn't for her!

Maddie felt a tear slip from the corner of her eye and slowly travel down her cheek. The darkness seemed to be closing in on her again, causing the fine hairs on the back of her neck to stand up. She'd never been afraid of the dark before, and her fear now substantiated the drastic changes in herself since her accident.

Drawing a nervous breath, she wished ardently that she had stayed in Texas. She could have boarded Fanny in a good stable—there were some excellent facilities in the Austin area—and moved her truck and trailer into a RV park. She would have been comfortably set and probably farther along on the road to full recovery if she hadn't taken that horribly long and trying drive to Montana.

She heard Noah in the hall, saw the glow of a flashlight through the doorway, and her heart nearly stopped. Her romantic mood was completely gone, and how did a woman explain such a drastic change of heart to a man?

He'd found a blanket, she saw with immense relief when he walked in, because it was draped over his shoulders and hung down to his knees. Without his nudity to contend with, she felt somewhat braver.

"I have two flashlights, one from my medical bag and one that I found in a kitchen drawer," Noah said. "I'll put one on the night stand for your use, all right?"

"Thank you." She tried very hard to sound normal, but her voice came out weak and wispy.

Noah caught on at once. Timing was crucial to great sex, and that brief break in their passion had eroded Maddie's into oblivion. He felt a biting mixture of disappointment and relief. He would still love to *make* love with her, but he knew it was best if he didn't. She wasn't just any woman, she was Mark's sister.

Still, he wasn't quite ready to say good-night, and he sat on the edge of her bed. "Don't worry, I would never pressure you or any other woman into doing something she didn't want," he said quietly. "But something's been bothering me. Would you mind talking a little?"

His perception was astounding to Maddie, also his calm acceptance of something he'd figured out the second he'd entered the room. Her overall opinion of Dr. Noah Martin rose dramatically. Men with Noah's understanding didn't come along every day, and Maddie couldn't help being impressed. *Very* impressed.

"No, I wouldn't mind at all," she said in a much stronger voice than she'd spoken in a second before.

"Is it all right if I sit here?"

"Yes, of course," she murmured. Truth was she was glad he was there. The beam of the flashlight was better than no light in such total darkness, but it wasn't very comforting emotionally. Only the presence of another human being had that power. Noah had that power at the moment, and Maddie hoped he would sit with her for the rest of the night, even though she knew that was a rather childish wish.

"How did you get your truck and trailer from Texas to Montana?" Noah asked.

Maddie frowned. She could see only the faintest details of Noah's face. Neither of them was directly in the flashlight's beam, and so she was certain he could see no more of her than she could of him, which was not the cause of her frown. It was his question, which struck her as inane when the answer was so obvious. "I drove it here."

"Alone?"

"Well, Fanny was with me, of course, but she's not a very good driver." Maddie couldn't help smiling at the visual that comment created in her mind.

But her sense of humor and Noah's sense of humor didn't coincide. "That's not funny, Maddie," he said sternly. "You were taking painkillers, and you should not have been driving."

"For heaven's sake, do you think I'm a complete moron? I didn't take those pills during the day. I knew better than that."

"You, uh, took them at night?" Noah was thinking of the residual effects of taking a strong painkiller at night that could easily affect a person the following day. Especially a person with Maddie's sensitivity to pain medication.

"Yes, I took one after I stopped for the day. It was a long and very tiring trip. I drove only a few hundred miles each day, and then I had to take care of Fanny. She needed to get out of the trailer and walk around a bit, and then, of course, she had to be fed and watered. If I felt badly during the driving part of the day, I took over-the-counter pain relievers. They helped."

"Did a doctor okay that long trip?"

"Well, no, but you see I didn't make an appointment to see Dr. Upton in his office, like he told me to do before I left the hospital."

"Why not?"

Talking in the dark was nice—or it could be—and Maddie was still glad that she wasn't alone. But Noah wasn't just chatting; he was grilling her!

There was a chilly note in her voice when she replied, "Let me tell you the whole story, although I know in advance that you will disapprove of everything I did. But here it is to do with as you will. When I came to in the hospital, my first thoughts were of Fanny. Was she all right? Where was she?"

"Back up a second. Was Fanny involved in your accident?"

"Was she involved? I was on her back when she went down. Of course she was involved."

"I guess no one ever told me what you do in rodeo."

"Do you know what barrel racing is?"

"Oh, you're a...um, a barrel racer."

"Don't make it sound like a deadly disease, for God's sake. I make a very good living. Last year I won a total of ninety-six thousand dollars, and since I've been making good money for five years I own my truck and trailer outright and I have a pretty impressive savings account. I rent storage space in Austin, Texas, and in Billings, and whenever I'm in either area I unload all the trophies I've collected since my last trip. Aside from all of that, I love what I'm doing."

"I can tell. And Fanny is an integral part of your life and career?"

"She's the reason I'm successful. I don't know if you realize the role one's horse plays in barrel racing, but believe me, it's crucial to have a well-trained horse. Fanny knows what to do in the arena as well as I do. Let me add one thing more about Fanny. I raised her from a foal, I trained her myself and I love her. So, you see, when I woke up in a hospital and remembered that both Fanny and I went down, I became more than a little concerned. You might say that I got a bit hysterical...I think. Actually, that was an awful day, and there are portions of it that I don't recall at all.''

"You were in the hospital only one day? How'd you accomplish that?''

"One day and one night. They wanted me to stay another night, but I had to make sure Fanny was all right.''

"Like you did today.''

"Well, it wasn't storming in Austin, but yes, it was a similar situation. Someone, Dr. Upton, I think, told me that Fanny was stabled at the rodeo grounds, but I really had to see her for myself.''

"Maddie, have you always done exactly as you pleased and to hell with the consequences?''

She bristled. "You're a fine one to talk!''

"I'm stubborn and independent, too, I grant you that, but you're worse…or better…I'm not sure which word to use in describing your temperament.''

"You fit that old saying, the pan calling the kettle black, if anyone ever did,'' Maddie snapped. "There's not a damn thing wrong with my temperament! Worry about your own.''

"I have been…since I met you.''

Maddie was momentarily lost for a comeback, but recovered quickly. "In other words, you believed you were perfect before meeting a woman who proved you weren't?''

"I never thought I was perfect…I doubt anyone is…but I was satisfied with who I was and with the life I've made since moving to Whitehorn.''

"Which brings to mind a question or two,'' Maddie drawled. "For one, where did you live *before* Whitehorn?''

He hesitated because he never talked about himself, and Maddie was blatantly prying. After a few moments, however, he found himself saying, "San Francisco,'' and then wondered why he was so different with Maddie than he was with anyone else.

"Obviously you left San Francisco for a reason," she said. "People rarely make a move of that magnitude without a strong and compelling reason."

"I had a damn good reason, or so I thought at the time."

"Does that bit of insight into your psyche mean that now you're not so sure that you did the right thing by moving to Montana?"

"To be honest I don't know what I meant with that comment, and it was hardly an open door to my psyche. You have quite a vivid imagination."

"Not vivid enough to imagine what drove you out of San Francisco and to a small town in Montana. Are you going to enlighten me, or are you going to leave me hanging?"

"I doubt that you'd lose much sleep over it." Noah got off the bed and shone the beam of the flashlight on and around the night table next to Maddie's bed.

"What on earth are you looking for?" she asked.

"For the note I wrote when I left you alone today."

"What did you write?"

"That I was going to my house to pick up some personal items I would need for the night. You really didn't see it?"

"No, I really didn't see it."

Noah found it just under the edge of the bed. "I propped it against the lamp. I wonder how it got knocked off the stand."

"I didn't see it, Noah, so don't sound so accusing!"

"Well, here it is. Do you want to read it now so you will forever know that I'm a man of his word?"

"Is that something you'd *like* me to believe?"

He was standing very close to the head of the bed, and though he felt rather silly wrapped in a blanket, he realized that the situation was not silly, nor were the feelings that Maddie Kincaid had brought back to life after his long period of emotional stagnation.

He acted on impulse, bent over and nuzzled Maddie's face until his lips found hers. It was a soft, tender little kiss that stole Maddie's breath and made her heart pound.

Noah broke the kiss but his lips remained a breath away from hers. "I don't know what I'd like you to believe," he whispered. "But you're the first woman who's made me feel like a man in a very long time. I wasn't looking for any such thing and I don't think you were, either. But something happened the minute we met, and maybe we...each of us...should try to figure out what it was. What do you say?"

Maddie's mouth was dry as dust. "I...I think it's something that should be thought about in the clear light of day. This darkness conceals a variety of...of pitfalls and hurdles."

"You're right. Good night." He grazed her lips with his...a fleeting connection that again took Maddie's breath...then stood up and away from her. He put the flashlight in her hand, and with the second light in *his* hand he left her bedroom.

It was hours before Maddie fell asleep again.

Chapter Eight

Changes were in the air when Maddie got up the next morning. Snow was still falling, but the wind had died down. Without that driving force, yesterday's fierce blizzard was now a rather peaceful snowfall. There were horrendous drifts everywhere, of course, but Maddie knew that without the wind the plows would have a much better chance of clearing the roads today.

The house was silent, and walking from her bedroom, Maddie felt a peculiar pang. It was *too* quiet; Noah must have gone somewhere. He could be just outside, she thought, and hurried to the kitchen to check the driveway. It had been shoveled and was vacant! A chill walked Maddie's spine, though she had no idea why Noah's absence would affect her so adversely. She should be glad that he'd finally decided to resume his own life, instead of living in the middle of hers.

Turning away from the window with a stiff-upper-lip attitude—heavens, she certainly could survive without

Noah Martin's exasperating bossiness—she smelled coffee and saw the almost-full pot in the coffeemaker. She also saw a sheet of white paper in the middle of the kitchen table, held down on each of its four corners by a can of tomato soup. There were also two small packets that Maddie assumed contained pills, the new ones that Noah had given her yesterday and had worked so well.

Maddie eyed the note warily, strongly suspecting that Noah's bossiness hadn't vanished when he had. He'd left a note and made certain that she wouldn't miss seeing it, as she had yesterday.

Accepting her fate, Maddie poured a cup of coffee, added milk and then brought it to the table and sat down. Moving the cans of soup off the paper, she slid it over to reside on the table just in front of her. Then she took a few swallows of coffee and began reading.

Maddie,
First, let me apologize for last night. I was way out of line, and all I can say is that it won't happen again.

Yesterday was a day off for me, which is the reason I could spend so much time here. Today is a workday with a busy schedule, and I have no choice but to leave you alone. I hope you're feeling well this morning. I saw overall improvement yesterday, due entirely, I feel certain, to the change of your medications. Continue to use that antibiotic ointment as you've been doing, although any abrasions and cuts that might have caused infection appear to be nicely healed.

The electricity is back on, which you've probably already discovered for yourself, but as I write this message we still do not have phone service. Should that occur, I will call to make sure you're all right. Since I can't imagine a reason for your going anywhere, I'm going to count on your common sense to keep you inside. Talk to you later.

Noah

Maddie put down the note and picked up her cup. Sipping coffee, she frowned, pondered Noah's apology for kissing her *and* obviously expecting more than a kiss, and realized that she wasn't all that thrilled with his contrition. True, she was the one who'd called a halt to the whole thing, but why did he feel that he had to apologize for something that was no more his fault than hers? And he certainly hadn't seemed apologetic during those tender little good-night kisses, had he? Plus, no one had forced him to sit on the bed and instigate conversation. Obviously, curiosity had gotten the best of him and he'd had to ask her a few questions, but why would a man who kept his inner self in a lock-box be that curious about someone else, in the first place?

So, what happened in the night? Had he lain awake and worried that she might read too much into an unexpected interlude that could only be described as passion-gone-wild? Had he then decided at some point that he could eradicate the entire episode with an apology and a half-baked promise about it not happening again?

He's a lowdown coward, that's what he is, writing this…this insulting message instead of telling me to my face that he really doesn't want a personal association with me. Guess I was just too damned handy last night!

Seared by humiliation and anger, Maddie finished her coffee, then forced herself to read what Noah had written on each of the little packets. One contained an antibiotic, the other a painkiller and each bore instructions that she should take one after breakfast and one after dinner.

Sullenly Maddie tossed the packets back on the table. She'd take his damn pills because he was right about her overall improvement yesterday, plus the fact that she felt so much better this morning than she had on any other morning since the accident.

Well, there was little to be gained by sitting there fuming and fussing over something she could do nothing about, so she might as well busy herself with making some breakfast. After that she would find something else to do. She wasn't used to being cooped up like this, and now that she was feeling human again she was also feeling imprisoned. She needed fresh air and a hearty walk, and she needed to see Fanny.

A glance outside dashed those thoughts. Her truck was stuck miles from town, and she was stuck in this house! She might as well face facts, frustrating though they were—she wasn't going anywhere today!

With a heavily weighted, put-upon sigh, Maddie rose and left the table to scare up some breakfast.

Noah's work schedule had huge gaps. His patients were not braving the elements to keep their appointments, and could he blame them? His drive from Mark's house had been precarious and just plain dangerous. Without four-wheel drive, a vehicle stood no chance at all of getting around, and even with it Noah hadn't felt completely in control of his SUV. He'd been grateful for the exceptionally light traffic, for he'd skidded around more than one corner during that short trip.

With so much spare time on his hands, he drank too much coffee and stared out windows at the ongoing snow-fall too often. He walked through the hospital twice, talked briefly with other physicians about nothing important, and then, on his second tour, ran into Dr. Herrera, the orthopedic specialist he'd mentioned to Maddie.

After explaining Maddie's hand injury, he said, "But I'm more concerned with her knee, which she claims was not impaired by her fall but only recently began bothering her. I want her to see you."

"Fine," Dr. Herrera agreed. "With so many people staying home in this weather, as the highway patrol suggested they do, I have free time today. Does she have a way to get to my office?"

Noah frowned. Maddie didn't have a way to get *anywhere!* Without her truck, she was left high and dry, which was a good thing considering her tendency to act on impulse. Hopefully she was calm and resting, but somehow Noah doubted it.

"Yes, she has a way," he told Dr. Herrera. "Any particular time?"

"Anytime after four. I know for a fact that my appointment book is clear after four."

"Thanks. She'll be there."

Noah returned to his own office and tried the phone again. No luck, the line was still dead. His receptionist hadn't come in, and Noah didn't need to be told why she hadn't. She and her husband lived five miles out of town on an isolated dirt road that would be one of the last to be plowed, and without phone service there was no way she could have let him know. It was the same story all over Whitehorn, Noah knew, because he'd heard complaints on that score from everyone with whom he'd come in contact.

He still hadn't found his cell phone, but it wouldn't have done much good, anyhow. Some area residents carried cell phones, but that form of telecommunication was still spotty in Whitehorn. Besides, with so much turbulence in the air from the seemingly never-ending snowfall, Noah suspected that reception between two cell phones would be clogged with static.

Checking his appointment schedule once again, Noah saw that he was booked all afternoon. He'd been booked all morning, too, and one person had made it in. He decided that he would hang around until three, just in case a patient did keep his appointment, then he would put a Closed sign on his door and hope no one did come in.

The day dragged for Maddie. With her mind clear and her aches and pains minimized to practically nothing by Noah's miracle pain pill—which she'd taken after breakfast, as instructed—she felt much too good to sit and do nothing. For a while she walked around with a soft cloth and dusted the furniture. She thought of running the vacuum over the carpets, but it was a heavy old thing and she didn't want to test her newly found and much appreciated strength quite that much. Besides, the carpets weren't soiled. Before leaving on their honeymoon, Darcy and Mark had made sure that everything had been thoroughly cleaned.

Making her bed with one hand wasn't easy, but Maddie managed to put it in a reasonable semblance of good order. She looked in on Mark and Darcy's room, the one Noah had used last night, and saw the bed *neatly* made. Apparently Noah Martin understood household duties, because he could cook and make a bed as well as any woman. Oddly, that smooth, perfectly made bed annoyed Maddie, and she walked back down the hall toward the living room with her lips drawn into a peeved line.

Finally she switched on the TV, sat in a comfortable chair and began flipping channels. Nothing looked good and in mere minutes, she turned it off again. Sighing from utter misery, as though the weight of the world rested on her shoulders, Maddie reflected on last night's events.

She'd behaved so uncharacteristically—feverishly kissing and cuddling with Noah—and the memories caused her to wince. But the memories also delivered a sensual wallop to those areas of her body that had actually quivered with passion last night, and her imagination took flight without a dram of conscious effort from her brain.

If she'd waited breathlessly for Noah instead of getting all rueful and righteous... If she'd welcomed him back with opened arms... If she wasn't such a damned prude about personal relationships... If...if...if. Closing her eyes, Maddie licked her dry lips and visualized the wonders she *might* have experienced last night.

"Darn," she whispered, not exactly wishing things had turned out differently last night but certainly wishing for something. *Yearning* for something was more like it, she realized. There was a deep pocket of yearning in the pit of her stomach that certainly had not nagged at her before Noah Martin barged into her life!

It dawned on her then that she could have an affair with Dr. Sweet-Lips Martin. Regardless of his nonsensical apology and promise that he wouldn't make another pass—or words to that effect—she could easily lead him down the garden path, should she choose to do so.

Maddie stirred uneasily in her chair. She'd never knowingly led a man on. Why was she even contemplating something so shocking? As surely as grass was green, her imagination was creating the perfect setting for heartbreak, and since her libido responded so hungrily to Noah's call of the wild, so to speak, *she* was the most likely candidate to suffer that awful torment. In truth, she couldn't picture Noah in the throes of broken-heart syndrome at all, and it was very easy for her to see herself with that particular malady.

No, she most definitely would not lead Noah anywhere, or flirtatiously if subtly coax him into an affair. All she wanted was to get through her healing process, load Fanny into the trailer and get the heck out of Montana. Get far away from bad weather and…and yes, she might as well admit it—getting away from a man who could kiss her breathless and still give her absolutely nothing of his inner self only made good sense.

And thus Maddie whiled away the long, dreary day.

Noah scowled at the snow that had again piled up in Mark's driveway. Parking in the street, he went into the garage for the snow shovel and set to work. He flung snow right and left, moving fast and eventually breathing hard from the exertion. But he cleared the driveway in about ten minutes, then put away the shovel and drove his SUV off the street.

Inside the house, Maddie thought she heard something

going on outside and she went to the kitchen window to see what it was. She sucked in a big breath when she saw Noah, and she had absolutely no control over the totally female palpitations of her heart and pulse. Nor could she stop herself from being overwhelmingly impressed by his size and strength. He was dressed in a woolen sheepskin-lined jacket, dark pants and boots. There was a forest-green scarf wound around his neck and black gloves on his hands, and he was so handsome and so graceful with that shovel that Maddie just stood there and stared at him as though she'd lost all of her normal connections with reality.

The bottom line, she knew in her soul, was that she was glad he'd come back. The long day alone had been horrible. If Noah had come to spend the night again and if something happened between them—no, she wasn't going to *cause* something to happen—but if it did, all on its own as it had last night, maybe, just maybe she wouldn't allow her common sense to interfere this time.

Oh, you silly fool! The voice in Maddie's head was smarter than the rest of her, and she knew it, too, but still she couldn't help the rush of elation she felt over Noah's return.

He finally finished up outside and headed for the kitchen door to go in. Maddie's heart skipped a beat, and she twisted around to make a dash for the living room so he wouldn't know she'd been watching him. Her left knee gave out, and she moaned in pain as she plopped down on the floor, seat first.

Noah walked in at that exact moment and, with a look of alarm on his face, ran over to her. Kneeling, he asked rather anxiously, "What happened?"

Maddie could hardly look into his vivid-blue eyes, which seemed even bluer than usual, probably because he'd been working outdoors. There were snowflakes in his hair and on his clothing, and he even smelled of snow.

"I guess I turned around wrong...or something," she mumbled. "My knee gave out."

"Your left knee?"

"Yes."

Noah took off his gloves and laid his hand on her knee, which brought him even closer to her, and she dizzily inhaled the scent of his shaving lotion or cologne or whatever that deliciously masculine smell was.

"It...it's all right now," she said, the worry over how strongly he affected her—even the way he smelled, for heaven's sake—showing in the unsteadiness of her voice.

Noah noticed something amiss with the way she was speaking, but he thought it was due to her knee.

"Are you in pain?" he asked.

"It did hurt...my knee, I mean...but it's not hurting now. Not very much, anyway."

Noah took back his hand and looked into Maddie's eyes. "I have an appointment with Dr. Herrera for you. He's the orthopedic specialist I mentioned yesterday. We have to leave right away."

"This minute? Are you sure I need a bone specialist? My hand feels fine."

"I'm sure you're hand *is* fine, but that knee isn't." Noah got to his feet and offered his hand to help her up. "Come on, Maddie. We have to get going."

She looked at his hand, realized how truly beautiful it was—wide in the palm with long fingers—and then remembered how it had felt on her body last night.

Stop thinking about it! What's wrong with you? Clearing her throat, Maddie extended her good hand and laid it in his.

Noah frowned because her hand was so small compared to his. Small and warm. *She* was small and warm...all of her...every inch of her. The potency of last night's collision and very hot aftermath suddenly gripped his senses again, and he wondered uneasily what in the devil was going on with him these days.

And, pray tell, why was he standing there holding hands with her instead of getting them both out of this house and on their way to Dr. Herrera's office?

"Hold on," he said gruffly. "You shouldn't be pulled up until we find out a little more about that knee. Stay put and let me do the work." Noah released her hand, then bent down and lifted her by her waist. "Try putting your weight on your left foot," he instructed.

Maddie did as told for she could do nothing else. She was all tingly inside and knew now that eventually it was going to happen between them, however often she told herself differently. There was too much electricity or chemistry or whatever it was that drew two people to-gether for it *not* to happen. Unless, of course, Noah re-alized the same thing, fervently decided against any such liaison and then stayed completely away from this house and her.

But he was here now, Maddie thought, and he'd be here again and again until either Maddie was fully recovered or Mark and Darcy were back.

"My knee feels fine," she said softly, standing on both feet and looking up into Noah's eyes. His hands were still on her waist, and there was a gap of mere inches sepa-rating them. "As I said before, I probably just twisted it when I turned around."

"It shouldn't hurt to turn around, Maddie," Noah said quietly, though his heart was pounding from this incred-ibly intimate moment. But he didn't want any intimate moments with any woman! He abruptly stepped back and dropped his hands from Maddie's waist.

She saw it happen with her own eyes...the very first time since meeting this very private, very guarded man...she saw through his behavior. He'd just gotten de-liciously ensnared in an extremely tender moment with her, realized it, became alarmed and then deliberately bro-ken the spell.

"I'll get my jacket...and things. They're in my bedroom,'' Maddie said, and walked away nursing her left knee only a little. Her mind raced as she went. Noah had a reason for backing off today. Was it because she'd turned off on him last night, or was his passion last night a fluke that he really did regret because...because he was involved with someone else?

It was a startling idea for Maddie. Until that moment she hadn't placed Dr. Noah Martin with a woman, and it had been a foolish oversight because a man with his extraordinary good looks would have more women than he could possibly juggle hot on his heels. Then there was his profession. Doctors, especially good-looking doctors, were always in high demand. Cowboys, the men with whom Maddie normally associated, were idolized by cowgirls, or sometimes by girls who were merely attracted to a bull- or bronc rider's undeniable masculinity.

Maddie understood that world—her own world—but she was a fish out of water in Noah Martin's world. Any way she looked at it, thought Maddie with a sinking sensation, to let herself do anything but admire from a safe distance Noah Martin's looks, profession, intelligence and sex appeal was just asking for trouble.

That kind of trouble she *didn't* need! Wasn't she already in the biggest mess of her adult life? God, some thief or vandal could be out there stripping her truck and trailer even as she got into her jacket and wound a warm scarf around her neck. Her heart leaped in fear. She shouldn't be thinking of something like that when she couldn't do one darned thing about rescuing two of her three most valuable possessions.

Or could she? Maddie's narrowed her eyes to think. Maybe she couldn't convince anyone to pull her truck and trailer to safety until the storm had passed. But wouldn't seeing for herself that her things were still intact greatly relieve her mind? Yes, it most certainly would, she decided, and since there was only one way to get out there, she would have to be especially nice and cooperative with Noah.

Not that she'd been anything else since he got there, she thought wryly. He was the one who'd made it pretty clear—though she doubted he knew how easily she'd read him today, surprising even herself—that he'd just as soon keep things cool between them. Thinking that it was time to test her acting skills again, she left her bedroom and walked into the kitchen with a blank but not unfriendly expression. "I'm ready."

Noah opened the outside door for her and when she stepped through it, he said gruffly, "Don't move."

She could tell he was making sure the door was locked, and she smiled sweetly when she would just as soon have pushed him into the deep pile of snow next to the stoop for issuing orders in that sort of overbearing voice.

He is one mixed up guy, for some reason, and now he's got you just as confused as he is. He wants you, he doesn't want you, and you could alternately kiss and kick him. Mighty strange goings on, if you ask me!

Noah took her good arm in his hand. "Oh, you wanted me to stand still until you could lead me to your car," Maddie said in the very nicest voice she could muster. "How gallant."

Noah shot her a suspicious look. "I don't want you falling again. It's slippery as hell in some spots, which you can't see because they're under too much snow."

"Yes, that's exactly how I would describe all this white stuff. Too much snow."

Noah pulled open the passenger door of his SUV. "You're playing with me and it's not fair because I don't know the game."

She settled onto the seat, then turned her head and gave him a dazzling smile. "Oh, I doubt there are very many games at which you're not only extremely adept but range in the expert category," she purred.

Frowning darkly, Noah shut her in and trudged around

the back of his SUV. She was up to something, and he couldn't imagine what it was. Apparently, she could flirt with the best of them, which was definitely a surprise, as she'd done everything but stand on her head to show him how much she resented his very existence.

Except for when he kissed her. She was hot in a clinch, that much was certain. Of course, in her case it wasn't wise to leave her hanging for even a few minutes because she cooled down fast.

Not that he intended any rematches of last night's main event.

Climbing into the driver's seat, Noah groaned silently. Good intentions be damned, that little woman had gotten under his skin and in his blood, and the biology of making love, fitting his body to hers and feeling their commingled heat would not leave his mind, however much he preferred things be as they'd been before meeting Maddie.

He started the engine and was about to put the shifting lever in reverse when Maddie exclaimed, "My purse! I forgot my purse, and I'll have to have my insurance card for the doctor."

Noah tried to appear patient and understanding, neither of which he was feeling. Of course she needed her insurance information. She should have thought of that when they were still in the house.

"I'll get it for you," he said as calmly as he could manage. "Where will I find it?"

Maddie didn't put up an argument about his getting her purse, for the sake of peace. But she also felt that he would be quicker getting her purse while she had a bad— well, slightly bad—knee and an almost useless hand to contend with. Besides, the car was warming up and she was buckled in and ready to go. If he wanted to play knight-in-shining-armor to her damsel-in-distress plight, it was fine with her.

"It's either in one of the bureau drawers in my bedroom or on the top shelf of my closet," she told him.

Noah bounded out of the driver's seat, pushed the door closed behind him and hurried back to the house. Maddie watched him disappear inside, then heaved a big sigh. She didn't want to see a doctor, she wanted to see her truck and trailer!

In the next instant, thinking of Fanny, Maddie's heart nearly broke. Noah had told her that Fanny was being kept inside and receiving good care, but some people's ideas of good care didn't even come close to hers.

And however nice she was to Noah, would he take her to see either her truck and trailer or Fanny?

"No, he will not," Maddie mumbled. All he was going to do was drive her to see his doctor friend, and even if she kissed his feet that was *still* all he would do.

She had an opportunity to do something that was far more urgent than having another doctor look at her hand and knee, and was she going to take it?

Maddie's heart began pounding with an adrenaline rush. She peered at the house. Noah would be appearing at any moment, and her opportunity would be gone. Quickly she unlatched her seat belt, then climbed over the console separating the passenger and driver seats. Hooking *that* seat belt, she slammed the shifting lever into Reverse and backed out of the driveway. In seconds she was a block from Mark's house. Noah would throw a fit, but she didn't care. *She* was going to see Fanny and would deal with Noah's temper when she got back.

Noah walked out of the house with Maddie's purse in his left hand. He blinked, not believing his eyes. His SUV was gone!

He stood there dumbfounded, then fury erupted within him, and he threw Maddie's purse into the house and slammed the door hard enough to rattle the windows. Huddling deeper into his jacket and scarf, he set out walking. He was going to report his SUV as stolen if he had to walk all the way to the police station! And he would press charges when the law caught up with her, too, even if she was Mark's sister. A cop's sister. She was a damned disgrace. Poor Mark. And poor Darcy for having such a screwball sister-in-law.

Maddie loved Noah's big SUV, but the seat was much too far away from the floor pedals. A couple of blocks from the house, she pulled over and stopped so she could figure out how to adjust the seat to fit her height.

"Much better," she murmured and took a look in the large mirror just outside the window to see if the street was clear, so she could get going again. Someone was walking very fast, coming her way. "It's Noah," she whispered, and with butterflies tearing up her stomach she pressed on the gas pedal and took off.

She had to admit that she was nervous about this—taking a person's car without permission was a serious offense—but no one, least of all Noah Martin, understood what Fanny meant to her. She'd take her lumps like a grown-up when she got back, but once she saw Fanny her heart and soul would be at peace. If Fanny was in a clean, dry stall with hay in a food trough and all the water she needed, that is. If the mare wasn't being cared for in that manner, Maddie knew that she would shriek so loudly that Mark would hear her in Europe.

"Concentrate on your driving," she told herself out loud. "You know how to find the Braddock ranch, and the roads are much better tonight than they were last night. You'll make it without a speck of trouble if you keep your mind on driving instead of on Fanny."

She was right. Maddie reached a large sign announcing the turnoff to the Braddock ranch without a bit of trouble. In fact, it looked to her as though it wasn't snowing nearly as hard as it had for two days now. The storm was passing, in its final throes, Maddie realized, positive of her analysis from having grown up with this kind of winter weather.

It took about five minutes after the turn for Maddie to

reach some buildings. One was a very nice house constructed of heavy wood beams and redwood siding, quite modern in architectural design and not an inexpensive dwelling. The other buildings appeared to be stables and storage barns.

Maddie parked, left the engine running and got out. A bright light came on when she approached the front door, which made it a simple matter for Maddie to locate the doorbell. She pushed it and heard reverberating chimes from within the house.

A pretty, thirty-something woman opened the door and smiled. "Hello."

"Hello," Maddie replied. "I'm sorry to bother you, but I believe my brother, Mark Kincaid, brought my horse out here. Are you boarding a gray quarter horse mare with the name of Fanchon or Fanny?"

"Yes, I am. Would you like to see her?"

Maddie breathed a sigh of relief. "Very much, thank you."

"Step inside while I get my coat and boots," the woman said. Maddie did so, and the woman went into the foyer closet and took out snow boots and a long woolen coat. "I'm Denise Hunter."

"I'm Maddie Kincaid. I thought you might be a Braddock."

"No, I just work for them." Bundled up, she led Maddie outside and together they strode toward the outbuildings. "We have an excellent stable and training center," Denise said, then gave a small laugh. "Most of which is under snow right now. But you'll have to come out and see the place when the snow melts."

"I'd love to," Maddie replied earnestly, for she was beginning to believe that Fanny was truly in good hands. Maddie's knee gave her a twinge with every step she took, but she never let on. "This is all new to me. I grew up in Whitehorn, but I've been mostly gone for five years now. My visits have been pretty short, so I haven't kept up with the area's growth."

"This is the stable," Denise said as they approached a long building with lights spaced all along its front.

Maddie followed Denise inside and felt all of her worries about Fanny's care totally vanish. It was a beautifully designed home for horses, and it was warmer than outside by at least thirty degrees. Hearing Fanny's whinny, Maddie laughed. "She knows I'm here," she told Denise.

"She's in stall number ten."

Maddie ignored her protesting knee and hurried along to number ten. Fanny stuck her head over the door, and Maddie threw her arms around the mare's neck.

"Oh, Fanny…Fanny," she said softly. She petted her beloved Fanchon's neck and nose and even kissed her.

"I can tell you don't like Fanchon at all," Denise said with a laugh.

"She means the world to me."

"Well, none of the horses have been getting enough exercise, but they will when the weather permits. This storm has everyone on edge. I hate being cooped up in the house, and having no phone service has been a real hardship."

"Yes, if I could have called, I would have," Maddie agreed.

"You and about ten other people who have horses stabled here."

"Well, she's warm, dry, fat and sassy," Maddie said with a big smile. "I had to find out for myself."

"I understand," Denise said.

Maddie positively glowed all the way back to town. She didn't even try to find the spot where her truck and trailer were stuck, although she had a pretty good idea of the location. But once she'd seen Fanny, she'd decided that she had better return Noah's vehicle before he called the police.

Hopefully his anger—which Maddie knew must be nearly eating him alive—wouldn't have taken him that far.

Chapter Nine

Maddie pulled into the driveway of her brother's home and saw that most of the windows of the house gleamed with warm, yellowish light. Her high spirits over seeing Fanny and finally knowing for certain that the mare was in good hands deflated like a pricked balloon. Noah was inside, of course, furiously awaiting her return with an arsenal of invective.

She turned off the ignition, removed Noah's ring of keys and sat there wondering if she really was going to take her lumps, as she'd previously told herself. Taking guff from anyone, even if she was in the wrong, went so against her grain that the mere thought of meekly accepting a dressing down created what felt like a tension-filled ball of burning fire in her stomach.

But Noah had a right to *some* anger, she reasoned, striving for rationale. After all, she'd blithely driven his car right from under his nose, and she could probably never convince him that she hadn't deliberately left her purse in

the house, figuring that he would offer to go back inside
and get it. What she'd done had been completely spon-
taneous, and in all honesty she wasn't a bit sorry about
it.

If she went in with that attitude, though, Noah would
probably explode and maybe, just maybe, he had a right
to unmitigated fury. On the other hand...

Maddie's heart sank. There was no *other hand.* If someone had done to her what she'd done to Noah, she would
have notified the sheriff's department, the state patrol and
the National Guard to chase down and arrest the wretch!

Releasing a suddenly anxious breath, Maddie opened
the door and got out. She would do her best to stay cool,
no matter what Noah said to her. She held her chin high
while walking from the driveway to the house. One thing
she wouldn't do was act cowed. Nor would she go in
reeking of remorse or looking timid or cowardly.

She opened the outside door and there was Noah, eating
at the kitchen table. He turned a hard, steady gaze on her,
and she widened her eyes at him, letting him know that
she was no cupcake to be taken apart piece by piece.

"Having dinner?" she asked merely to break the ice,
at the same time dropping his keys on the table.

"Such as it is."

He sounded colder than the snow outside, and a definite
chill went up Maddie's spine. This could be worse than
she'd expected, which had been an instant attack the second she walked in. Noah obviously wasn't one of those
people who expressed anger by shouting, cussing and calling names. Oh no, *he* simmered internally, which wasn't
to say that he wouldn't let her have it in his own controlled and calculated way.

With her head still held high, Maddie left the kitchen
and went to her bedroom, where she took off her outdoor
gear and put it in her closet. Her stomach was fluttering
so wildly that it felt invaded by butterflies. She could have
handled some verbal abuse from Noah better than that

granite-like silence. Actually, she sort of felt as though her head was on the chopping block and she was waiting for the ax to fall.

Shaping a sickly smile at her reflection in the bathroom mirror, she brushed her hair and realized that she looked pretty awful. She needed a hot shower and a shampoo, and since she would rather not join Noah at the dinner table, she would bathe, put on something clean and eat later.

Noah finished his plate of warmed-up stir-fry, left over from last night, and his salad. He'd made a large salad, far too much for one person, so obviously he'd made enough for Maddie's dinner, too. He hadn't done it consciously, and it irked the hell out of him now that he would do something nice for her. She didn't deserve anything even remotely nice from him. With her self-centered personality, she probably didn't deserve anything nice from anyone!

He heard the faint but unmistakable sound of the shower and decided angrily that Maddie was planning to hide out in her room for the rest of the evening. If she thought she was going to avoid him that easily, she'd better think again.

Wearing a smoldering, tight-lipped expression, Noah cleared the table, rinsed the dishes he'd used and placed them in the dishwasher. When the kitchen was clean, he took himself to the living room, sat down and waited for the shower to stop running. In minutes it did stop and then he could hear little rustling noises—Maddie drying off, obviously, and moving around the bathroom.

The images those tiny sounds evoked in Noah's brain actually stunned him. He didn't want to picture her naked, pink and dewy from the shower, and he scowled because he couldn't think of anything else.

"Dammit!" he cried explosively, and jumped up from the chair. Striding straight to the bathroom door, he pounded on it with his fist. "I want to talk to you, so don't think you're going to tiptoe from room to room and ignore me!''

Maddie's jaw dropped. *Now* he was really mad! Why? Because she hadn't stayed in the kitchen and taken her licks like a good little girl? Holding the towel in front of her, as though he could see through the door, she yelled back, ''Cool down, sport! I don't plan on doing any tiptoeing because of you. I certainly hope you're not thinking that I'm afraid to face you!''

''Oh, yeah, I forgot that you're not afraid of anything!''

''You've got that right, buster. Now move away from the door and let me finish up in here. I'll be out to continue this exhilarating discussion in about ten minutes.''

''See that you are!'' Walking away, Noah felt good about having had the last word.

Maddie was steamed, and not just from the shower. ''You arrogant jackass,'' she muttered toward the door. ''You just declared war, and if war is what you want, war is what you're going to get. I guarantee you'll say uncle before I do.'' Quickly she finished drying off, then brushed her wet hair back from her face and applied moisturizer. However furious a woman was, there were some things she couldn't ignore, things like moisturizer. And, in Maddie's case, antibiotic ointment.

She also took the time to hang up her wet towels, then, wrapped in the terry robe she kept on the bathroom door, she picked up the clothes she'd worn all day and left the bathroom. She nearly stumbled when she saw Noah standing in the hall near her bedroom door, with his back to the wall and his arms folded belligerently across his chest.

''Oh, honestly,'' she spat, and gave him the most disgusted look she could muster as she went past him and into her room. It gave her great pleasure to slam the door really hard, and, in fact, she hoped the blast set his head to ringing.

''You child!'' Noah yelled.

''You jerk!'' she yelled back.

"At least I'm not a car thief!"

Maddie was wounded through and through, and her only defense was fury. She went to the door, yanked it open so she could kill him with a look and said acridly, "No, you're worse. You're a damned buttinsky! Did you ever hear *me* ask you to butt into my life and business?"

"I heard your brother ask me, you...you thieving in-grate!"

"I'm not a thief!" Maddie screeched so loudly that her throat hurt. She tried to give the door another killer slam but Noah caught it and held it open. "Take your hands off my door," she shrieked.

"Good Lord, the good citizens of Billings are probably covering their ears," Noah said disgustedly.

Ruffled and somewhat embarrassed over screeching like a fishwife, Maddie drew a breath and spoke with more dignity. "Take your hands off my door, *please.*"

"That's much better," Noah said with so much male superiority that Maddie had to physically stop herself from scratching out his eyes. His blue, blue eyes that she'd admired far too many times, even during moments of intense resentment for his overbearing tactics.

She tossed her head instead and said with stinging sarcasm, "Believe me, your approval or *dis*approval of anything I might do or say means zip to me, so why don't you save your breath and my time and go do something for someone who gives a damn. Interfere in someone else's life, for a change."

"You don't give a damn? And you're proud of that? What in hell kind of person are you? Dr. Herrera was expecting us at four. I happen to value my reputation as a man of his word, although you probably don't even know the meaning of that concept. It's damned apparent you don't live by it, in any case."

Maddie's face flamed. It was always the truth that hurt the most, and the truth as Noah had just spelled it out was a sorry state of affairs. She'd never considered herself a thoughtless, selfish person, but that was precisely how she'd behaved today. What she'd done was terrible! She really was a thief and…and she was untrustworthy and ungrateful.

Maddie felt so awful about the whole thing that she was about to apologize with genuine sincerity when Noah said, with his eyes piercing holes in her, "Maybe you're totally self-centered because you live without a man."

Instead of the lovely apology she'd been about to deliver, she coldly asked, "Are you mentally deranged or merely obtuse? My God, you're a doctor! Did some moronic professor during your training actually lead you to believe that a woman can't function normally without having a man under her feet?"

"I was referring more to your not having a man in your bed than having one under your feet," Noah drawled.

"Oh, of course, you probably have a woman in *your* bed every night. How could I ever doubt it? And I'm sure you're a magnificent lover and every female in Whitehorn is waiting in line for her turn to sample the great Dr. Martin's technique." Maddie curled her lip. "Give me a break. You're just another man, and I don't—"

However she'd intended to finish that sentence Noah would never know, because he'd had enough of her smart-mouthed cracks. Maybe he should have run as fast as he could from Maddie's room and this house, but he grabbed her instead, pulled her up against himself and covered her lips with his in a kiss of utter and total possession.

It seemed to Maddie that her heart dropped clear to her toes. This was not how arguments ended! Arguments ended with vows to never speak to each other again and slammed doors. She *should* scratch out his eyes, and maybe she would if he ever got done kissing her!

But, oh, my, it did feel so…so… Maddie's thoughts drifted away as passion started sending waves of pleasurable yearning throughout her system. No one had ever kissed her in the same feverish, hungry way that Noah did, neither had she ever responded to another man as she did with Noah. She slid her arms up around his neck and kissed him back with all of the fire contained in her hot little body.

When Maddie's mood changed, Noah lost every connection with the real world. One thing mattered and *only* one, and he held Maddie's face in his hands and kissed her eyelids, her nose, her lips, again and again. Then he again enclosed her in a fiery embrace and concentrated solely on her mouth, which was without a doubt the sexiest, most sinful mouth he'd *ever* kissed.

Needing air, he broke their chain of kisses to grab a breath, and he gasped out, "You're driving me crazy. Do you know that?"

Maddie was breathing hard. "I know that I can say the same about you."

He looked at her long and hard, then said huskily, "Can you, Maddie, can you really?"

"Yes," she whispered, and traced the contours of his lips with her fingertips. "What's this power you have over me, Doc?"

"You're kidding around again."

"Maybe so, but who started this and how should I look at it? You're just fooling around, too, aren't you? I mean, there's nothing serious going on here, is there?"

Noah's jaw clenched for a moment, then he said gruffly, "That's a pretty tough question."

"Yes, isn't it?" Maddie murmured just before he kissed her again. She sighed and gave in completely. This time she wasn't going to halt anything. She wanted Dr. Know-It-All to make love to her, and since it was the very first time she'd wanted sex with such fervor, she knew in her soul that it would be a very special event.

So maybe this wasn't remotely serious for either of them, but it *was* imperative. And since nothing had ever seemed so necessary before, Maddie saw no good reason to play coy about it.

"Take me to bed," she whispered.

Noah was in no condition to refuse. Not that a refusal was lurking anywhere in his overheated brain. He was hard enough to break, and aching was part and parcel of that degree of arousal. Still, he was mindful of her injuries, and instead of swinging her up into his arms, as he would have liked to do, he led her to the bed. His eyes were hot and dark while he untied the sash of her robe and slid it from her shoulders.

"You're beautiful, Maddie," he said in a hoarse, unnatural voice.

"That's nice to hear, even if it isn't true."

"You're even going to argue with me about that?" He clasped his hands on each of her shoulders and looked deeply into her eyes. "Do you take umbrage with everything everyone says to you, or am I the unfortunate exception?"

She returned his gaze without blinking. "That's another tough question, Dr. Honey-Bear. Are you sure you want to delve into the answer right now, because I'd just as soon do something else. Later, of course, we can get ourselves into another lather and fight the night away."

Noah couldn't help laughing. "If I'm a honey bear, then you're my honey."

"Well, that's debatable. Or let's just agree for the time being that I'm your honey but that label isn't a permanent fixture." Maddie began unbuttoning his shirt. "You've had the advantage long enough, Dr. Way-Too-Handsome. I'm standing here stark naked and you've got on layers of clothing. Let's get rid of it."

Noah felt happiness bubble up within him, a joyful excitement that included the desire racking his body but also encompassed a sense of youthful exuberance, which, he was positive, he hadn't felt in years. He wasn't old—thirty-five wasn't old, was it?—but he'd been living as though anything fun, funny or even slightly enjoyable was ancient history. In spite of her larcenous streak Maddie was fun, and she was funny, even when she wasn't trying to be.

She was also sexy, brazen and comfortable in her own skin, and he particularly liked that she could stand naked before him without embarrassment. Grinning, he started helping her undress him.

His rush to get naked didn't surprise Maddie, but the devilish little grin on his face did. He was so stunningly handsome that Maddie's head swam. People always said that beauty was only skin deep, and that might be precisely the case with Noah Martin, but it gave Maddie such pleasure to look at him that she really didn't care—not at that particular moment, at any rate. Maybe she'd care in the morning, maybe she'd be sick-to-her-stomach sorry in the morning, but right then, doing her finest to rid him of every garment covering his buff, sexy body, she had neither wish nor will to bring this to a screeching halt.

Noah threw back the covers of her bed. Together they lay down and then Noah pulled the covers over them. They snuggled and cuddled and kissed. Their desire grew with each caress, and Maddie couldn't keep quiet to save her soul. At first her sounds were tiny whimpers, but then they changed to moans that became louder and louder until anyone in the house would have heard her.

But considering the incredible sensations that Noah was arousing within her with his hand between her legs, she couldn't help herself.

"You...you know everything about...a woman...because you're a doctor," she gasped.

"I think most men know what pleasures a woman."

Maddie almost told him that he was wrong about that, but she really didn't want to invite any sort of discussion or even a comment about other men who might have shared her bed. But he *was* wrong. The men in her past—few as they'd been—certainly hadn't known what Dr. Nimble Fingers did about a woman's anatomy. How could a woman not love a man with Noah's expertise?

"Kiss me," she whispered raggedly. "Kiss me and never stop kissing me."

Noah obliged her with a long, hot, wet and passionately hungry kiss. She might be very appreciative of his knowledgeable caresses, but her hand encircling his manhood was bringing him to the brink very quickly. This time he was better prepared, and he broke away from her just long enough to reach to the floor and into a pocket of his pants.

Then he took care of business in two seconds flat and moved on top of her. Kissing her breasts, pacing himself as best he could so this would end as it should—he wanted her as satisfied as he knew he would be—he then kissed her mouth again. The sexy moans coming from deep in her throat increased the pressure building in his body. Sliding into her, joining their straining bodies intimately nearly finished him off, and he gritted his teeth and didn't move a muscle to maintain some self-control.

Maddie moved, though. She couldn't lie still with him inside her. He filled her so completely, and her need for fulfillment was bittersweet agony.

"Why did you stop?" she whispered.

"Had to or it would have been over before it began."

"Oh...I see."

"I doubt it. Just believe that it's been a while for me and let it go at that, okay?"

"Hmm," she murmured, extremely curious about Noah's statement. A man like him going without didn't seem possible. Were the women in Whitehorn blind? They didn't used to be. Maddie remembered her growing-up years very well, and Montana gals sure hadn't been shy in those days.

"Maddie, help me out here. Lie still, just for a minute or so," Noah groaned.

"I can't lie still. It feels so good and I need...I need... well, you know what I need. You need the same thing, don't you?"

"You are driving me crazy! Yes, I need the same thing,

but you're not going to get what you need if I don't take a short breather.''

Maddie's response to that observation was to slowly but steadily lift and lower her hips. ''Sorry,'' she whispered, ''but I can't help it.''

Groaning, Noah gave up and began moving with her. ''You are hotter than Hades,'' he growled in her ear. ''Hot and tight. Perfect…so damned perfect.''

''*You're* perfect,'' she panted. ''Big and hot and perfect. Oh, Noah, I—I've never…felt so much before.''

He covered her chatty little mouth with his own and kissed her senseless. Himself, as well. When they reached the pinnacle and cried out, they each realized it had happened at the same time, something of a miracle for first-time lovers.

In the afterglow of the most spectacular lovemaking of Maddie's life, she lay in Noah's arms. ''That was very special for me,'' she whispered after pressing a loving kiss to his chest.

It had been special for Noah, too, but he couldn't quite bring himself to say so. In truth he wasn't entirely contented, not in the same way that Maddie was. Oh, he was sexually satisfied, immensely so, in fact, but he didn't want Maddie thinking that what they'd just done together meant more than it did. She was acting all lovey-dovey and would probably swoon if he talked about how incredible it had really been for him.

What he was, he finally realized, was confused, addled. He had absolutely no intentions of falling in love, planning a wedding, et cetera, et cetera—God knew that one turn at bat in *that* ball field was enough for any man—but he would bet anything that Maddie's brain was full of romantic hearts and flowers, and that really concerned him. After all, Maddie was a country girl at heart, however much she'd traveled around because of her work.

In spite of so much concern, he couldn't deny that he'd connected with Maddie in a remarkable way. It would be damned tough to chalk this up to a one-night stand and never touch her again, especially when he already wanted her again. She was a sweet bundle of warm and pliable femininity all wrapped around him real cozy-like, and of course he wanted her again. The alternative was to get out of her bed, her brother's house and Maddie's life. If he stayed where he was, he was going to wear them both out.

No, he thought adamantly, he wasn't. He could never undo what had already occurred, but he was not going to compound one sin with repetition.

Stirring, he untangled himself from Maddy, turned on the bed and sat up with his feet on the floor.

Maddie lay there, wide-eyed and bewildered. She felt Noah's emotional withdrawal in her heart, her soul, and it struck her painfully and without mercy that while their lovemaking had been perfect and beautiful for her, it had disappointed him. *She* had disappointed him. After all, what did she know about pleasing a man?

"I—I'm sorry," she whispered, misery in every syllable.

"No, *I'm* sorry," Noah said gruffly, and got off the bed to get dressed. He didn't look at her while he yanked on his clothes and muttered, "I can't believe my own stupidity. What in hell kind of fool have I become?"

Maddie's eyes got even bigger. "You're angry at yourself? Why, for heaven's sake?"

He sent her a brief and granite-hard glance. "I took advantage of you, that's why!"

She sat up with a jerk. "That's crazy!"

"I fully agree."

"No, you're deliberately misinterpreting what I said! I meant your attitude *now* was crazy, not...not what we did."

"Not *we*, me."

"You were crazy but I wasn't? What are you trying to

do, make yourself out to be some sort of villain because you made love to a willing woman?''

"I made love to a child!''

"That's ridiculous. I'm twenty-three years old!''

"I didn't mean a child in terms of age.''

Maddie's mouth hung open while she digested the worst insult of her entire life. She wasn't good enough for Noah Martin, not intellectual enough or educated enough or sophisticated enough. Probably not pretty enough, either.

"You jerk,'' she croaked hoarsely. "Apparently you'd sleep with any woman. You proved it, so don't look all shocked and victimized because I spelled it out for you. But then, after you've had your kicks, you start judging her, and I didn't measure up, did I? With your nose-in-the-air, better-than-thou attitude, probably no woman measures up, so you're a strictly screw 'em and leave 'em guy!''

Noah felt sick to his stomach. Maddie might have a right to some anger, but she'd totally misinterpreted what *he'd* said, even while accusing him of misconstruing what *she'd* said. Actually he considered her country-girl charm vastly more desirable than the double-edged sword of sophistication with which women like Felicia skewered friends and enemies alike. But how did a man explain his kinder side to a hopping-mad woman whose blazing green eyes looked as though she'd love to destroy him on the spot?

"Forget it,'' he growled. "Just forget the whole damned thing.'' Grabbing his socks and boots off the floor he headed for the door.

"Which, I'm sure, you'll have no trouble doing! But some of us humans have a heart, you cold-blooded rat!''

Grim-lipped, Noah turned and looked at her. "Think about this. I could have led you on…and on…and on. Throughout the night without question and probably every damned day that you're in town. But I couldn't do it, not because of me, you ungrateful little witch, but because I didn't want you hurt. Are you capable of understanding that concept? I'd bet a million bucks that you—after making love only once—were up to your eyeballs in dreamy, romantic, candlelit scenarios. Where in hell would you end up after a whole night of lovemaking?''

Maddie forced herself to laugh, because it was either laugh or cry, for her. ''You have an ego problem, Dr. Ain't-I-Just-the-Cat's-Meow-in-Bed. I hope you're not laboring under the misconception that you were the best lover I've had, 'cause, Doc, it's just not true. Oh, you were pretty good, but the best? No way. So, my advice is to get over yourself and stop thinking that you could have had me throughout the night.'' Maddie forced another laugh. ''Frankly, I was starting to get bored…and quite sleepy. You saved me the trouble of kicking you out of my bed without hurting your sensitive little feelings. Oh, sorry, I forgot. You don't have any.''

Lying down again, Maddie turned to her side with her back to Noah. ''Please turn off the light before you go,'' she said. It was her final shot because she was tightly scrunching her eyes to keep them from spilling tears, and she didn't know how much longer she could fool Noah into thinking that she was tough and hard and as worthy an opponent as he'd ever run into. She was an independent soul, and she'd learned long ago how to take care of herself, but trading insults with a man she'd fallen pretty hard for—proving it to herself if not to him only minutes ago—hurt like the very devil.

The lights went off, relieving some of Maddie's anxiety, and then the room was completely silent, so Noah had apparently left quietly. She let the dam break then, and her tears drenched her pillow.

Noah sat in the living room with his boots next to his chair. He hurt all over. Maddie had been cruel, and he might have deserved some of the things she'd said but not all of them. She didn't know his past and she didn't know that he hadn't taken one woman to bed since moving to Whitehorn. To the contrary, she believed that he was a womanizer and would sleep with anything in skirts. Worse than that, she believed that he judged his bed partners. She was positive that he'd judged her and found her lacking!

He sighed heavily, despondently. He might not have been jumping-up-and-down happy before meeting Maddie Kincaid, but he'd carved himself out a routine in Whitehorn that had seemed reasonably satisfying. Now he knew the truth. He hadn't been contented or satisfied at all, and his celibate lifestyle had been a mistake—a very big mistake.

Well, it seemed pretty clear that Maddie preferred he not be there in the morning, so he might as well go home and leave her be. She didn't respect his efforts to help her, anyhow, so why was he bothering? Look how she'd blown off that appointment with Dr. Herrera.

And she really had stolen his SUV, Noah reminded himself. She had more bloody gall than anyone he'd ever known, and why should he spend one second worrying about a person who not only didn't appreciate anything he did for her but actually resented it?

With another long sigh, Noah reached for his boots and pulled them on. It took a few minutes to gather his things and to put on his warm, outside clothing, but the moment finally came when he was ready to go.

This time he would not leave a note. After switching off the lights he'd turned on earlier while waiting for Maddie to get back with his car—he'd come very close to finding a cop or deputy sheriff and demanding she be arrested, but he'd chickened out on that for Mark's sake— he finally left. Fuming between house and driveway, he asked himself if Maddie had appreciated his generosity in not bringing the law down on her treacherous head and answered out loud, "Not one damn bit." It irritated him still that she'd come waltzing into the house as though she hadn't done a thing wrong.

But he was worse than Maddie when it came right down to it. He was a sap and a sucker. When she got back he should have run, not walked but run, to his car and driven away as fast as he could under the icy conditions. Instead he'd hung around just aching to tell her off, and then when he had the chance to really give her hell he'd stupidly made a pass!

Reaching his vehicle, he suddenly realized something. It was no longer snowing, and a warm wind was blowing. It's a Chinook, he thought and lifted his face to the pleasant warmth on his skin. Chinooks were warm, dry winds that descended the eastern slopes of the Rocky Mountains. Sometimes they could be dangerously powerful and knocked down trees and anything else in their paths, but normally they were like this one was, a delight that warmed winter-burned skin and melted mountains of snow and ice in record time.

Of course, if a Chinook was too warm it melted the snow too fast and caused flooding. This one felt just about right to Noah, warm but not dangerous. The snow would be about half-gone by morning, and if the Chinook continued throughout tomorrow, Whitehorn would be pretty much snow free and back to normal. No one would be sorry about that, Noah thought as he climbed into his SUV.

He started the engine, then sat there and looked at the house. He wished to God that he hadn't laid a finger on Maddie, but the empty hole in his gut was proof of the futility of wishing for the impossible. He'd done a lot more than lay a finger on Mark's sister, and he wondered if he'd be able to ever look the man in the eye again.

Slapping the shifting lever in reverse, he backed from the driveway and drove away.

Inside, crying into her wet pillow, Maddie thought

about how fragile and easily hearts were broken. Hers felt totally and irreparably shattered.

"I hate him...I hate him," she sobbed, and then despised herself because it wasn't true. She didn't hate Noah Martin—Dr. Jerk-of-the-Year—she *loved* him!

"No-o-o-o," she moaned, because how could she be so traitorous to herself with such a self-destructive thought?

She *didn't* love him, she couldn't!

Chapter Ten

Maddie didn't have to hear Noah leave to know he was gone. She was so down in the dumps over their ridiculous argument that she couldn't sleep soundly all night. He'd hurt her feelings beyond belief, but she'd been even more hateful than he'd been, she decided morosely. Her own conscience kept tweaking her awake and then it would be almost an hour of self-castigation before she fell asleep again. The only pleasant thing about the night was the wind, which she recognized as a Chinook from memories going clear back to childhood.

When she was up and dressed the next morning, the extraordinary changes in the landscape were uplifting, even if little else was. The snow was rapidly disappearing, and icicles hung and dripped from every roof. The sun was shining, the sky was blue, and Maddie stepped outside to test the temperature for herself. It was a beautiful day, warmish with a fresh tang and very breezy, but the blizzard, thank heavens, was definitely over.

She was still outside when the phone rang. Elation that the phone service had been at last restored rushed through her as she hurried inside to answer the kitchen extension with an excited "Hello!"

"Maddie? Maddie Kincaid?"

"Yes, this is she."

"This is Ralph Burroughs with the county sheriff's department. We had a call about a truck and trailer stuck in the snow out on county road 34. The rig was locked, but we ran the plates and your name came up as owner. You must be Mark's sister. Heard you were in town."

"Of course you did," Maddie said with a laugh. "If Whitehorn is the same as it used to be, everyone in town has heard I'm here."

"Well, you used to play with my kids. That was before you moved in with your aunt June. Do you remember Sissy and Thad Burroughs?"

"Yes, I do. As a matter of fact, I remember you and Mrs. Burroughs. How is everyone?"

"Fine, real fine. Both the kids are married. Sissy lives in Great Falls and Thad's all involved with computers and lives in California. My wife was getting a little stir crazy once the kids left home, so she went out and got herself a job at the bank. I'll be sure and tell them all I talked to you. You're somewhat of a celebrity, you know."

"Hardly," Maddie said with another laugh.

"Well, you're the town's biggest rodeo star, Maddie. Lots of folks put rodeo right up there with football and making movies, you know."

"That's very nice to hear, thank you."

"Maddie, what happened to your truck and trailer? Were you in an accident during the blizzard? Was another vehicle involved?"

"No one else was involved, and it really wasn't an accident…not what one normally thinks of as a road accident, anyhow. To be perfectly honest, Mr. Burroughs, I was out driving when I shouldn't have been. Before Mark and Darcy left for Europe, Mark boarded my horse at the Braddock stables. Since I knew nothing about the Braddocks or their facilities, I decided to drive out there and check on Fanny. I couldn't have picked a worse time to do it. The blizzard was so bad I couldn't see where the road ended and the fields began. To make a long story short, I missed the curve, drove straight into that grove of trees and got my truck stuck."

"Were you hurt?"

"Just my pride, Mr. Burroughs, just my pride."

Ralph chuckled in her ear. "You still have your sense of humor, I see. You were a funny little kid, always cutting up and making your little friends laugh. You were a good kid, though. I don't recall your ever getting into trouble."

"You're right, I was a good kid. Aunt June thought so, anyhow. I was so lucky to have her."

"She was a good woman, Maddie."

"The best," Maddie said softly.

"Okay, let's get down to business. I've got Joe Mahoney and his tow truck all lined up to get your truck out of that pickle it's in, but he'd like to have a key to the door and ignition. Can I send him by?"

"Oh, yes, please do. I'll write him a check to pay for his time and equipment, Mr. Burroughs. I really appreciate this. Isn't the weather today just grand?"

"We're having typical Montana weather, Maddie. A ferocious blizzard one day and sunshine the next. Nothing surprises us Montanans, does it?"

"Not much," she agreed. "I'll watch for Joe."

"Talk to you later, Maddie."

"Thanks, Mr. Burroughs."

Maddie was high as a kite by the time she hung up. She felt good—except for that weird little pain that shot through her left knee every so often—she was getting her truck and trailer back sometime today, and the weather had done a complete turnabout. Other than the foolish mistake she'd made last night with Noah…?

"Oh, damn," she whispered, wishing for a lapse of memory as far as last night and Noah Martin went. She might have gone too far in telling him off, but he was a heartless opportunist, and she would wager her soul that Mark believed in and trusted Noah completely. Knowing Mark as she did, she was positive that he would not have asked Noah to look in on her if he'd heard even one word of gossip about his friend being a wolf in sheep's clothing.

Frowning suddenly, Maddie plopped into one of the chairs around the table, struck by the piercing accuracy of that conclusion. If there had ever been the slightest hint of gossip about Noah and women, Mark would not have asked him to check on her!

Groaning, Maddie rested her head on the back of the chair and stared at the ceiling. What in heaven's name should she believe about Noah? If he was a womanizer, then he was managing to do something very few people did in a small town—keep his personal life a secret.

But if he wasn't that sort of man, what was he, and why had he chosen her to help him tarnish an apparently spotless reputation?

All day long, every time Noah thought of yesterday's session in Maddie's bed, their lovemaking seemed hotter and more erotic. Thoughts of that sort were very damaging to his stolid, unsmiling, dedicated physician's countenance. In truth, it was difficult for him to keep his mind where it belonged—on whichever patient he was treating. They had come in droves today, and Noah didn't have the time for a real lunch break. He ate a sandwich on the run, a bite here, a bite there, and caught himself wondering far too often if Maddie was all right.

It was almost seven when the last patient left, and Noah slumped in his desk chair. He was tired and would have liked to go directly home, but he still had to visit some patients in the hospital, and only when that very important duty was behind him could he call it a day.

Wondering wryly why he'd grown up thinking that a doctor's life just had to be the greatest career in the world, never once realizing that a doctor's work was never done, Noah stretched and yawned.

He knew the phones were working again because they hadn't stopped ringing all day. Until now, that is. With everyone else gone, his medical quarters were quiet and peaceful, and he really would have liked to stretch out on the couch in his office and catch a nap. But a short nap wouldn't do it, and if he fell asleep now, he'd never come to enough to make his hospital rounds.

And so he sat at his desk, stared at the telephone and thought once again about last night and Maddie. What if she *wasn't* okay? He was her doctor—however many times she'd bristled over that idea—which made him responsible for her well-being.

The very word *responsible* and the knowledge of how far he'd strayed ethically were tough nuts to swallow. After all, he'd done the unthinkable—slept with a patient—and he could lose his license to practice medicine over that one foolish mistake. The AMA and the Montana State Medical Association gave lecherous physicians very little sympathy, and if Maddie should take a notion to file a complaint against him, his goose would be cooked.

Even with that appalling fate hanging over his head, Noah couldn't forget his promise to Mark. Not that Mark would thank him for making love to his sister—if he ever found out about it, of course—but putting that aspect of the mess he'd created himself aside for the moment, Noah still felt bound by that promise. After all, Mark had left town believing that Maddie was in good hands.

Of course, he'd also believed that Maddie was much better off than she'd really been. The little fake had deliberately misled her brother into thinking she was fine, when she hadn't been fine at all. Okay, so she'd lied for an unselfish reason, so Mark wouldn't cancel his honeymoon and stay home to care for her. But that was probably the first unselfish thing Maddie Kincaid had ever done!

Weary of trying to figure out Maddie—easily the most confusing woman he'd ever known—Noah left his office and walked the short distance to the hospital. The Chinook was still blowing, and the night air was delightfully warm on his face. Noah recalled the first time he'd witnessed the Chinook phenomenon. His second winter in Whitehorn had been harsh and bitter, and after a two-week stretch of almost constant snowfall, he'd awakened during a night to a strong wind that sounded different from any he'd ever heard.

He'd been astounded in the morning to see that a good four feet of snow—on the level—had shrunk by half. Later someone had told him what to call that rather eerie, warm wind; it was a Chinook, and the person had been happy to explain how it developed on the eastern slopes of the Rockies. ''But that's what the scientists and weather experts claim,'' the fellow had added with a teasing, tongue-in-cheek grin and then delivered more information. It seemed that some of the area's Native Americans still believed that the magical warm wind was a gift from the gods.

Noah gave his head a wry little shake as he later entered the hospital, thinking that he had some truly down-to-earth problems to deal with. Maddie couldn't be more of a dilemma, nor could the topsy-turvy feelings he had for and about her. One thing he'd stated to her last night actually said it all: she was driving him crazy!

Noah's rounds at the hospital only took about an hour. Driving home he was glad to see that the restaurants were open again, and he stopped at the China House for some takeout as he was too done in to even think about cooking dinner for himself. Then, just before ordering, he wondered if Maddie had felt well enough today to cook anything, and he found himself ordering enough for two.

Carrying a large sack of what he knew to be delicious Chinese food, he returned to his car and headed for Mark's house. He gaped when he got there because Maddie's white truck was parked in the driveway!

If she'd managed that on her own today, she certainly must have felt well enough to fix herself something to eat, he thought, feeling a little silly over buying far more Chinese food than he could eat himself. Besides, she wasn't apt to receive him with a smile, not after everything that had occurred between them last night. That thought caused Noah to heave a long, confused sigh. Why couldn't he just put her out of his mind once and for all?

Well he'd bought far more food than he could eat, he had it with him and he was there. He might as well ask Maddie if she wanted to eat with him, even though it was getting late and odds were that she'd had dinner hours ago. Then, too, if she started yelling the second she saw him, he could turn around and hightail it out of the house, but there was a slim chance that she wouldn't. It was possible, after all, that she had some regrets about last night, same as him. At least he was big enough to try to make amends. The rest, of course, would be up to her.

Feeling rather charitable for forgiving Maddie's insults last night and offering her another chance to appreciate his steadfast fidelity for a promise made, Noah got out of his rig, took the sack of food, strode to the kitchen door and knocked. Nothing happened. He knocked again, then tried the knob. The door wasn't locked and he stuck his head in and called, "Maddie?"

Either she wasn't there or she didn't plan on seeing him in any capacity. Frowning, Noah stood on the stoop and pondered the situation. If she really didn't want to see him and was, say, waiting somewhere in the house for him to take the hint and leave, then he shouldn't just walk in. Not now. Not like he'd done before. Things weren't the same as they'd been the first time he'd walked into this house uninvited.

Deciding to just leave, Noah turned, and that was when he saw Maddie's trailer behind the garage again—very similar to the first time that had happened—only this time the windows all glowed with light. That was where Maddie was, inside her trailer!

Noah left the stoop and walked toward the trailer. The Chinook rattled the sack in his arms as well as the leafless limbs of the trees in Mark's yard, creating sounds that could be construed as eerie if one were so inclined. Noah wasn't. He was deeply focused on Maddie and how she would take his dropping in again—even though he'd decided only minutes ago that she might appreciate an opportunity to dispel the painfully negative aspects of last night—although he was unquestionably aware of the hard, gusting wind at the same time. How could he not be when it was tossing his hair and tearing at his clothes?

Rounding the front of the trailer, he reached its entrance door, paused for a breath to appease the sudden spurt of nervousness that gave him a serious jolt, admitted in his heart of hearts that maybe he *shouldn't* be here again tonight and then forced himself to knock. He could hear movement inside, and his pulse rate increased dramatically. Then there was the closing of a drawer or something and light footsteps, and finally the door was pushed open and electric light spilled out. Maddie regarded him with a solemn, emotionless expression, Noah saw with intense relief. At least she didn't look to be on the verge of braining him.

"Hi," Noah said quietly. "I've got a ton of Chinese food here. How about helping me eat it?"

Although Maddie loved Chinese food, she didn't jump for joy over one more of Noah's nervy intrusions. And yet, as much as she hated facing it, some secret place within her erupted with joy over seeing him again. It was an odd sort of joy, however, as this exact moment was undeniable proof of the ambiguity she'd suffered all day because of this man. She knew in her soul that any relationship with Noah, including simple friendship, would be complicated and uncompromising because *he* was complicated and uncompromising.

And still she was glad to see him. She wilted internally when she realized that she just might be starting to understand both of them, and it was always scary when a woman realized that she could be falling for a man whose only feelings for her were below his belt.

"How about it?" Noah asked, wondering what in devil was happening behind her gorgeous green eyes. Obviously, she was doing some heavy-duty thinking, but how much mental mauling did a simple invitation to eat Chinese food require? "The China House puts out great food," he added, hoping to whet her appetite.

Maddie delayed giving him an answer for another few moments, during which she lamented his stunning good looks. Along with that, did he have to *exude* sex appeal? Put simply, Dr. Noah Martin was a lot for her to cope with, especially when she recalled how easily he'd seduced her last night. Was she dimwitted enough to play with fire again after getting burned once? Lord above, she wasn't hoping for a rematch, was she?

No way! In fact, she would just love for him to make another pass so she could put him in his place once and for all.

Oh, yeah. That possibility and its accompanying imagery were just too inviting to pass up. There was that ambiguity again, she realized. She was glad to see him and would still love the chance to slap him down to size! Noah wasn't the only complicated person in this part of the world, obviously.

In the next instant Maddie felt drained. She couldn't think of anything worse than another mean-minded fight with Noah Martin or anyone else. As for slapping him down to size, or putting him in his place, she simply didn't have the heart or the energy for either. And so she gathered all of her best emotional components and became the grown-up that she'd been before meeting Dr. Noah Martin.

"I love Chinese food. Come on in," she said with such cool self-confidence that she mentally patted herself on the back.

Noah was both surprised by and appreciative of her poise, and he climbed the two steps into the trailer, noting that Maddie squeezed herself against the wall so he wouldn't brush against her on his way in. Her behavior was fine with him, for he wasn't there to pressure, lure or sweet-talk her into anything. While she pulled the door closed, he set the sack on the dinette table.

"There are chopsticks in the sack, but I'd rather have a fork," he said, speaking casually so she would understand that he was in exactly the same place that she was, as far as anything even remotely personal went between them. There remained a question in his mind about whether he'd done any pressuring last night—it seemed to him as though the responsibility for last night's affair should be divided equally—but Maddie could think he'd come back for more lovemaking and that simply wasn't the case. "Would you happen to have a fork or two out here?"

Maddie gave him an incredulous look. "What do you think I eat with, ice cream or swizzle sticks? I *live* in this trailer."

Noah frowned slightly. "You told me that before, didn't you?"

"I believe I did. Do you doubt it?" Maddie went into a drawer for some cutlery and paper napkins. "You're ordinarily so positive about everything that I find it hard to believe you would ever doubt your own memory."

Noah tried to study her on the sly while taking the cartons of food from the sack. He'd admired Maddie's aplomb only moments ago, but had it all been an act? Was she as angry with him tonight as she'd been last night and pretending—or trying to pretend—that everything was forgotten and fine?

"Actually, Maddie, I'm not positive about much of anything where you're concerned."

Maddie was laying out the napkins and forks. She looked up from the table and straight into Noah's eyes. "Now why on earth would you be positive about everything else and uncertain about me?" she asked with a slightly disdainful toss of her head as she returned to her cabinets for two plates and some large spoons.

"You don't quite believe me, do you?" Noah took off his jacket and then didn't know what to do with it in this small place.

"Put it on the bed," Maddie told him. "It's through that door."

Noah walked through the door and found himself in an efficiently planned bathroom. That small room opened onto the bedroom, and he saw a good-size bed bearing a soft-looking blue comforter with matching pillowcases and what appeared to be a long closet behind mirrored doors. Laying his jacket on the bed, he hurried back to the kitchen area of the trailer.

"This is really nice," he said sincerely. "It has everything."

"Yes, I'm very comfortable traveling and calling this home. Sit down. Everything's ready."

Noah slid into one side of the dining booth, and Maddie took the other side. They both took servings from the cartons, then began eating.

"Oh!" Maddie exclaimed. "Would you like something to drink? I shopped today, so there's milk, iced tea and soft drinks. And water, of course."

"I'll have the tea, thanks," Noah said.

Maddie got up for the tea and two glasses. Seated again, she began eating. "This *is* good Chinese," she said. "You called the restaurant the China House?"

"Yes. It's over on Third Street, near the bowling alley. Apparently it wasn't there when you lived here."

"No, it wasn't."

They ate without speaking a while, then Noah said, "You didn't answer my question, Maddie."

"What question?"

"I asked if you believed that I wasn't positive about anything where you're concerned."

She shrugged. "It shouldn't matter if I do or do not believe that."

"No, I guess it shouldn't." Noah gave her a long look. "I say things to you that sometimes don't make a whole lot of sense."

"You do things that don't make much sense, either."

"If you're talking about last night, you did everything I did."

"Except treat you like Typhoid Mary after it was over," she said flatly.

Noah was appalled. "Maddie, if I did that I'm more sorry than I can say!"

"You did worse than that, Noah. You said you'd made love to a child and you weren't talking about age!"

He looked regretful and rather helpless. "You're so young."

"You're hardly ancient," she retorted.

"I'm thirty-five."

"Okay, so you're twelve years older than I am, but that wasn't at the heart of what you said last night. I know I'm not educated the way you are, and I have no doubt at all that you've lived a much different life than I have. But I don't deserve any slams over our differences."

"You're right, you don't, and I swear I didn't mean what I said the way you took it. Maddie, you convey the kind of innocence that vanishes with time. Hell, I sure don't have that quality anymore, and neither do most people my age. Every year takes its toll on a person, and so does every bad experience."

Maddie laid down her fork and took a drink of tea before saying, "You've hinted at having had a bad experience before."

Noah looked surprised because he truly believed that he'd never given anyone in Whitehorn so much as a dram of personal information. "I have?" he asked doubtfully. "Are you sure?"

"I didn't make it up, Doc."

Noah grinned. "See? A comeback like that is exactly what I meant when I said you possessed a charming innocence."

"You said the word *charming?* No, I don't think you did."

"All right, I'm saying it now."

"Let's put my 'charming innocence' on hold for a few minutes while you tell me about your bad experience," Maddie said. "Only a suggestion, of course, but I'm naturally nosy, and I would love to hear what caused that sourpuss expression you usually walk around with."

"Thanks for sharing that complimentary opinion," he retorted dryly. "Does my heart good to be put down every so often."

"Was that a put-down?" Maddie deliberately shaped a thoughtful, speculative expression on her face, then said, "Maybe it made you feel sort of the way I felt last night when you told me I wasn't good enough for you."

"My God, I never said that!"

"I'll forget you *did* say it if you tell me about your bad experience."

"Maddie, I never said you weren't good enough for me. Do you think I run around the country sleeping with women whom I truly believe don't come up to my standards?"

Maddie put her elbow on the table, her chin in her hand and then batted her eyelashes at him. "Goodness, but I do like your gentlemanly manner of turning a phrase, I really do." Again her eyelashes fluttered.

"You're being silly."

"That's my charming innocence at play, Doc." Maddie dropped the act and picked up her fork. "Apparently you're not going to tell me anything about yourself, which is fine. After all, I don't really want anything from you, and it's a dead certainty that you don't want anything from me. Except for, maybe, another roll in the sack."

Shocked, Noah stared across the dinette table at her. "That's not fair, Maddie."

"Not very ladylike, either, right? Well, put this in your pipe and smoke it, Doc. I know a word that I would bet almost anything has never entered your mind."

"That's absurd."

"No, it's commitment."

"You're saying I don't know the meaning of the word *commitment?* Maddie, the little you know about me wouldn't cover the head of a pin."

She regarded him calmly. "I agree. Fix it, Doctor. Make it all better."

"Yeah, by telling you things about myself that no one in Montana knows. I happen to like my privacy, which I wouldn't have for five minutes if I told my history to even one person in this gossipy little town."

"Don't put me in that category, Noah. I may be a lot of things, but a gossip isn't one of them. Besides, I won't be around Whitehorn for very much longer."

Noah felt as though he'd just received an electrical shock. He'd known all along that her time in Whitehorn was limited—been glad of it in several memorable instances, to be honest. But at the present startling moment, envisioning the town, his work and every other facet of his life without Maddie, her problems, her brass and sass and her big green eyes caused a bleak and empty sensation in his gut. When he added the memory of last night's steamy lovemaking and then Maddie's ability to make him laugh to the mix, that empty feeling became so huge that Noah's gentler emotions—the ones that governed his tear ducts—threatened to overcome him. Deeply shaken over something so unexpected and rare as an urge to shed tears, he blinked several times and then stared numbly across the table at Maddie.

She felt the massive change in the way he was looking at her. It was as though he'd suddenly taken on a different personality and become a man she'd never met!

"Uh," she stammered. "Did I suddenly sprout horns or something? I mean, you're looking at me in a very strange way."

Noah was battling the worst emotional upheaval he'd suffered in years and asking himself what had brought on so much distress. Maddie's mentioning something he already knew seemed like a pretty lame excuse to get maudlin and self-pitying. Life would go on after Maddie Kincaid left town, after all.

But he realized that was the crux of this whole thing— life would go on. Exactly as it had been before Maddie's rather tornado-like explosion into his humdrum existence. When she was no longer around he would get up early every morning and go to work. He'd return home at night, read or watch a little TV and go to bed. When time and scheduling permitted, he would drive to the gym at the high school and work himself into a sweat with the facility's state-of-the-art exercise equipment or by taking a good long run around its indoor track.

And the really stressful part of examining his daily routine at this particular moment was that there was nothing wrong with it, other than its incompleteness. It was like a fishing line without a hook, a bow without an arrow, a road with no destination. Granted, he could blame no one but himself for what he knew now was an imperfect, inadequate way of life, but that didn't make this sudden spate of knowledge any less painful.

He cleared his throat. "You don't have the horns, I do."

Maddie's eyes widened. "Invisible horns?"

"Internal horns, Maddie. Look, if you're still interested in my past, I'm prepared to fill you in."

She regretted pushing him into this and reached across the table to touch his wrist, a simple gesture that, from her point of view, indicated remorse. "Noah, you don't have to tell me anything," she said quietly. To her intense surprise, he covered her hand with his own.

"Touching you wasn't a pass," she said.

"Neither is my touching you at this moment," Noah said. "I don't know how you did it…or maybe I just don't know the whys and what-fors of the whole thing…but you've changed me."

Their gazes locked. "And just how did I do that?" she asked softly.

"By being you, I suppose."

"Just by being my own charming, innocent self, I changed you into…into what, Noah?"

"You're not taking me seriously."

Maddie pulled her hand back and sat up straighter. "Do you *want* me to take you seriously?" There was intensity in his eyes that shook her foundation. "I…I guess I don't know what's going on here." Her voice wasn't altogether steady, but she'd not seen this side of Noah before, and it unnerved her.

Noah's gaze never strayed from her face. "Would you like to know? I think I would. Maddie, it's obvious that neither of us really understands why we did what we did last night. And I sure as hell don't comprehend my behavior—" Noah paused to clear his throat again, proving to Maddie that he was as unnerved as she was by this discussion "—after it was over."

"I comprehend it. You so regretted seducing me that your only recourse was cruelty."

"You're not really putting all the blame for last night on me, are you? I didn't seduce you. The whole thing was by mutual consent and, uh, participation. Maddie, you were hot to trot. No more so than I was, but then I'm willing to share the responsibility and you're not.''

Maddie's face flamed. "Could you be any cruder? I was *not* hot to trot! I've never been hot to trot in my life.''

"Damn it, don't fly off the handle over semantics. Maddie, any way we look at it, or whatever either of us calls it, you can't deny that we were hot for each other last night.''

She tore her gaze from his. "Let's change the subject. You said you were ready to talk about your past, so I— I'm ready to listen.''

Noah drew a long breath. He'd said it all right, but was he really ready to talk to anyone about Felicia? But he'd been truthful when he'd said that he would like to know what was happening between him and Maddie, and maybe the place to start that learning process was years in his past.

"All right,'' he said in a very low but not completely controlled voice. "I'll talk about myself, but I'd like you to do the same. Will you?''

"I have no deep dark secrets, Noah, but if you'd like to hear all about the adventures of a rodeo queen, I'll bare my soul.''

"You're making fun of me.''

"No, I'm making fun of *me!* Heavens, don't you have a funny bone? Didn't you catch my 'rodeo queen' reference?''

"Are you a rodeo queen? I mean, I've never even attended a rodeo. I'm not sure what a rodeo queen is.''

Maddie shook her head in exaggerated dismay. "You poor dear. Obviously your education was sorely lacking in fun and excitement. Promise me one thing. There are rodeos all over Montana during good weather. Go and see one this spring. Do you think you can do that?''

"To hear you talk, I might even enjoy it.''

"You will, I guarantee it. Now, let's finish eating while you tell me all about Noah Martin.'' Maddie looked across the table and into his eyes once again. "I really am interested, Noah."

The fact that he honestly believed her—a surprise in itself—loosened Noah's tongue, and he began talking.

Chapter Eleven

Noah began his narration with a brief reference to having had "loving and affluent parents." By the time Noah had reached his middle teens, his father had owned a chain of new-car agencies throughout California. "Dad worked himself to death, and Mother lived only two short years longer. She simply had no wish to go on after he died. I was in my senior year of college when I lost her."

Maddie thought of her own sad past. Losing both parents in a car crash at age thirteen was actually much worse than Noah's loss. At least he'd been an adult. She'd been a child, a frightened little girl that only partially understood the blow she'd received.

But she said nothing about her own sorrow—said nothing at all, in fact—and pushed around the remaining food on her plate with her eyes on the fork in her hand. This was Noah's time to speak, although she couldn't figure out for the life of her why he wanted to. She'd taunted him about that "bad experience" he'd supposedly suffered, but she hadn't done it maliciously, nor with a serious wish to hear his entire life story.

"I'd chosen medicine for my career when I was still in grade school and never once wavered from that decision," Noah said, embarking on that particular chapter of his story.

Maddie continued to listen without interruption, but other than losing his parents—indeed a tragedy, but one that everyone has to endure at some point—Noah had lived like a prince! The best schools, the best cars, the best of everything! In fact, the more Maddie heard of Noah's college and medical school days and nights—the long tedious days in classrooms and *so* much reading and studying—the harder became her heart. Compared to her life, Noah's had been a walk in the park.

But then she realized that Noah wasn't telling all. Was he deliberately omitting some of the more interesting details of those years? More precisely, he hadn't mentioned girls even once, and no college or med student with his looks and money to spend had to go without female companionship, to put it nicely.

Maddie held up her hand, and Noah broke off in midsentence. "What about girls?" Maddie asked bluntly.

"Well…sure…there were girls," Noah admitted. "No one important, though."

"No one important. Not ever?"

Noah's stomach sank. He didn't want to tell Maddie about Felicia, even though he'd been working up to doing exactly that. Now, suddenly, the very thought of committing such emotional suicide nauseated him. What was wrong with him tonight? If a man had any feelings at all for a woman, he didn't talk about *other* women. For certain he didn't go into detail about the one big love of his life and how crushed he'd been when it was over. That kind of story might be told after a man and woman were solid with each other, trusting in each other's love and unafraid of his or her partner's old memories, but even then it was an iffy subject. He and Maddie Kincaid had hardly reached that golden stage of trust and candor. What's more, did he even *want* to attain that all-inclusive status with Maddie?

What he was was a damned mess, he decided, not knowing what he wanted from anyone or anything. So what if he wasn't happy? What was so great about walking around with a silly grin on your face? Well, this confession session had certainly come to a screeching halt, and thank God it had.

"Not ever," he said with such stoic sincerity that Maddie knew he was lying.

She sighed. Noah's body language revealed the truth, even if he'd changed his mind about relating it to her. She was disappointed enough to cry, because his "bad experience" was only a woman, and who gave a damn how many women he'd romanced through the years? She already knew that he was the love-'em-and-leave-'em kind of guy, so this was no revelation.

Actually, she would have enjoyed telling him to get out of her trailer and her life, but she'd been there and done that quite a few times already, and he hadn't paid the slightest attention to her demands.

But she was not going to sit there and listen to any more of his self-pitying version of a past that most people would give their eyeteeth to have lived. And if there was any way to accomplish it, she was going to put him on the spot about his so-called "bad experience" and not feel guilty about doing it, either.

"Please. Go on with your story," she said softly, hoping to lead him into the trap he so richly deserved, the big liar.

Noah's mind raced. Without the Felicia segment, how would he explain leaving San Francisco and moving to Whitehorn?

"Are you having trouble sifting through your memories to exclude the parts you don't want me to know?" Maddie asked in the most sickeningly sweet voice she could devise. Her phony smile was equally as saccharine.

Noah's face became crimson, and he mumbled, ''I don't know what you're talking about.''

Maddie widened her eyes. ''You really don't? Well, I suppose I might have misjudged you. Very well, why don't you just skip to that bad experience, which was actually the only thing I had any curiosity about, if you'd care to remember the beginning of this conversation. I mean, your hell-raising college days aren't of much interest to me, and why would they be? Oh, wait, I forgot. All you did in college and med school was study, study, study and put up with dull and boring classes all day every day. I'm such a ninny, but you probably knew that before now.''

Noah knew when he was the butt of someone's joke, and Maddie was sitting across the dinette table and making fun of him right to his face.

''You're especially good at making a man feel like a fool, aren't you?'' he said.

''If I am, that's the first I heard of it,'' Maddie replied dryly. ''Are you going to finish your story or not?''

''It's finished,'' Noah said flatly, and started to slide from the center of the bench seat to the open end to get up, but then he changed his mind. ''Maybe it's your turn.''

Maddie shrugged. ''Fine with me. I believe I said before that I have nothing to hide, so is there anything in particular you'd like to know?''

Noah looked at her for a long time while wondering what he was really doing in Maddie's face tonight. Did he want to know about the men who'd preceded him in her bed? She hadn't been a virgin last night, so there had definitely been at least one guy, and with her career and independent attitude, the list could be long. No, he didn't want to know anything about that, not one damned thing.

Shaking his head, he got up from the booth. ''No more

conversation tonight, okay? I'm tired and it's time I went home.''

Though surprised by his abrupt change of pace, Maddie turned her thoughts back to the mundane. "There's a lot of food left in these cartons. Take it with you."

"No, thanks. If you don't want it, just throw it out."

Maddie slid from the booth and stood, as well. "By the way, I called Dr. Herrera's office and made an appointment to see him."

"Glad to hear it. I should have asked sooner, but how are you feeling?"

"Other than the painful twinges in my left knee, I feel fully recovered. Can I stop wrapping my hand?"

"Wait and see what Dr. Herrera says about that." Noah took a step toward the door, then stopped for another question. "How did you get your truck and trailer back so soon?"

Maddie explained what had occurred in brief terms and then remarked, "If this Chinook blows all night, there'll hardly be any snow left by morning."

"I won't miss it." He gave her a hard look. "Are you really feeling all right?"

"Do you think I'm lying?"

"You've lied before."

Her eyes suddenly blazed. "And you haven't?"

It was the challenge in her voice that caused Noah to do what happened next. Taking the one long step separating them in that small space, he wrapped his arm completely around her neck and then bent forward a little to press his lips to hers. It was a long kiss that went from simple to complex in two seconds, and after that got both of them so worked up and breathless that they clung to each other for support.

It finally ended because they had to have air. Maddie gasped, "Why did you do that?"

"Good question," Noah said. Much taller than she, he had to look down to probe the depths of her eyes. "I don't have all the answers…yet…but a few things are beginning to add up. For one, the time between med school and the present was a meaningless void, and strange as it might seem to you, I just now realized it. You opened my eyes, Maddie, and what I'd like to know is how someone I didn't know a week ago…less than that…could alter my outlook on life and on a few specifics that seemed earth-shaking and weren't. What did you do to cause such a transformation?''

With her head tilted back against his arm, Maddie returned his penetrating gaze. "You're giving me too much credit…or too much blame. I'm not sure which," she said in a low and husky voice. Her insides felt liquid and soft, a sensual sensation caused by his ongoing embrace, from which she could have freed herself and didn't. "But believe this. I never set out to do anything to you. If you've lost emotional contact with events that directed the course of your life, such as the reason you moved to Whitehorn, that's rather sad, but I didn't cause it."

"Don't take this wrong but I'm afraid you did. I was a starving man before meeting you."

Maddie frowned. "You're speaking Greek."

Noah smiled just a little. "It sort of sounds like Greek to me, too, and I'm not sure how to translate it." His smile faded. "I wasn't going physically hungry, Maddie, I was on an emotionally barren plateau. You brought me down to earth again."

"And exactly how did I do that?"

"You're not buying into a word I'm saying, are you?"

"Obviously I sounded dubious."

"Very. Okay, let's drop it for now." Noah gave her a quick but sweet kiss on the mouth, then backed away from her. "When is your appointment with Herrera?"

Though she was reeling a bit from kisses and conversation she didn't understand, along with emotionally perturbing feelings, Maddie managed a reasonably intelligent reply. "Day after tomorrow. In the morning."

"Good." Noah again started for the door, and again he turned around before opening it. "May I drop in tomorrow night?"

"You're asking?"

"And your eyes are big as saucers because I did. Guess it's best for me to stay in character and just barge in," Noah said dryly. He started to leave for a third time, and stopped himself again. "Do you know that you left the house unlocked?"

"I have the key with me, so I must have thought I'd locked it. I was only going to do a few things out here and that was hours and hours ago. I guess time got away from me. You know, I love it when the wind rocks the trailer at night, so I think I'll sleep out here. Would you mind locking the house on the way to your car?"

"You'd rather stay out here than in the house?" Noah looked rather incredulous.

"I just keep throwing you curves, don't I? Well, relax and chalk that one up to another of Maddie Kincaid's quirky personality traits."

She looked so damned cute that Noah almost went back for another kiss. He stayed where he was, though, because this time a kiss might not be enough. "I'm kind of quirky, too, you know," he said. "Right now I'm quirky as hell over you."

Maddie sucked in a sudden breath, because that was a flirtatiously cute pass if she'd ever heard one, and if he really pressed her to make love with him again, she'd probably do it. She spoke pertly but firmly, as though her stomach hadn't just taken a drop and her thoughts weren't in the bedroom.

"Good night, Dr. Half-and-Half."

Noah cocked his head. "And that means?"

"Half-forthright, half-evasive. Don't worry, it's not a fatal disease or a sin. My diagnosis is that you'll be back to your normal unsmiling self by morning."

"My *unsmiling* self?" He looked wounded.

"Oh, for pity sake, don't try that con on me, Doc. You hardly ever smile and you know it."

His rebuttal was a big, bright smile that showed off his perfect teeth and lit up his incredible blue eyes. "What d'ya call this?" he asked.

"It's a smile, but you really should check your face for cracks, 'cause it's sure not the norm."

"You're the sassiest little chick I've ever known."

"*Chick!* Now there's a shock. If anyone had ever asked me if you used such a juvenile term for the fairer sex, I would have denied it to the death."

Chuckling—surprising Maddie again—Noah finally left. Maddie returned to the dinette and resumed the seat she'd used during dinner. She was overloaded with questions that she maybe *should* have asked, but she could only pry so much, which, of course, left her perplexed and uneasily mystified about Noah Martin. He'd been emotionally starved before meeting her? What in heaven's name was *that* supposed to mean?

The wind rocked the trailer most of the night just as Maddie had looked forward to, but it didn't lull her into the lovely sleep it always had before. Rather, she slept restlessly, waking up over and over and then lying there for what seemed ages before drifting off again. The problem, she finally decided, was that she had far too much on her mind to sleep soundly.

For one thing, she'd rarely had to see a doctor during her twenty-three years, and since the accident, that was practically all she did. Not that she'd invited Noah to stick his nose into her medical problems, but however innocent his initial involvement had been, there he was. She really had to see Dr. Herrera as her knee worried her more than had all of her other injuries combined, so she wasn't through with medical professionals yet.

Then, of course, there was that other thing with Dr. Noah Martin, the intimate and personal thing between them, and Maddie wondered what Aunt June would have said about her niece sleeping with a man she hardly knew.

Maddie sighed over that, recalling again how positively Aunt June had believed that people knew in their hearts when they fell in love. Maddie tried to figure out what, if anything, was in her heart and came up blank. She seemed to be putty in Noah Martin's hands when it came to feverish feelings of sexual desire, but was that love? Maybe love in disguise? Maddie would prefer being in love with a man if she was going to *make* love with him, but how did one make sure that love preceded lust?

All in all it wasn't a good night, and Maddie was glad when it was over. She'd torn herself, Noah and the present course of her life to shreds, and she was happy to think of something else, if only her normal morning routine. She went to the house to bathe, dress and eat breakfast, and during the short walk from her trailer she came alive. Almost all of the snow was gone and the Chinook had died down, leaving behind a pleasantly warm day with a bright sun shining in a cloudless blue sky.

She decided at once that she was not going to waste a rare February day like this one, and as soon as she was ready, she got in her truck and drove away. She noticed that the gas gauge was below the half-full mark, so, as was her habit, she stopped to fill the tank at the Easy-In convenience store and gas station.

Because of the glorious weather, she was even enjoying pumping gas, and she smiled when a car pulled up right behind her truck and Melissa North got out.

"Maddie!" Melissa called, and walked over to Maddie to give her a hug. "How are you doing? I heard you were home."

"I'm fine, Melissa."

"But you did have an accident?"

"Yes, I took a fall in the arena. I have makeup on my face, but there are still some traces of bruising, if you look closely. My whole right side was pretty banged up."

"And your hand?" Melissa's gaze dropped to Maddie's wrapped hand and the sling around her neck, which she wore all the time even if she didn't keep her hand in it constantly.

"I broke a few small bones, but it's pretty much healed now."

"Well, I'm glad you're all right. You know how rumors are. I will never understand how a few simple facts can get so blown out of proportion, but I even heard that you were in a body cast."

Maddie couldn't help laughing. "Well, as you can see, 'the rumors of my death are greatly exaggerated.'"

Melissa laughed. "I love that quote. I apologize for not calling you before the storm, which put the whole town and my good intentions on hold, but in all honesty, Maddie, I felt that you must be much better than some rumormongers had you, or Mark and Darcy would not have left you alone."

"And you were right." As they chatted, Maddie was remembering some things Mark had told her about Melissa. For one, the diner she owned, the Hip Hop Café had been burned to the ground by an arsonist a few weeks ago. Someone had poured gasoline throughout the restaurant and lit a match. If that weren't enough to spook a person, Melissa had been poisoned at Mark and Darcy's wedding. Since she was the only one who'd gotten ill, it had obviously been a deliberate attempt on Melissa's life. Maddie had known that Melissa had become ill at the reception, but she'd left town before the diagnosis had been made, and Mark had told her about it during a telephone call. Of course Maddie had had to do some prodding on the subject as her brother was hardly a chatterbox.

At any rate, talking to Melissa now, Maddie couldn't help being curious about the awful events hanging over Melissa's head. Actually, *dangerous* was a better word than *awful,* because it was apparent that someone wanted to harm Melissa, but Maddie couldn't quite bring herself to ask questions. Melissa was as pretty as she'd always been, with her black hair, deep-blue eyes and slender figure. She and her husband, Wyatt, were a good-looking couple, as Wyatt North was a truly handsome man.

Melissa smiled. "I have to get my gas and be on my way. Maddie, it was great seeing you. Do you know how long you'll be here?"

"No longer than I have to be," Maddie said frankly. "As soon as I'm able, I'll be on the road again."

"In that case, I'll leave it up to you. If you find yourself with some spare time on your hands, give Wyatt and me a call, and we'll get together for dinner or something. It was good seeing you, Maddie." Melissa returned to her own car and began the process of filling its gas tank.

Maddie finished up, waved goodbye to Melissa and got in her truck. As she drove away she found herself hoping that whoever it was that was trying to harm Melissa North, the culprit wasn't a member of the Kincaid family. Whitehorn's history was heavily laden with Kincaid scandals, from mayhem to murder, and while there were some good and decent Kincaids—Mark and herself, for instance— there was definitely a felonious, greedy streak running through the family.

Maddie headed straight for the Braddock ranch, but even while looking forward to seeing Fanny, she couldn't forget Melissa. If Noah *did* come by tonight, she was going to ask him the numerous questions she hadn't had the nerve to ask Melissa, Maddie finally decided.

If Noah came by. Maddie found herself mentally repeating that phrase. To her dismay, once that seed was planted she couldn't think of much else. As hard as it was to face and admit, she knew in her soul that if she didn't get away from Whitehorn and Noah Martin very soon, she was going to be in big trouble.

"Damn," she whispered.

Denise Hunter seemed glad to see Maddie. Denise was wearing rubber boots that reached her knees, faded jeans and a bulky, pullover red sweater. Her cheeks were pink from working outdoors in the fresh air, and Maddie liked the way she'd pinned up her long dark hair—all haphazard-like, as though she'd just grabbed bunches of it and secured it without any sort of design in mind.

"Isn't this a fantastic day?" Denise called out while Maddie was walking toward her.

"It's days like this that keep Montana's residents from leaving en masse after a blizzard," Maddie returned with a laugh.

"True enough."

The two women met near the stables. "I put all the horses in the fenced area right behind the stable," Denise said. "They needed exercise, and I needed them gone so I could clean house."

"Thus, the rubber boots. You've been mucking out stalls."

"I'm almost done. I'll probably leave the horses outside for most of the day, though. They've been cooped up far too long. Are you planning to ride Fanchon today?"

"No, this is just a visit."

"How about a cup of coffee at the house after your visit. I should be finished out here in another fifteen, twenty minutes. Then I need to clean up a bit myself. Coffee should be ready in about half an hour."

Maddie was pleased by the invitation. Denise Hunter was an interesting woman, and Maddie would like to know her better.

"Thanks, I'll come to the house after I see Fanny."

"Okay, great. See you later."

Maddie hiked around the building, and there were the horses in a small fenced field. There was very little to graze on—what remained of last year's grass crop was brown and soaked in standing though shallow water from the quick thaw of so much snow—but there was hay spread out on the ground, so the animals had plenty to eat. Some of the small herd was eating and some were wandering.

Spotting Fanny, Maddie whistled softly. The mare lifted her head, pricked up her ears, saw Maddie and began trotting toward her. But, to Maddie's surprise, she only trotted a few steps then slowed to a walk, and she wasn't walking straight!

"Oh, my God, what happened to you?" Maddie whispered. But she knew what had happened. Fanny had gone down in the arena, same as Maddie had, and because the mare hadn't immediately shown signs of injury, no one had checked her over. Even when Maddie had left the hospital early to make sure Fanny was all right she hadn't been concerned that Fanny might have been hurt in the accident. No one had been concerned, and Fanny *had* been injured!

The mare reached the fence and with tears in her eyes Maddie put her arms around Fanny's neck and hugged her. Fanny whinnied softly and nuzzled Maddie's shoulder. Those were signs, Maddie knew, that the mare was glad to see her. Maddie cried harder.

Finally she broke away, went to the gate and walked into the pasture and over to Fanny. Bending down, Maddie ran her good hand up and down Fanny's legs. She could tell there was swelling and tenderness around the mare's knees, which could have been caused by numerous problems, some minor, some very serious. Fanny needed a veterinarian.

Telling the mare goodbye with another hug, Maddie exited the small pasture and slowly plodded to the house with her head down. Her heart felt as though it weighed a ton in her chest. She tried not to think the worst, but it wasn't possible to convince herself that this was just a trivial little injury. A horse's legs, particularly its front legs, took the brunt of competition, be it speed racing or barrel racing.

But what really brought Maddie to the brink was how

badly she'd neglected Fanny. Yes, she'd been injured herself, but she should have called a vet from her hospital bed and had him go to the rodeo grounds and give Fanny a complete examination. Why hadn't she thought of it?

Suffering a throat full of tears, Maddie rang the house's doorbell and heard from inside, "Coming!"

Denise opened the door with a smile that faded away when she saw Maddie's crestfallen face. "What's wrong?"

"Something's wrong with Fanny's front legs. May I use your phone to call a vet?"

"Of course. Come in."

Denise brought Maddie to the kitchen, where she sat her at the table, and brought her a telephone. "I have an office, but I like making my calls in here. I'll get you some coffee. Cream and sugar?"

"Just cream...or milk...whatever you have. Denise, I don't know the vets around here anymore. Who do you use?"

"Dr. Riley Pierce. I have his card right here." Denise took out a stack of business cards from a drawer and easily located the one she wanted, which she passed to Maddie.

"Is he good? You've used him for serious problems? Please don't think I'm judging you in any way, but I have to have the best for Fanny. She...she's so...important to...me." Maddie broke down and cried. Embarrassed, she covered her eyes with her hand.

Denise brought over a box of tissues. "Don't you dare be embarrassed about caring enough for your horse. To answer your question, he's the best I've found in the area, after trying two others. As for a truly serious problem, no, I haven't had to call him for anything life threatening or crippling on any of the Braddock horses. But Riley Pierce is young and up-to-the-minute on the latest treatments and techniques. I don't think you would be disappointed with his work."

Maddie dried her eyes. "Thank you." She placed the call and after explaining Fanny's condition to the lady who'd answered the phone, was told that Dr. Pierce would be free to drive to the Braddock stables tomorrow afternoon. His approximate arrival time would be three o'clock.

When the call was over, Maddie related the appointment time to Denise, took a swallow of coffee, then got to her feet. "I'm going to spend a little more time with Fanny." She saw that Denise was frowning and looking uncomfortable. "Denise, I'm not blaming you."

"No, but I am. When I heard you recite Fanny's symptoms, I wondered why I hadn't noticed anything. Maddie, it's part of my job...an important part...to make sure my charges stay healthy."

"Look, I hauled her clear from Texas and noticed nothing wrong. You're not to blame, so please stop thinking that way."

"Would you mind if I came with you and took a look at Fanny's legs?"

"Of course I wouldn't mind." They left the house together.

It was hours later that Maddie drove home. She was worried sick. After examining Fanny's legs, Denise had become quite concerned. They had discussed all sorts of awful problems that involved bones, tendons, nerves and muscles, but neither of them could do more than guess at the cause of Fanny's condition.

Denise had insisted Maddie have lunch with her, and Maddie now felt that she had made a new friend. After lunch she'd helped Denise lead the horses into their stalls in the freshly cleaned stable, and finally she had spent another fifteen minutes with Fanny, talking softly to the mare and stroking her neck and nose.

Now she was paying for so much walking and standing. There was a constant ache in her left knee, and she'd also used her injured hand too much, causing a dull ache in it, as well.

Her life had gone all to hell, she thought while wiping away a self-pitying tear. She'd always been strong and healthy and so had Fanny. Now they were both under the weather, and God only knew what diagnosis she'd hear from Dr. Herrera about herself and from Dr. Pierce about Fanny.

Maddie suddenly wished for her brother. Just to talk to, to unload her ton of worries to someone who cared. Mark had always been there for her, not geographically, but she'd always been able to call him when she'd needed contact with family, if only by telephone.

She could probably find him, considering that he'd left a copy of his and Darcy's itinerary at the house, but disrupt their honeymoon just to cry on her brother's shoulder? No, she couldn't do that. She would get through this troubling time by herself. After all, she wasn't some wet-behind-the-ears girl who'd seen nothing of the world and had never been on her own. Why, she'd traveled thousands of miles by herself, met countless people, supported herself financially and had loved every minute of it.

Then, without warning, the fear that Maddie had fought for hours was suddenly stronger than her will. If Fanny was seriously maimed and could no longer compete, then Maddie's career was over. She would never find another horse like Fanny, not one she could afford to buy. And starting completely over with a young foal and training it the way she'd trained Fanny would take years.

And so Maddie drove home with a heart full of pain. She alternated between wonderful but poignant memories of Fanny and herself, and enormous, heartbreaking worries about the future. Rodeo was all she knew. What on earth would she do to make a living if Fanny could no longer compete?

Chapter Twelve

Noah barely had a break all day. He did, however, manage to squeeze in a couple of phone calls to Maddie, and when she didn't answer, logic told him that she was out in her trailer again. His messages recorded on Mark and Darcy's voice mail were brief and to the point. "I'll call again later."

In truth Noah was so busy with back-to-back patient appointments that he didn't wonder too much about Maddie's unavailability until late afternoon. At that point, her being so consistently out of touch all day felt wrong. Noah became anxious to reach the end of his workday so he could go by Mark's house and make sure she was all right.

Somewhere within the organized chaos of the day he became aware of the grand weather warming Whitehorn's winter-weary residents. With that knowledge Noah's concern of Maddie subsided a bit, as anyone who didn't have to stay inside would surely be outside. Still, one would think that she would have answered the phone at least once.

Shortly after four, Noah's plan to go directly to Mark's house after work went flying because of a phone call from the hospital's emergency room doctor. It was the E.R. doctor's opinion that a patient required immediate surgery to survive. Would Noah drop everything and waste no time in getting there?

Noah put down the phone, tersely told his nurse the situation and ran from his office to the hospital. He studied X rays and the result of a cat scan in the E.R., then scrubbed for surgery.

It was after eleven when the emergency was over—the patient was doing fine—and after a shower Noah all but collapsed on a chair in the doctor's lounge. He wearily rubbed the back of his neck and for the first time in almost seven hours thought of Maddie. At the same time Felicia entered his mind, Felicia and the many, many times he'd disappointed her because of medical emergencies. She had complained about it, nicely at first and then not so nicely. According to her, she couldn't live with never being able to count on his presence on a daily, routine basis. Noah had always known that a physician's wife had to have abnormal patience and understanding, and he also came to realize that Felicia had neither. But thinking about it now, years after their breakup, was she the only one to blame?

For the first time ever Noah asked himself which of them, Felicia or he, had been the most selfish. Granted, he'd only been doing his job, just as he'd done tonight, but maybe his expecting her to cancel dinner parties and other social functions without resentment had been unfair. Felicia's friends were a large part of San Francisco's A-list, and those sophisticated, wealthy, mostly carefree patrons of the arts took their social obligations quite seriously.

Frowning, Noah pondered that chapter of his life and

realized he no longer harbored any ill will toward Felicia. It was an astonishing revelation and led him into a much clearer understanding of what had really happened between the two of them.

For a while he'd been blinded by her astounding beauty, which he'd ultimately learned had taken up a great deal of her time to maintain. He remembered that she would never leave the house unless everything was perfect—her hair, her makeup, her clothes. Eventually her worldly sophistication, her insistence that everything be as *she* wanted it and her obsessive need to be the center of attention had worn thin. As a responsible physician he hadn't always been able to perform on Felicia's command, but even with so many problems with which to contend, he'd still believed he loved her.

And he'd kept on believing it until…until meeting Maddie Kincaid!

"My God," he whispered, shaken by so much unexpected clarity. He didn't love Felicia, he hadn't loved her in ages; he was in love with Maddie, who couldn't be more opposite to Felicia and to the kind of women that had attracted his attention before Felicia. What force of nature had changed him so drastically that he was head over heels for a fiery little woman who couldn't care less if her hair was a mess? A bit of a girl who made him laugh and had proved that she would protect her honor with whatever weapon was on hand—if only a silly little paperweight. That was a day he wouldn't forget—it could still make him laugh—if he lived to be a hundred.

He loved Maddie Kincaid. Admitting and thinking about it made him feel lighthearted and happy. He let his mind wander and began picturing a life with Maddie—marriage, kids, the works. What a fantastic fantasy!

But what about her career in rodeo? And after I answer that one, I should ask myself what clues she's given to make me think that she might be in love with me!

The joy in which Noah had been basking drained from

his system. Maddie was going to leave Montana as soon as her health permitted, and the only thing that had happened to make him hope she might have feelings for him was their one time in bed. Using one sexual encounter as a barometer was an unrealistic approach to a question as serious as "does she or doesn't she love me?"

Without one credible answer to the questions now hounding him and a sinking sensation in his gut because facing his feelings for Maddie had opened a Pandora's box of problems, Noah got up and went over to the wall telephone. He knew it was late, but he wouldn't be able to sleep until he heard from Maddie's own lips that she was all right. He dialed the number to Mark's house.

Maddie only partially came awake and she reached for the phone on her bedstand without opening her eyes. "Hello," she mumbled.

"Maddie?"

Her eyes flew open and were instantly teary. "Mark! Oh, Mark, I'm so glad you called." She began sobbing.

Noah was stunned. "Maddie, it's not Mark. It's Noah."

"Wha-what?"

"It's Noah. Why are you crying? What's wrong?" He heard panic in his own voice and told himself to calm down. But something terrible must have happened to make Maddie almost hysterical in the middle of the night. "Maddie?" he said questioningly when she said nothing for far too long.

"You big jerk! Why did you call and pretend you were Mark?" She slammed down the phone.

Noah hung up with every nerve in his body jangling. Exactly how much undeserved abuse did a man have to take from a woman, even if he *was* in love with her? Angrily grabbing his jacket, he hurriedly left the lounge and then the hospital. Running to where he'd parked his vehicle early that morning, he got in, started the engine and then broke the speed limit on Whitehorn's dark and empty streets to get to Mark and Darcy's house.

Parking in the driveway, he strode to the house like a man with a mission. After unlocking the door with the key Mark had given him, he went inside and switched on the kitchen light. He made no special effort to be quiet, because if Maddie was sleeping again he was going to wake her up and ask her just who in hell she thought she was. All he'd done since Mark left town was grovel at Miss Pain-in-the-Neck Maddie's feet and try to keep his promise to her brother. Well, he'd had his fill of her ungrateful sass, and it was time she found out that the world didn't revolve around self-centered rodeo queens!

Noah reached her bedroom door, which was wide open, and the little night-light plugged into a wall outlet cast enough light for him to make out Maddie's form under the blankets. She appeared to be in deep slumber.

He stood there looking at her and felt the anger vanishing from his system. He didn't want to yell at her; he wanted to love her. To hold her and plead with her to tell him why she'd been crying. To say out loud that he wanted her in his life, to talk out things that might cause bumps in their relationship, such as their short acquaintance, and then to ask if she could be contented living in Whitehorn as the wife of a doctor. That was an especially crucial question, and Maddie's feelings on that subject could make or break any chance they had of attaining a successful and permanent relationship.

It struck Noah very hard, however, that what he would really be asking was for Maddie to give up everything for him, a career she loved, a way of life she loved. How could anyone ask so much of another person?

He couldn't. No one should. Sick at heart he decided to leave her be. She was doing fine now—medically speaking—and by her own words she didn't need or want anything else from him. In truth, she hadn't even wanted medical attention from him. She'd considered him as nothing but an intruder from the first, which he would be wise to keep in mind while he went on his way and lived out his own life.

He would leave, but first…? Tiptoeing to the bed, he leaned over and tenderly kissed her forehead. For Noah it was a goodbye kiss; he would not bother her again.

But it didn't turn out that way. Maddie's arms were suddenly around his neck, and her mouth was seeking his. Noah's heartbeat went wild. "Are you awake?" he whispered, afraid that this might go beyond a kiss and she wouldn't remember it because she'd slept through the whole thing.

"I'm very awake," she said low and huskily. "Sensually awake."

He thought of asking now why she'd been crying when he called, but destroying her sensuous mood with a reality question seemed just *too* unselfish. There was a limit to a man's generosity, after all, and this was the woman he loved.

And so he pushed everything else from his mind and kissed her soft, pliant lips until both he and Maddie were a little bit crazy.

"Undress," she gasped, and tugged at his clothes. "Get under the covers with me."

How could he get all noble and chivalrous at this point? She was hot and needy; *he* was hot and needy. So be it.

Tearing off his clothes and watching her shed her nightgown, he then got into bed and drew her into a fiery embrace. "Maddie, sweetheart," he whispered raggedly, and began kissing her face, her throat, her breasts.

"Oh, yes, do that," she moaned when he took a nipple into his mouth and sucked gently.

"And this, too?" He slid his hand down to that special spot between her legs and began a sure, slow and very gentle stroke.

"Yes…yes…that, too. Noah…Noah."

There were so many facets to making love, and just the

fact of Maddie saying his name when she was so sexually aroused meant the world to Noah. His every touch, kiss and movement conveyed the love he felt for her, and although he wished he could say the words *I love you,* he knew he couldn't. Maybe he was wrong about the importance of rodeo to her, but he knew in his soul that it was wrong to offer himself as an alternative. If only she was in Whitehorn to stay, things would be different, not nearly as complicated. He would have the time for a long courtship, which he certainly didn't have as things stood now.

Maddie was on cloud nine, somewhere in outer space and reaching for the moon. She *had* to be in love with Noah, she thought within the vagaries of her passion-dazed brain. She could not feel so much for a man without love.

But there was Fanny and rodeo and her own injuries and so many things to worry about. How could she be thinking about loving a man who had both feet firmly planted in one place when she was a nomad? While she lingered in Whitehorn, her career was passing her by. Every missed competition meant a less profitable year, but how could she even be thinking of money when Fanny wasn't hale and hardy?

She gave her head a shake to dislodge the worry and concentrate again on Noah and his magic. She loved the varied textures of his skin and the utter maleness of his body.

"You're very handsome," she whispered.

"And you're very beautiful. Oh, Maddie, if you only knew."

"Knew what?" she asked dreamily.

"Nothing," he mumbled, for what else could he say? He moved on top of her.

Their passion exploded, and neither thought at all for an incredibly long time. Everything was hot, molten physical sensation as they moved together, each striving for the ultimate pleasure but thoroughly immersed in the aching pleasure derived from the ride to the finish line. Feverish and flushed, they cried out mere seconds apart. It had been glorious…for both of them.

And then, only moments after it was over—Noah was seeking a comfortable position on the bed next to her—Maddie embarrassed herself with a seemingly unstoppable flood of tears. She tried to hide what was happening, but when she began choking on sobs, Noah caught on. He sat up, took her chin and turned her face toward him.

"What's wrong?" he asked gently, for she was weeping as though her heart were broken, and her terrible grief brought tears to his own eyes. "Maddie, you were crying when I called, and now you're crying again. Talk to me, please."

"I—I've become a…tramp," she stammered between great gulping sobs.

Noah nearly fell over from shock. "Maddie, what in hell ever put that notion into your head?"

"Oh, just listen…to…to…the man's surprise," she gasped out, then viciously turned on him. "It's your fault, and you know it, too, don't you?"

"Uh…okay…fine. I'll take the blame…but would you mind telling me what blame it is that I'm accepting?"

"For my being a tramp! Do you think I sleep with just anybody? You have the most uncanny knack for catching me with my…my…guard down."

"I thought you were going to say 'with my pants down,'" Noah drawled. "Maddie, you couldn't be what you called yourself if you tried. The word is so insulting and so far from the truth that I can't even say it. Listen for a minute. The reason you drop your guard with me is because you're falling in love." He knew he was taking a huge chance with those words, but he was so full of words that he wanted to say to her, and maybe he had to risk part of himself to gain all of her.

"*What?*" Maddie bolted to a sitting position and gaped

at him with tears still dripping down her face, her hair all askew and apparently unaware that she'd left the blankets behind and she was naked to the waist.

Noah's gaze dropped and lingered on her perfect little breasts. "Would that be so terrible?" he asked softly, and lifted his hand to gently cup the back of her neck. "I rather like the idea."

She was truly stunned, mostly because she'd been thinking so much about love while they'd been *making* love. But he'd only said that *she* was falling in love, and that hurt her.

"Just because you seem to have some kind of sexual influence that makes me behave like a…a…you know…doesn't mean I'm falling in love. Your ego is getting just a bit out of hand, Dr. I'm-Just-Too-Cute-To-Resist."

"Well, obviously you can't."

"Can't what? Resist you? That's absurd!" She shook his hand away from her neck, noticed the sagging blankets and yanked them up to cover her breasts.

"Maddie, you just said yourself that— Well, you know what you said, and the bottom line is that now you're not being honest with me."

"And you, of course, are the heart and soul of honesty," she retorted sarcastically.

"I'd like to be. With you, I'd like very much to be totally honest."

"Oh, sure, that's the reason you inserted that huge void in your soap opera tale of young Dr. Martin's life between his medical school years and the present. Do you think I'm stupid enough to believe that nothing important happened during those years? I believe you used the word *meaningless*. Well, something damned meaningful transported your ass from San Francisco to Whitehorn, buster, so if you're suddenly all holy and full of grace over honesty, start talking!"

"All right, I will. But will you tell me something first?"

"Tell you what?"

"Why you were crying when I called."

Maddie looked at him a moment, then sighed and lay down again. "I thought you were Mark."

"I realize that, but do you usually cry when he calls?"

"Of course not. But today was…awful…and I came to bed wishing I could talk to Mark about it. He's more than just my brother. He's my best friend…my confidant…the one person I can tell anything to. I apologize for yelling at you…for accusing you of pretending to be Mark. That was ridiculous, and I knew it was even while I was saying it, but I was just so upset over the day, and then being awakened by the phone in the middle of the night and…well, I'm sure you get the picture."

"Pretty much, yes, except for what happened that made the day so awful."

Maddie's eyes filled again. "Something's wrong with Fanny. I spent most of the day at the Braddock stable with her, and there's something wrong with her legs. I have a veterinarian going out there tomorrow, and…"

"You have an appointment with Dr. Herrera tomorrow."

"I know I do! Good Lord, give me *some* credit. My appointment with Herrera is in the morning, and the vet, a Dr. Riley Pierce, is going to the ranch around three in the afternoon. I plan to be there when he is, and I *will* be if I have to cut every corner in the book."

"I'm sorry, Maddie, maybe I spoke out of turn, but I happen to think that your health is more important than a horse's."

"How dare you say that to me? You don't know the first thing about my feelings for Fanny. I couldn't bear anything serious happening to her. She's the reason I've been successful in rodeo. I love her more than myself, and what's more, I couldn't earn a living without her.

We're a team. You probably don't understand how crucial teamwork between a rider and her horse is in barrel racing, but take my word for it, no one wins without it.''

Noah listened to Maddie's every word, but he was also realizing something astounding while she talked. If she couldn't compete anymore, she would probably stay in Whitehorn!

Oh, my God, he thought as hope blossomed within him. In the next heartbeat, guilt hit him with all the power of a battering ram. Maddie adored her horse, and he had never been a cruel person, certainly not cruel enough to wish for the demise of an innocent horse so he could have what *he* wanted—its owner!

Noah snuggled himself around her. ''Let's believe that both you and Fanny are fine,'' he said quietly. ''Maddie, may I stay here with you tonight?''

''I should say no.''

''Because?''

''Because…because we're both getting deeper and deeper into something that could and probably will end up with one of us…probably me…getting hurt.''

He brought her head to his shoulder and sighed. ''Maddie, I'm more apt to be the one who gets hurt. Remember that I'm not planning to go anywhere, and you are.''

Maddie became very still. His warmth surrounded her, and it was truly wonderful to be so close to someone in bed at night. She'd slept alone all of her life. Even the few romances in her past had not included sleeping all night with a man. But along with that realization came another. For the first time she saw whatever it was that was going on between her and Noah from his point of view. At least she caught a glimmer of how he might be feeling about everything.

She was hardly your average, everyday woman. Take their first meeting, for instance, when he'd nearly laughed himself to death over her bravado with a paperweight. After that she had to have been one shock after another for him to absorb—her career, for one thing, her lifestyle for another. She lived in a trailer with a horse! She'd never thought so, but Noah, who had grown up in a perfect family and had lived a perfect life—until the VOID, which she still didn't comprehend—even to attending the perfect schools, probably couldn't think of her choice of home and roommate as anything but bizarre.

But all that could be over, Maddie thought with tears stinging her eyes again. If Fanny couldn't compete anymore, everything would change. Could she ever adjust to an ordinary way of life? Be an ordinary woman who worked at some boring job and lived in a regular house? A house without wheels? She would be *so* stuck, *so* rooted.

On the other hand, if Fanny was all right, they would be leaving Whitehorn, possibly very soon, which also meant saying goodbye to Noah.

Maddie's heart began aching so badly that she could hardly bear it. She knew then, just as Aunt June had said she would, that she was madly, deeply and eternally in love with Dr. Noah Martin.

"Noah," she whispered emotionally. "I have to tell you something. You were right. I…I do love you. I just now realized it. I love you, I really do."

"Hmm, that's…good. I love you, too, Maddie."

He sounded odd, and Maddie turned her head to peer at his face. He was sound asleep! Had he really heard what she'd said and knew what *he'd* said? Would he remember in the morning that they had each confessed love for the other?

Maddie quietly cried herself to sleep. Normally an optimist, she couldn't find one single thing in her life to be optimistic about. Nothing was right, not one damned thing.

Very early the next morning Noah got up, gathered his clothes, dressed in the living room and noiselessly left the house. When Maddie woke up several hours later, the only evidence that he'd really been there during the night were the scrunched indentations in the pillow he'd used. She had no idea what time it had been when he'd gone, but she wished that he had kissed her and told her that he loved her before he went. It would have been much easier to believe if he'd said it when they were both wide awake.

The cloudy gray sky that morning did nothing to lift Maddie's downcast spirit. Obviously yesterday had been a fluke—one glorious day of sunshine and warmth—before true February weather blanketed the area again. The sky didn't look like another heavy snowfall to Maddie, though, but she felt that rain was a strong possibility.

She arrived at Dr. Herrera's office fifteen minutes ahead of her appointment to take care of the paperwork physicians always required of a new patient. An hour *after* her appointment time she was ushered into an examination room, where she impatiently waited another twenty minutes for the doctor. Worrying every second about being at the stable when Dr. Pierce examined Fanny, Maddie couldn't bring herself to smile at Dr. Herrera when he finally came in.

After thoroughly questioning her about her arena accident, then examining her hand, her knee and her reflexes in all of her limbs, the doctor called for his nurse and requested that she phone the radiology department at the hospital as he was sending Miss Maddie Kincaid over for some X rays.

"Wait a minute," Maddie said. "How long will that take?"

"I'm really not sure," the doctor said. "I hope you have the time for X rays today, Maddie. I believe your hand is healing as it should, but I'm quite concerned about your knee."

Maddie was suddenly terribly depressed. "I don't doubt it. In fact, the way things have been going lately, I'd be surprised if you weren't concerned."

"Let me explain. A sudden twisting of the knee may cause a ligament sprain or tear a meniscus...one or both of the disks of protective cartilage covering the surfaces of the two major bones in the human leg, the femur and the tibia. Now, that very well could have occurred when you fell from your horse. You also could have incurred severe damage to the knee joint, which can cause hemarthrosis, or bleeding into the joint. These are serious injuries, Maddie, and we must rule them out before considering more minor problems, such as inflammation of the joint lining. X rays are quite necessary, Maddie, and the sooner the better."

"And...if my injury is more serious than not...what then?" Maddie was shaken and showed it in the unsteadiness of her voice. "Take the worst-case scenario from those you told me, would I still be able to ride my horse?"

"You'll always be able to ride, Maddie," the doctor said gently. "You may not be able to compete, but you'll always be able to ride."

Maddie nodded numbly. Never be able to compete again? And that was *her!* Were both she and Fanny going to be put out to pasture today?

"All right," she said tremulously. "I'll get the X rays whenever you say."

"Wise decision." Dr. Herrera left the room to finalize Maddie's arrangement with the hospital's radiology department.

"I'm not wise, I'm desperate," she whispered.

Maddie didn't make it out to the Braddock ranch before three. She phoned Denise from the hospital at three-thirty. "I'm so upset I could spit," she told Denise. "I agreed to having some X rays taken, but then when I got over here to the radiology department, I found out that they'd put me on a standby list. Apparently they were booked solid and only agreed to squeeze me in, which, of course,

Dr. Herrera didn't tell me. Anyhow, is Dr. Pierce still there?''

"He just left. I'm sorry, Maddie."

"Well, he wasn't there very long."

"He was here about an hour."

"Then he got there *before* three!"

"Yes, he did. I told him you wanted to be here while he examined Fanchon, but he had other obligations and couldn't wait for you to arrive."

Maddie was afraid to ask, but she had to. "Did...did he tell you what's wrong with her?"

"It's a tendon problem, Maddie. Have you heard of bowed tendon?"

"Yes, it's a serious condition...mostly found in race-horses," Maddie said weakly. "Is that Fanny's problem?"

"Yes, but it's not as bad as it could be. Here, let me read what he wrote down to give to you. 'Tendons consist of numerous fibrils. The tendons involved in a bowed tendon condition are the deep flexor tendons located behind the cannon bone that runs from knee to fetlock. The condition is most common in the front legs. The bow is caused by swelling fibrils, oozing inflammatory fluid and by capillary hemorrhage. The severity of the condition depends on the number of fibrils stretched or torn, and on the position of the injury.'"

Denise continued. "He also wrote his treatment recommendation. Do you want to hear that, too?"

"Yes, please," Maddie said in a near whisper. She was shaking all over and knew that if she were someplace alone, instead of in a public place, she would break down and wail out loud. Her heart felt shattered, and the horrible guilt engulfing her over her neglect in not having Fanny checked out immediately after the accident was almost more than she could bear.

Denise read, "'Rest is crucial. Do not exercise the horse. Apply ice packs to the swellings, then wrap legs firmly from knee to the fetlock joint. Repeat daily.' Maddie, he said that he'd drop in every few days to give her an anti-inflammatory injection.''

''Do you have time to apply the ice packs and wrappings?''

''No, but I know a young man who adores horses and is constantly hounding me for odd jobs. If I show him once what to do, he'll take it from there.''

''I'll pay his wage, of course. Denise, you said it wasn't as bad as it could be. Was that Dr. Pierce's opinion?''

''Maddie, he sort of beat around the bush about that, to be honest, but he clearly stated that he'd treated horses that were a lot worse off than Fanny. If you take that into consideration along with his calm appraisal of the situation, I think Fanny will be okay in time.''

''How much time, Denise? Did he say?''

''No, he didn't.''

''I've heard of horses being spelled in a paddock for months and months,'' Maddie said sadly. ''I'm sure you have, too.''

''Fanny's not that bad off, Maddie. Even I can see that, and Dr. Pierce did come right out and say that the swelling of Fanchon's legs was minimal. Please don't think the worst. I'm betting she'll be fine in just a few weeks.''

''Fine enough for competition? You don't have to answer that. At this point I don't know if *I'll* be fine enough for competition in a few weeks. Denise, thanks for everything you did today. I'll contact Dr. Pierce's office and find out when he'll be out there again. I really would like to talk to him.''

''Of course you would. You said you're in line for some X rays?''

''It's my left knee, Denise. Fanny's not the only Kincaid with leg problems,'' she added in a feeble attempt to lighten the situation.

''Let me know how you are,'' Denise said quietly.

''I will. Thanks again.''

* * *

It was drizzling rain when Maddie finally drove home. She could not have been in a more despondent frame of mind. She'd been told in radiology that her X rays would be read, documented and sent to Dr. Herrera, probably tomorrow, but while she was understandably concerned about her own physical well-being, it was Fanny's condition that had Maddie so down in the dumps.

Because of the dismal atmosphere of rain, heavy cloud cover and an early nightfall, the streetlights were on and creating eerie yellow globes in the pewter-like twilight. Maddie drove like an automaton, heeding stop signs and other vehicles through sheer habit, not because her mind was where it should be.

But, dear God, how could her life have become such a disrupted, discordant and probably irreconcilable mess in so short a time?

A sob threatened to escape her throat, but she refused to shed another tear today. In fact, she was fed up and angry, mostly with herself, but the world in general wasn't all that great, either. Actually she was ticked off at pretty much everything and everyone—Noah Martin included! Maybe Noah Martin especially! After all, other men hadn't taken advantage of the frail little woman she'd become since the accident, had they? No, sir, he was the only unscrupulous rogue she knew, and she wasn't going to pace away the evening frustrated and steaming mad.

Maddie suddenly turned her truck around and headed back to the medical center. It didn't take long for her to locate Noah's office and to find a parking place. When she walked into his waiting room and saw no one but the receptionist, she knew she'd come to spew her wrath at exactly the right time.

"Hello," the receptionist said with a pleasant smile.

"Hello. I need to see Dr. Martin."

"Do you have an appointment?"

"No, but I know he'll see me. Just tell him that Maddie Kincaid is pacing in his waiting room."

"Ms. Kincaid, he's with a patient. But I'll speak to his nurse. Please have a seat."

Noah was just finishing up with his last patient of the day when Norma, his nurse, knocked, then opened the door and stuck her head into the room.

"Could I see you for just a moment?" she asked.

Noah sensed something amiss in her voice. "I'll be right out. Mr. Jenkens was just about to leave anyhow." He walked out with Mr. Jenkens and then veered over to where the nurse was standing and looking anxious.

The second Noah walked up to her she whispered, "There's a woman in the waiting room who is demanding to see you, and the way she looks and talks alarmed Belva. Her name is Maddie Kincaid and—"

Noah knew that his grin surprised his nurse, because she didn't usually stop speaking in the middle of a sentence with a rather stunned, inquisitive expression on her face.

"I know Miss Kincaid, Norma. Please bring her to my office and tell her that I'll be in shortly."

He was still grinning when Norma hurried away to impart the information she'd just collected to Belva, the receptionist.

"And that's how a seed of gossip is planted," Noah murmured under his breath.

Chapter Thirteen

The door had no more than closed behind Nurse Norma—Maddie had noticed her name tag—than the steam driving Maddie to do something so totally outlandish began draining away. Noah would think she'd lost her mind, walking in as though she owned the place and then demanding to see him.

Groaning quietly, Maddie perched herself on the edge of the chair situated at the front of an impressive mahogany desk. Noah's office was tastefully appointed, and Maddie's nervously darting eyes took it all in. Framed documents adorned the wall behind the desk, and a marvelous landscape painting hung over a long, hunter-green sofa with a decorative pillow at one end and a green and gray afghan folded along its back. Finally there were several attractive brass lamps and, of course, the various items that one would expect to see in any office.

All of that was fine. Any doctor worth his salt should have a decent office, but what in God's name was she doing in Noah's? Her bravado and bluster were completely gone, and she truly felt like a naughty child who was very soon to be nabbed and chastised.

Maddie rose from the chair with one intention—getting out of there before Noah came in. She was almost to the door when it opened, and when she saw him, her insides turned to mush and she stopped in her tracks. He was so handsome, so tall and straight and clean, and so professional looking in his white coat that any doubts still cluttering her mind about whether or not she had fallen in love with him began vanishing like puffs of smoke.

He smiled. "Hello. This is a nice surprise." He put his arms around her and tried to draw her into a close embrace.

"No...wait...please," she stammered, and escaped his hug.

Noah frowned slightly. She had to be there for a reason, but if it wasn't to nurture the development of their personal relationship, what was it?

"Go ahead and sit down," he said, gesturing toward the chair she had just vacated. He walked around the desk and took his own chair. "I sense that all is not well," he said quietly. "Did you see Dr. Herrera?"

And that one bit of kindness was all it took to break the dam holding back her emotions. Covering her face with her hands, Maddie moaned, "Oh, Noah. I've had the most horrible day."

Noah got up for a box of tissues, which he placed on her lap. Instead of returning to his chair, he sat on the edge of the desk, not more than a foot away from her.

She humiliated herself by crying like a baby, using the tissues to sop up her flow of tears. "I'm...so sorry," she finally got out.

"Don't apologize for being human," Noah said gently. "Tell me about today."

Maddie sighed, wiped her eyes one more time and shook her head. "I didn't come here to cry on your shoulder.'' She tried very hard to laugh. ''Actually, I don't know why I'm here.''

''Could it be because you needed to talk to someone?''

''Not, uh, entirely. I mean, when I turned around to come here, I was horribly angry and wanted to lash out at something...or someone.''

''Hmm. It's interesting that you would think of me when you felt the need to climb someone's frame.''

''I'm miserably sorry.''

''Yes, I can see that. Hey, how about you and me having some dinner together?''

Maddie blinked her sodden eyes at him. ''After this you still want to be friends?''

''Since I don't think you're in the mood to hear anything else right now, let me say, yes, Maddie, I still want to be friends, and leave it at that, okay?''

''You're perplexing me again.''

''Ditto, sweetheart. Let's go have a good dinner and see if we can relax and straighten out the snarl we've made of what should have been a perfectly normal relationship all along.'' Noah took off his white coat, went into a small closet for his outside jacket and put it on. Returning to where Maddie was sitting, he held out his hand. ''Come on, let's go.''

Was this the real reason that destiny or fate had brought her here today? she wondered uneasily. To take Noah's strong, warm hand, eat dinner with him and then undoubtedly end up in bed together again? To her dismay, just thinking of his kisses and of his hard body controlling and pleasuring hers made her breathless.

Oh, this had to be love, she thought as her last niggling doubt on that point vanished, never to return. She knew it with every fiber of her being. If by some miracle both she and Fanny were given a clean bill of health tomorrow, she would not pack up and leave Whitehorn and Noah. She had found her true love, her true mate, and she knew it in her heart, just as Aunt June had said she would.

She took his hand and let him help her up. Something told her this was going to be a very special evening, and the adoring smile she gave him as thanks made Noah question his eyesight. She looked like...my Lord, she looked like a woman in love!

He couldn't stop himself from pulling her close and kissing her lips with all of the love and desire he felt for her. She kissed him back, moving her mouth on his so seductively that he *never* wanted the kiss to end. Breathing hard, he ran his hands up and down the female curves of her back and hips. He had completely overturned his previous opinion on what features made a woman beautiful, and Maddie, with her small stature and big green eyes was without a doubt the most beautiful, the sexiest and the most delightfully entertaining woman he'd ever known.

He whispered, "I want you so much I hurt."

She felt the same. "Right now? Here?"

"Everyone's gone home. We're alone."

"You're positive?"

"I'll check and make sure." He let go of her and hurried out.

Maddie looked at that long green sofa against the wall and felt the flames grow hotter in the pit of her stomach. Oh, yes, she needed Noah, needed what only he could make her feel. He'd brought her to life. He'd made her a real woman, and how could she *not* love him?

Quickly she undressed, taking off her stylish taupe trench coat, then her boots, her slacks and her sweater. Two seconds later her panties and bra were on the chair with her other things and she shook out the afghan, lay down on the sofa and covered herself with the afghan. It was very soft—cashmere, probably—and snuggly warm. With the pillow under her head she was wonderfully comfortable, but it was an external comfort. Only one thing would ease her internal aches, and there he was now!

Noah walked in and laughed when he saw her. "You

are a doll." He took off his jacket and laid it on his desk. "Do you realize that I hadn't really laughed from the time I left San Francisco until the day you decided that murder by paperweight made perfect sense?" He took off his shirt, feverishly aware of Maddie's unwavering gaze. She wanted to see him naked, the little imp.

"Since you're usually very stingy with your smiles, I don't doubt it," she said dryly. "You know, I thought you were there to burgle the house, and I simply was not going to lie on that couch and watch you steal Mark and Darcy's things. Then, when you laughed so hard that you got hysterical, I wondered if you weren't a mental case."

"Anyone would have laughed that day, sweetheart." Noah unbuttoned and unzipped his pants. "That was the funniest thing I'd ever seen."

"*I* was the funniest thing you'd ever seen?" She pretended to be deeply offended, but that act lasted only a second because he'd pushed down his shorts and there he was, in all of his masculine splendor. "Has anyone ever called you Dr. Big?" she asked innocently.

Noah roared with laughter. She laughed, too, but in a very few minutes no one was laughing. He was on top of her and the afghan was gone. Neither noticed its absence, for a chill wasn't possible with so much heat between them.

"Noah...Noah...there's nothing else like this," she moaned as he thrust in and out of her hot body.

"I know, babe. Believe me, I know."

"But you don't know...I mean, I never...not with either—" She stopped and started over. "You must know I wasn't a virgin, but there were only two men...one time with each...and I never felt...I never had...oh, damn."

"Don't be embarrassed. Are you trying to tell me you never had an orgasm before making love with me?"

"Yes," she whispered. "You know things other men don't. Things about a woman's body."

"Sweetheart, it's not knowledge you and I have together, it's chemistry."

Chemistry, Maddie thought to herself, and love.

"I can tell you that I'm scared to death you're going to load your horse in that trailer and leave town without telling me," he whispered.

She touched his face. "I wouldn't do that."

"In other words you'll tell me about it and *then* leave town." He began kissing her roughly, passionately, possessively, and moving faster and going deeper.

His explosive ardor completely disarmed Maddie. She lost all sight of herself and became an extension of him, and their final rush to completion was powerful and overwhelming for both of them.

Lying with her eyes closed and gradually catching her breath, Maddie became aware of Noah staring at her. She opened her eyes and saw tears in his. Tenderly she laid her hand on his cheek.

Noah was physically satisfied and strangely unnerved. He knew they had a lot of talking to do, but he probably shouldn't have mentioned her leaving Montana during lovemaking. It wasn't that he wanted to hurt her at all; at least he didn't think about what he said in that way. But the second he quipped, "How was that for chemistry, baby?" he could tell by the stunned expression on her face that he'd said the wrong thing.

She replied in kind, drawling sarcastically, "Are you going to feed me now or bore me to tears with typical ego-building, macho questions?"

It was not a good moment. They got off the sofa and dressed with their backs to each other, with Maddie seriously considering just going home and letting the big jerk eat dinner alone.

But she loved that big jerk, and maybe love wasn't always sweet and kind. After all, how would she know *what* people in love felt or did? Besides, everything else in life was a play-it-by-ear guessing game, and why would love be any different?

Noah's thoughts were so heavy, so distressing that he was frankly miserable. Looking at Maddie alleviated some of his discomfort. He'd behaved like an ass, but surely he could turn things around with a little diplomacy.

When they were both fully dressed, he picked up Maddie's coat and held it up for her to slip into. Then he put his hands on her shoulders—her back was to him—his cheek next to hers and whispered raggedly, "Tell me you don't hate me. Or tell me if you do." Whether that was diplomacy or desperation was an arguable subject, but Noah knew he was too jarred at the moment to recognize the difference.

Maddie's breath caught. Discussing feelings in their present down-in-the-mouth moods was a frightening prospect. There was no peace or contentment in the room, as maybe there should have been. She wanted very much to believe that a couple in love became softer, gentler people after they made love and the fires of urgency had been quenched. But it was difficult to cling to romantic notions that might be nothing more than hopeful delusions when each step she took with Noah was her first.

She truly could not give him an honest answer at the moment, and maybe she wouldn't if it was tickling the tip of her tongue. "May we talk later?" she asked rather coolly.

"We can do anything you want to do." He was so relieved that "later" was an option for her that he went to the door and opened it. "Shall we go?"

They left the building, and Noah led her to his vehicle. Maddie hesitated at the passenger door. "Maybe I should take my truck."

"Please ride with me. I'll bring you back here anytime you say the word."

"But if I had my truck I could go directly home from the restaurant."

You could also go directly home from here. Right now! He could actually visualize her getting into her truck, changing her mind about having dinner with him and then veering off in another direction once they were both under way.

But he couldn't insist that she ride with him and undoubtedly bring about another argument. In truth he didn't want another disagreement with Maddie over anything. She was an independent, outspoken, self-sufficient young woman, and deep down he knew that he wouldn't change her if he could. Besides, relationships between people who lacked respect for each other's differences didn't stand much of a chance of surviving.

"Suit yourself," he said quietly.

His acquiescence startled Maddie, but it also pleased her. So much, in fact, that she reversed herself and said, "My truck will be fine in the parking lot. I'll ride with you."

Acting as though she hadn't just surprised the breath out of him, Noah helped her into his SUV, then walked around the front of it to get into the driver's seat. His heart raced with a sudden burst of knowledge: Maddie *hated* being told what to do! And damned if he hadn't started issuing orders the very day they'd met! Was it any wonder they constantly crossed swords?

Noah felt so good over discovering something so crucial about the two of them that he completely changed his plans for the evening. A restaurant was out. They needed time alone together, not a meal with conversation that might be stilted because the next table was occupied and people could hear.

Maddie noticed that they had entered Whitehorn's most upscale residential area, but she decided that Noah could be taking a shortcut to a part of town that had several restaurants, so she said nothing about it.

Neither did Noah, not until he pulled into a circular driveway and turned off the engine. "This is my home."

Maddie gawked at the beautiful, sprawling ranch-style house. It had a three-car garage, and even in the dead of winter she could tell that the yard had been professionally landscaped. It occurred to her that she had never once wondered about Noah's financial status. Obviously, he worked steadily, and everyone knew that most doctors made a good living. But this was easily a half-million-dollar house, and in Whitehorn, a small town with only a handful of truly imposing homes, that meant something.

Thinking of Noah as wealthy made Maddie very nervous. And now there was another factor—money—in the already convoluted equation of their relationship. If she could never compete again, either because of Fanny's injury or her own, and she and Noah actually made a go of…of…what? Their affair? Their lusty sexual appetite for each other? Dear God, she had actually decided that she could not leave Noah behind, even if both she and Fanny were fine and she *could* compete! But no one would ever get the story right, and people would think she had quit rodeo and married Noah for the financial security she could no longer provide for herself!

"No-o-o-o," she moaned, and lowered her head to cover her eyes with her hand.

Noah was afraid to ask what was wrong now, so he hurriedly got out and rushed around his car to open Maddie's door.

"Come on, darlin'," he said while offering her his hand. "I'm going to pour you a nice glass of wine, turn on the gas fireplace to warm your toes and then order the best pizza in town. How does that sound?"

It sounded wonderful and…dangerous! But she simply didn't have the heart or the strength for another rebellion, so she gave him her hand and got out of the vehicle. He kept hold of her hand until they'd reached the front door, at which time he kissed her full on the lips—startling her again—then backed off, smiled and unlocked the door.

Inside, Noah pushed what was obviously some sort of

main switch, because lights came on all over the place. Maddie tried very hard to not look girlishly impressed, but she was. From the foyer she could see into the living room. This was definitely a bachelor's home, decorated with leather couches and chairs, heavy wood and glass tables, brass lamps and wildlife paintings and statuary, but it was still absolutely beautiful.

Noah took her coat, hung it along with his own in the foyer closet, then brought her to the living room, where he immediately turned on the gas and ignited the masonry logs in the fireplace.

"Sit anywhere," he told her. "I'm going to phone for the pizza and open a bottle of wine. Oh, you're not taking any pain medication, are you?"

"Hardly," she said dryly. "Have you forgotten that you destroyed my only supply?"

"Well, I gave you a few pills."

"Very few. They're long gone, believe me."

"Fine. Mixing alcohol and pills is bad business. I'll be back in a flash. Sit where you want." He walked out.

Sighing, Maddie sat on a chair that was near the fireplace. The dancing flames and the bit of warmth they threw were soothing to her troubled mind, but not so soothing as to eradicate her many worries. For one thing, it couldn't be more obvious that she hadn't yet reached the end of her run of bad luck. Oh, sure, she could toss her head and say to hell with gossip, but what if sometime in the future Noah got angry for whatever reason—everyone did once in a while, after all—and he accused her of only marrying him because she couldn't compete anymore? She would defend herself with the truth, of course, but angry people didn't always recognize and accept the truth.

Sighing heavily, Maddie put her head back and asked herself why she kept thinking about marriage. Had Noah ever said the word? No, he had not.

Had *she* held out for marriage? You couldn't have been easier!

Life was the pits, and it had been since she'd taken that fall in the arena. Self-pitying or not, she'd gone through hell after that.

Noah returned with an uncorked bottle of red wine and two glasses. Pouring the wine, he said, "You're looking very pensive. Penny for your thoughts."

"That's about what they're worth. I was remembering that miserable, long drive from Texas, for one thing," Maddie replied.

Noah brought her a glass of wine, which she took, then touched it with his glass. It made a pleasant little *clink,* and he said, "Shall we drink to more enjoyable drives?"

The toast dug a smile out of Maddie. "Sounds good to me." She took a swallow and found the wine delicious.

Noah sat on the carpet in front of the fireplace. "The pizza should be here in about thirty minutes. Do you like this wine?"

"Yes."

"Tell me about that miserable, long drive from Texas."

"There's really nothing to tell. It was miserable because *I* felt miserable, and no one could disagree that fifteen hundred miles isn't a long drive."

"I can't figure out how you managed to drive at all when you were so drugged."

"I wasn't drugged during the day, for heaven's sake. I know better than that. The only time I took a prescription pain pill was after I had stopped driving for the day *and* after I had fed, watered and cared for Fanny. If I felt really horrible while I was driving, I used over-the-counter pain medication. It helped."

"You've got guts, kiddo."

"Always have had, kiddo," she retorted. It was the unmitigated truth, and hadn't she been forgetting the hard times—her parents' fatal accident, for one earthshaking example—that she'd gotten through by the grace of God and her own courage? She would get through whatever fate had in store for her now, too, and if that included never competing again and *didn't* include marriage with the man she'd come to love in so short a time, she would survive.

The wine was relaxing the tension she'd arrived with, and it felt so very good to just let go and stop worrying, even if it was only a temporary respite from the emotional gridlock she would again be facing when this evening was over.

"I like your house," she said. "But if I may be honest, I'm not fond of its location. When I buy a house someday, it's going to be situated on at least a hundred acres." She knew she sounded as though she had the means to buy that dream home tonight if she wished, and in a way she did. Certainly her savings account would more than cover a down payment and closing costs. But what on earth would she do to earn enough money to make monthly payments for twenty or thirty years?

"I made a real deal on this house," Noah said. "The owner had it built because he and his wife had fallen in love with Montana during a summer vacation, and they had the money to construct the kind of home they were accustomed to living in in California. Well, as I've seen happen more than once around here, one winter was all it took for the missus to say uncle. Her other complaint was that Whitehorn had no shopping malls, which, of course, it doesn't. Anyhow, I was at the gym one day and overheard the man telling a friend that if he didn't sell fast and get his wife back to California, she was going to leave him. I was living in an apartment complex at the time and I hated it. People coming and going at all hours, noise of some kind going on *all* the time and very little privacy.

"Anyway, I butted into the conversation and asked the fellow if I could see his place. He was visibly overjoyed to just show the house, and after I saw it and he named a price so low I could hardly believe my ears, I became a homeowner.''

"Lucky you."

"It *was* luck, very good luck, because, guess what— One of my patients is an elderly man who happens to own a six-hundred-acre ranch about fifteen miles from town. He and his wife have reached the age where maintaining and operating even a small ranch is simply too much work, and they have no children who might want the place. Anyway, they would like to move to Whitehorn and he told me that they would trade for this house, straight across.''

Maddie nearly hyperventilated from a momentous burst of instantaneous excitement. "Are…are you going to do it?''

"I might." Noah got up for the bottle of wine and poured some into Maddie's empty glass. Standing before her, he topped off his own, then stood there sipping from his glass and looking at her. "Do you think I should?''

"Uh…I would…but why, uh, would you want a ranch?''

Grinning rather slyly, Noah turned and resumed his seat on the carpet by the fire. He startled Maddie with a complete change of subject.

"You heard about the chest of gold and jewels, I'm sure.''

She wanted to talk about that ranch so much she hurt, and besides why on earth was he rambling on about gold and jewels?

"I'm surprised the Braddocks didn't buy your patient's six hundred acres. Didn't you tell me that the Braddock family was buying land all over the area?''

"My patient hasn't advertised his intentions, so the Braddocks probably haven't heard about the availability of that ranch. Besides it's small potatoes for them, according to rumor. About that chest of gold and valuable jewelry…''

Maddie sighed impatiently. "What about it?"

"You did hear about it, didn't you?"

"I'm afraid not."

"It was found in the old foundation of the Hip Hop Café during the arson investigation."

"Oh, maybe Mark did mention something about it."

"Well, no one knew where it had come from or who had buried it there, so it was sent to a lab for investigation. I heard today that the investigators did a darned good job and put the gold together with some old memoirs left by…you'll never guess…one of your very own ancestors. A Kincaid."

"Now why doesn't that surprise me?" Maddie drawled dryly before taking another swallow of wine. "I swear that nothing happens in this entire county that doesn't involve at least one Kincaid. Are you aware of Kincaid history? Some of them were terrible people…dishonest, greedy, you name it, they did it."

"And some of them were and *are* terrific people," Noah said softly. "You're a Kincaid and so is Mark."

Maddie arched her eyebrow. "Oh? Are you saying I'm a terrific person?"

"Terrific, exciting, beautiful, funny, intelligent and dare I add mouthwateringly sexy?"

"I think you'd dare anything, Dr. Smooth-Talker."

Noah's laughter made Maddie smile. "I amuse you very easily, don't I?"

The doorbell rang and Noah got to his feet. "That's our pizza." He went to Maddie's chair, bent over and kissed her lips. "No one *ever* amused me the way you do, Miss Cutie-Pants."

Maddie could hardly believe that he'd made up a name for her the way she'd been doing for him ever since they'd met. "Times, they are achangin', and so are you, Doc," she said under her breath as happiness—and good wine—warmed her through and through. He'd told her about that ranch for a reason, and maybe they wouldn't get to the rest of it tonight—such as a discussion about marriage and their commingled futures—but eventually they would.

No, she couldn't leave Whitehorn ever again, not to compete, not for any excuse or reason.

Noah came in with the pizza box, two plates and a stack of paper napkins. "I consider pizza to be finger food, but would you like a fork?" He set everything on the coffee table.

"Nope. I eat it the same way you do, but I had the impression that you only ate fruits and vegetables."

"That impression was mostly right, sweetheart." Noah sent her a broad grin. "This is vegetarian pizza."

"You scoundrel," she scolded. "*Your* name should be Kincaid."

Laughing, Maddie moved to sit on the sofa with him, and they began eating, and, of course, they washed down the delicious vegetarian pizza with delicious wine.

"So," Maddie said after a few bites. "What's going to happen to the gold and jewels? Or didn't Whitehorn's thriving grapevine carry that message yet?"

"It belongs to Jennifer McCallum, of course. What is she, about eight or nine now? An adorable child that everyone seems to love. She's known as the darling of Whitehorn, you know. Anyhow, since she inherited the original Kincaid empire, the chest is hers, but the biggest news of all is that when she was told about it, she said that *every* Kincaid should have a piece of the pie. Apparently she plans to divide it up among all of you Kincaids."

Maddie lowered her piece of pizza. "You're not serious."

"It's what I heard."

"From whom?"

"My nurse."

"Well, if Nurse Norma is that deeply involved in Whitehorn's mainstream, imagine what she'll say about my coming to your office today."

Noah nodded with a tongue-in-cheek expression on his face. "Oh, she'll say a lot."

"You think you're teasing, but it's not funny, Noah."

"Sure it is. Do you really give a damn what anyone says about you?"

"Well…no, actually."

"Good, that makes two of us." Noah took a big swallow of his wine and looked at Maddie with his eyes twinkling. "So, maybe you're going to be a rich woman."

"Yeah, right. I'll believe that when it happens. There are so many Kincaids, that chest would have to be the size of Texas to make any one of us really rich."

"A bit of an exaggeration, but I get your point." Noah added softly after a moment, "Will you stay with me tonight?"

Maddie's pulse went wild. "You really don't care what people might say, do you?"

"Told you I don't. Maddie, listen. It's starting to rain again. Stay here tonight. We'll open another bottle of wine and lie together in front of the fire. We'll cuddle and talk and cuddle and…"

Laughing, Maddie slapped him on the arm. "You can stop with the 'cuddles,' Dr. Sweetie-Honey, I got the message loud and clear."

"Sweetie-Honey?"

"Yes," she said softly. "Tonight you feel like my sweetie-honey."

Noah was so moved he could barely speak. After clearing his throat he managed one simple question. "And tomorrow?"

Tomorrow she was going to talk to Dr. Herrera and to Dr. Pierce. Tomorrow could be a bright and wonderful day—even *with* rain—or it could be dreadful beyond imagination.

"I won't know anything about tomorrow *until* tomorrow," she said with a sudden mist of tears in her eyes.

Emotional with compassion for her troubles, he took

her glass from her hand and set it with his on the table. Then he put his arms around her and held her for a very long time.

Both of them knew they could not be any closer to each other than they were during those lovely minutes, though neither said so. The time wasn't yet perfect for saying what was in their minds, but it would be. Soon, very soon.

Chapter Fourteen

Early the following morning Noah drove Maddie to her truck. After a tender parting kiss, he asked, "Will you call me after you talk to Dr. Herrera?"

"I...guess so."

Noah was insistent. "Better still, would you give *me* permission to talk to him?" He playfully touched the tip of Maddie's nose and smiled. "I am your primary physician, you know."

"Completely your decision, I could remind you at this point," she replied pertly.

"You needed someone to look out for you, sweetheart. I just happened to be that someone and I just happened to be a doctor. That was good luck for both of us, I'd have to say."

"Oh, you would. Your life must have been terribly boring before I came along if you think our meeting brought you any good luck."

"My life was boring beyond belief."

Maddie still didn't know for certain why Noah had labeled so many years of his life a "void." She suspected a woman had brought him a lot of misery, but that theory was strictly guesswork. Be that as it may, it was difficult for her to look at Noah, see him for the handsome, intelligent man that he was, and accept that he'd lived a boring-beyond-belief existence. His work couldn't possibly be that uninteresting to him, so he obviously was referring to his personal life.

Well, had hers been so great that she could doubt anyone else's portrayal of life in the slow lane? The truth of the matter, of course, was that interaction with people you liked, admired, were drawn to by personality or hormones was perhaps the most profound distinction between "boring" and "exciting." Obviously Noah hadn't been doing much interacting.

It moved Maddie that he'd found her interesting enough to change his loner ways, and she laid her hand on Noah's cheek and wished she could say everything that was in her heart. She couldn't, though. Last night had been wonderful. They had made love, laughed together over silly things and talked and talked. But Maddie knew they'd both been holding back, because neither of them had really opened up about feelings or hopes for the future.

Maybe they were both hopeless misfits, but there was no way she could ignore her very serious problems, and it was entirely possible that neither could Noah ignore them. After all, what did she have to bring to a permanent relationship besides problems?

"Gotta go," she said, striving to sound upbeat instead of as sad as she suddenly felt inside.

"Wait and let me help you out." Noah stepped to the ground, hurried around to her side of his vehicle and opened the passenger door.

"Thanks, Doc," Maddie quipped, still making that effort to appear unruffled and certainly in control of herself. But she couldn't hide everything behind a bright facade.

For instance, her old response to offers of unneeded assistance from a guy had usually been a clearly stated, "Thanks, but I can do it myself." However, considering her bad knee and the fact that Noah's SUV was so high off the ground—he didn't have the extra little step that she'd had installed on her truck—she genuinely appreciated his assistance.

"See you later?" he said, putting what he apparently wanted to happen in the form of a question.

Maddie nodded. "I'm sure you will." She crossed the street to reach her truck, unlocked it and got into the driver's seat. Looking out the side window, she waved and he waved back. Then they each drove away, going in opposite directions. The symbolism did not escape Maddie's notice. Their individual paths through life could very well have crossed this one time, never to be repeated again.

Aren't you getting a bit melodramatic?

Well, hell's bells! If I'm fine and Fanny's fine, what excuse could I possibly come up with to hang around Whitehorn? If I'm so darned interesting that he's no longer bored, why not come right out and say that he doesn't want me to go anywhere?

He did.

Uh, guess he did say something to that effect, didn't he?

Truth was, they'd both hinted and beaten around the bush way too much.

But did she have the nerve to do anything else?

"Not really," she whispered just as she drove into Mark's driveway. Sighing heavily, she got out of her truck and went into the house.

Noah received a surprise that morning. While making his rounds at the hospital, he ran into Dr. Clark, chief of hospital administration. The older man fell into step with Noah, and they discussed various patients and diagnoses until they reached a fork in the corridor, where they stopped to chat further.

"Noah, we're losing Dr. Franklin to retirement. As you know, he's been an important member of the hospital's board for a long time. We must replace him, of course, and I would like to submit your name to the remaining board members for consideration. How does that strike you? It's quite an honor, you know."

Noah didn't want to appear ungrateful, because many physicians *did* consider board membership at a fine hospital an honor, but did he want to take on the additional work? Also, he'd always done his best to avoid hospital politics, and with an appointment to the board, he would be diving headfirst into the fray.

"May I think about it for a day or so, Dr. Clark?" he asked politely.

"Of course, but I would like an answer as soon as possible."

"I understand."

By two that afternoon numerous telephone calls had taken place: Maddie and Dr. Herrera, Maddie and Dr. Pierce, Noah and Dr. Herrera, and Maddie and Denise Hunter. Notably absent was a call between Maddie and Noah, because that was going to be one very difficult conversation for her.

A weak sun was shining, the temperature was mild, and Maddie left the house wearing jeans, boots and a heavily ribbed, hand-knitted, green wool sweater. She tossed a jacket into the cab of her truck, just in case, but her sweater was warm and probably all she would need. She drove straight to the Braddock stable, got out and went inside the building to hug and stroke Fanny. Try as she might, she could no longer hold back the tears that had stung her eyes and nose all the way from town.

After a few minutes of crying on Fanny's warm neck, Maddie began consoling herself by speaking softly to her beloved horse. "I will always take care of you. You're my darling, and after you're well you'll take me for long rides and we'll explore together. You'll always have a good home, I promise you. Oh, Fanny…Fanny." Emotion overcame her.

"Maddie?"

She wiped her eyes and turned to look at Denise. "I'm all right."

"I'm so sorry. I really wish Dr. Pierce had been as frank with me that day as he was with you on the telephone today."

"He couldn't be. I understand his code of ethics. The things he wrote down for you to tell me were the barebones medical facts of Fanny's injuries. The rest of it…his opinion that she should not compete again…could only be said to me, Fanny's owner. Before he said that, he let me know that I *could* race her, it was really up to me. Some people would, he said, even though another fall and further injury to her legs could cripple her." Maddie stroked Fanny's neck. "I'll never race her again. I wouldn't put her in that kind of jeopardy."

"Oh, Maddie," Denise said with a saddened sigh. "I'll leave you alone again. I just wanted to let you know how badly I feel about this. If you'd like to talk later on, come to the house and I'll make some tea…or coffee."

"Thank you, Denise." Maddie stayed with Fanny for a long time, petting her, stroking her soft nose and talking to her as though the mare could comprehend the promises she made to always care for her, to never let anything bad happen to her again.

When she finally left, Maddie went directly to her truck. She needed to be alone, and she was certain that Denise would understand why she didn't stop by the house. Driving away from the ranch, Maddie felt as burdened as she would have with a ton of bricks on her shoulders.

Noah probably had talked to Dr. Herrera by now and

knew that she would be just fine after approximately six weeks of physical therapy. But he didn't know about Fanny, and to Maddie, Fanny's forced retirement from competition was the end of an era. It was the end of her career in rodeo, which she'd truly loved, and while she had begun worrying about that very thing the second she'd realized something was wrong with Fanny's legs, deep down she really hadn't believed it would happen.

Well, it *had* happened, and she was now floating in the wind like a piece of dandelion fuzz, or a solitary leaf struggling to cling to a limb that wasn't offering even a tiny bit of help. What should she do? *What should she do?*

The really terrible thing was that all of her promises to Fanny were completely groundless, because she couldn't afford to board Fanny at the Braddock ranch indefinitely. She would have to find a job that paid enough to support herself *and* Fanny, but what kind of job? What did she know besides rodeo? Who would be stupid enough to hire her?

Realizing that she was approaching the curve in the road that bordered the big field where she'd gotten her truck stuck during that record-breaking blizzard, Maddie wondered if she had lost her cell phone somewhere out there. She needed that phone, and the field was pretty with so many huge old trees. She could walk around and look for her phone while she did some more thinking, she decided. There was no oncoming traffic and she made a left turn onto the field.

Just about the time that Maddie was caressing and talking to Fanny in the Braddock stable, Noah's concern about Maddie became serious. She wasn't answering the phone again, and he'd left numerous messages on Mark's voice mail for her to call him at his office. He had anticipated a call from her all day, especially after he'd talked to Dr. Herrera and heard what Noah considered to be good

news about her knee. Six weeks of physical therapy
wasn't a cakewalk, but it was a long way from a complicated diagnosis that could result in a wide variety of treatments, some of them not exactly pleasant.

At 3:00, Noah packed it in and did something he *never*
did. He told his nurse a lie about not feeling at all well
and that he had to go home and get off his feet. Feeling
guilty as hell about it, but too worried about Maddie to
let anything—even a guilty conscience—stop him, he left
Norma and the receptionist to deal with the patients still
in the waiting room.

By the time he reached his car he had devised a plan
of action. He would drive by Mark's house first, because
that was the logical place to start looking for Maddie. But
deep down he suspected that she'd again gone out to the
Braddock ranch to see Fanny. He felt an urgency to talk
to Maddie and wasn't sure what was behind it, except for
one niggling concern that she might not have completely
grasped Dr. Herrera's diagnosis and thought it was worse
than it was.

Then, too, he couldn't deny the possibility of his feeling
another form of guilt over being glad that she would be
tied to Whitehorn for the next six weeks for her physical
therapy. Not to say that she couldn't receive the same
treatment elsewhere, but it made sense to Noah that she
would stay right where she was for the duration. That
would be more than enough time for the two of them to
figure out the true nature of their relationship and agree
on an outcome.

Whatever was behind the persistent ache in his gut that
demanded he find Maddie and see for himself that she
was all right with Herrera's diagnosis, Noah couldn't
overcome or ignore it. Something was wrong and it involved Maddie; he knew it as surely as he knew his name,
and so help him Hannah he was going to find out what it
was and help her get past it.

* * *

Maddie took the ruts and bumps in the field very slowly and still her truck rolled right and left as she drove toward the grove of trees where she'd gotten so stuck during that storm. Looking around, she realized how different the area looked without a two-foot blanket of snow on everything. For one thing there were huge patches of winter-bare brush that would be quite beautiful when leafed out, but made it impossible to see the entire field. In fact, one could have concealed a herd of elephants in all that tall brush, Maddie thought wryly, if a person was so inclined, of course.

Thinking something so silly alleviated some of Maddie's emotional pain, and she parked within the grove of trees and got out to look for her phone, feeling a little better.

Walking around, Maddie breathed deeply of the clean, fresh air and listened to the songs of the hardy little birds that resided in Montana during the winter months. And suddenly, right before her own very next footstep, was her telephone!

"Well, I'll be darned," she murmured, and bent down to pick it up. It was dirty and the battery was dead, but Maddie had hopes of reviving it. Carrying it with her, she found a pretty patch of grass next to a big tree and sat down. Putting her head back, she pondered the twists and turns of her life since that day in the arena in Austin when she had sat on Fanny and waited for Janie Weston to run her race. A person never knew when disaster was going to strike, and even Maddie hadn't realized how truly disastrous that accident had been.

Troubled again, Maddie tried to make sense of her relationship with Noah. She was in love with him and maybe he loved her, too, but were his feelings for her as deeply everlasting as hers were for him?

"Aunt June," Maddie whispered, "I know now what's in my heart, but how does a woman know what's in a man's heart? We never talked about that, did we?"

The sound of an angry, shrill voice shattered Maddie's reverie, and she leaped to her feet with such speed that she hurt her bad knee. "Oh, damn," she mumbled, then put her discomfort aside to listen again. The shouting was easily heard, but Maddie couldn't see a soul.

Finally, however, she pinpointed its direction. It was a woman's voice, and she was clearly shrieking at someone who wasn't fighting back, or if they were, they were speaking too quietly for Maddie to hear.

Maddie's heart began pounding, because there was something creepy about this. What in heaven's name was going on over there behind that thick stand of brush? Who would come way out here to screech and yell?

Maddie glanced back to her truck and realized that she could just barely see it. Just as the brushy terrain concealed that screeching woman, so did it almost completely camouflage her truck.

The next burst of shrillness from beyond the thicket contained a perceptible phase. "Wyatt North wants me, not that namby-pamby wife of his!"

Maddie gaped with her mouth open. This was *worse* than creepy, it was downright scary. Some deranged woman believed and apparently was trying to make someone else believe that Melissa's husband, Wyatt, wanted her instead of Melissa!

Maddie looked helplessly at the phone in her hand and wished that it were working. She should call the police. *Someone* should call the police.

But there was no one but her to do anything, and she couldn't stay hidden—or creep away to her truck—if someone was in danger. Considering the fury in the woman's voice, whomever she was shrieking at could very well be in grave danger.

Maddie began walking toward the thicket. She told herself that she would just get close enough to see through the brush. Maybe using her eyes instead of her ears on the situation would eradicate her concern.

The shouting went on…and on…and the closer Maddie got to its source, the clearer became the language. "He's never loved Melissa. He's always wanted me. Oh, why didn't that poison I put in her drink at that boring wedding party kill her? Or why wasn't she in her wretched little excuse for a restaurant when I burned it to the ground? She would have been toast, and Wyatt and I would be together by now!"

"Oh, my God," Maddie whispered. Her need to identify the terrible person who was doing all the yelling became more urgent, and when she reached the thicket, she crowded into its prickly little limbs and twiggy branches in an effort to gain a better view.

There was a light-blue van parked in the field. Its wide side door had been left open, and an old man with long gray hair and beard sat in the opening with his feet on the ground. Before Maddie's very eyes the tall, not unattractive blond woman ran over to him and slapped him alongside the head.

"Ouch," the old man said sadly, and he rubbed the sore spot.

"You old fool. I'm so tired of looking at your ugly face. I'm so tired of playing nursemaid to an idiot, when I should be living with my true love. I'll get Melissa yet, you just wait and see."

Maddie was unnerved enough to cry. For one thing, she recognized the old man. He was Homer Gilmore, and he'd been considered the town eccentric for as long as Maddie could remember. Obviously, someone had decided that he needed a caregiver, but he sure as hell didn't need one that slapped and abused him!

Maddie backed out of the thicket and shouted, "You leave Homer alone, you…you witch!" Rounding the heavy stand of brush, she came face-to-face with the woman, who looked angry enough to battle a grizzly.

Maddie gulped—the woman was much bigger than she

was, and she looked a whole lot healthier, besides—but she stood her ground.

"I saw you slap Homer, and I'm going to report—" Maddie dodged the blow coming her way, turned around and began running for her truck.

Screeching invectives and threats, the woman ran after her. Maddie could feel her only a few feet behind her. Her knee was hurting and her heart was beating like a jackhammer, but she kept on running because if that insane woman got her hands on her, she would kill her for sure!

But in the next instant Maddie's inborn sense of self-protection kicked in, and she ran around a tree, stopped and waited the few seconds for that horrible woman to catch up with her. When Maddie saw that twisted criminal face coming around the tree she swung the telephone as hard as she could and slammed it against the woman's temple.

She went down like a sack of potatoes. "Oh, no, I killed her," Maddie cried. Kneeling beside the unconscious woman, Maddie felt for a pulse. To her horror the woman came to, grabbed her ankle and held on.

"You interfering busybody," the woman snarled. "I'm going to cut you up in little pieces and bury you in this field. No one will ever find you."

Noah had just spotted Maddie's truck in almost the same place she'd gotten it stuck in the snow. He pulled off the road, drove to her truck and parked next to it. Getting out, he frowned, because there were voices coming from somewhere, *angry* voices! Maddie was here, but she wasn't alone!

Instantly alarmed, Noah took off running. In mere seconds he spotted two women fighting with each other and rolling around on the ground. One was Maddie and the other was— "Good Lord," he muttered, "that's Connie

Adams. What in hell is going on? Maddie! Maddie!'' he shouted.

Both women heard him, but his voice thrilled Maddie and apparently scared the tar out of Connie. She jumped up and ran. Fearing that she would get away, Maddie got up and chased after her.

"No, Maddie, leave her alone!'' Noah shouted, but Maddie kept going.

Connie went around the thicket screaming at Homer. "Get in the van, you old fool!''

Before *either* of them could get in the van, Maddie came barreling around the thicket and without so much as a first thought, let alone a second, she wound up and threw the phone at that evil woman. It was a perfect hit, and again Connie sank to the ground.

"You beaned 'er, you beaned 'er,'' Homer chanted while happily clapping his hands.

"Yes, I most certainly did,'' Maddie said with immense self-satisfaction. "Are you all right, Homer?''

"Aw, sure. Right as rain. Good as new.''

Recalling that Homer Gilmore had never seemed to be quite right in the head, Maddie smiled at him. "I'm glad.''

Noah ran up, saw Connie out cold on the ground and looked inquisitively at Maddie. "Did you do that?''

"She beaned 'er,'' Homer said.

"I beaned her,'' Maddie said solemnly.

"With what?''

"I found my cell phone.''

"You beaned her with a cell phone?'' Spotting the instrument on the ground, Noah went over, picked it up and took a look at it. "You didn't find *your* cell phone, you found mine,'' he said to Maddie.

"I most certainly did not find your phone, I found mine! That's my phone you're holding!''

"Nope, it's mine.'' Seeing Maddie bristling, he held up his hand. "Let's not argue about it now. What happened here? Why did you bean Connie Adams?'' He wanted to laugh over the word *bean,* but this all seemed a bit too serious to stand around and laugh at.

"Do you actually know this...this witch?"

"She's a nurse. Mostly does private work. She's been taking care of Homer here for quite some time."

"Well, she's terrible to him, and she should be locked up! I saw her slap Homer with my own eyes, and she was screeching and yelling all kinds of terrible things about having poisoned Melissa North and burning down her café so she could have Wyatt, Melissa's husband. She thinks Wyatt is in love with her. Did you ever hear anything so ridiculous? Well, I can tell you right now that Connie Adams is nuttier than a fruitcake."

Noah saw Connie starting to regain consciousness. "She needs to be restrained until this whole thing can be sorted out." He peered into the blue van and came out with a length of rope. "This should do it." Deftly he tied Connie's hands together behind her back, and then hobbled her ankles.

Maddie had been thinking about what he'd said. "Are you doubting my version of what took place here?" she asked him.

Noah stood up, leaving Connie tied up on the ground. "Not at all. All I meant was that it will be up to the authorities to sort it out."

"She threatened to kill me," Maddie said, realizing that both her courage and strength were deserting her and leaving her feeling weak and shaky. "I'm sorry, but...I have to sit down."

"She actually said she would kill you?" Noah put his arm around Maddie and led her to an ancient fallen tree. He sat on it with her and held her close to his heart. The whole thing was really sinking in now. Connie Adams had threatened Maddie's life! It was bizarre and one of those things that people found hard to believe, but Maddie wasn't making this up.

Noah suddenly felt rather shaky himself. "Maddie, she's so much bigger and stronger than you are."

"Size only counts in—" Maddie bit her tongue.

"In what?"

"Uh, in the clothes one buys."

Noah chuckled. "You weren't thinking of clothes, sweetheart. Maddie, one of us has to get to a telephone to call the police, but Homer fell asleep, and if Connie comes to enough to start yelling again I'll stuff my sock in her mouth. I've got a few things to say to you, and I don't plan on waiting to say them."

"Oh, really?"

"Yes, really. I talked to Dr. Herrera and I know you'll be up to speed again with six weeks of physical therapy. Maddie, I told you this before, but maybe not in the right way. This time I'm going to say it all. I love you, I want you for my wife and I *don't* want you even thinking about heading off for parts unknown to follow the rodeo circuit again."

Maddie backed away from him just enough to see his face. "Well, I guess this is as romantic a spot for a marriage proposal as any other."

Noah chuckled. "Anywhere you are is romantic to me, darlin'. In case you're considering saying anything but a resounding yes to my proposal, let me entice you with a few bribes. First, there's the ranch. I'll make the trade for my house and we'll live on that six hundred acres and raise horses and babies, or cattle and babies, or even hootie owls and babies, whichever you prefer."

"Apparently babies aren't an option?"

"You want babies, don't you?"

Maddie's heart was gradually filling with joy, but considering the way things had been going for her lately she was almost afraid to believe this was really happening.

"Yes," she said softly. "I want babies. Noah, there's something you *don't* know. I had already made up my mind to never compete again. Fanny...Fanny is disabled, and one can't compete in barrel racing without a horse.''

"Maddie, I'll buy you a good horse, if that's what you want to do. I didn't mean to tread on your toes about your career when I said I didn't want you even thinking about it. You have a right to do whatever you want. I hope with all my heart it's the same as I want, but if it's not, I'll buy you any horse you choose.''

Maddie's eyes misted over. ''I'll never forget you said that," she whispered emotionally. "But I'm through with rodeo. It's probably difficult for you to understand this, but no other horse could ever replace Fanny.''

"Honey, there must be plenty of good racing horses on the market.''

"I'm sure there are, but none of them is Fanny.''

"I'm sorry she was so badly hurt.''

Maddie looked away. There was Connie, the demon nurse, still tied up, still silent, and poor old Homer, sound asleep with his head against the side of the van. Maddie saw it all but none of it really registered. Noah had asked her to marry him. He'd said he loved her. Why was she hesitating?

"People will talk, you know," she said. "They'll say I married you for financial security because I couldn't compete anymore.''

Noah shrugged. "Let 'em talk. What you say and I say matters. Everyone else can talk themselves blue in the face and it wouldn't matter. Maddie, I've told you that before, and you agreed. What's bothering you now?''

"I...I guess I didn't know you were...wealthy," she stammered.

Noah threw back his head and roared with laughter. Then he hugged her closer to himself. "Listen, you little monkey, what good is money if you don't spend it? Now, I want you to close your eyes and picture a house...the kind of house you'd like us to build on our ranch.''

"It doesn't have a house?''

"Yes, but it's very old and sort of run-down."

"Well, I'd like to see it before you tear it down."

"Anything you say, sweetheart, as long as you say yes first. Will you be my wife?"

Maddie sucked in a long breath. "Yes…yes!"

Noah hugged and kissed her and whispered all sorts of erotic promises for later on, when they were finally rid of poor old Homer and his psychotic nurse, Connie.

"You know, I just realized something," he said. "With your aim, I wasn't safe at all the day I walked into Mark's house and you threatened me with that paperweight."

Maddie grinned impishly. "Right on, Dr. Husband-To-Be."

"You adorable doll!" He kissed her with so much love and passion they both became breathless. "I'd better stop that for the time being," he gasped.

"Save it, though. Don't lose it or throw any of it away."

"Never, sweetheart, never."

Then, out of the blue, Maddie said, "We could breed Fanny," and when Noah gave her a curious smile, she added, "On our ranch. Fanny and the right quarter horse stallion would make incredible babies."

"Sounds absolutely fantastic. We're going to make some beautiful babies ourselves. Okay, you sit here and dream up a whole bunch of great plans while I go find a telephone." Standing, he bent over for one last kiss before striking off toward their vehicles.

Maddie watched him for a moment, then called, "Noah! I love you with all my heart, but don't forget that's my cell phone you're carrying!"

"Like hell it is. It's mine!" he called back, and then he laughed all the way to his SUV. Life with Maddie was never going to be dull. One thing was certain. He was going to refuse that position Dr. Clark had offered on the hospital board. Any spare time he had now was going to be spent with his sweetheart of a wife.

Someday, of course, he'd tell her all about Felicia. Why wouldn't he? By then Maddie would be so saturated with his love he'd be able to tell her anything.

There was one question that he wished someone could answer for him, though. How in God's good name had he lived so long without Maddie Kincaid?

Shaking his head, he got into his vehicle and headed for town.

* * * * *

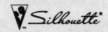

Silhouette®

INTIMATE MOMENTS™
is proud to present

Romancing
the Crown

With the help of their powerful allies,
the royal family of Montebello is determined
to find their missing heir. But the search for the
beloved prince is not without danger—or passion!

**This exciting twelve-book series begins in January and
continues throughout the year with these fabulous titles:**

Available at your favorite retail outlet.

Silhouette®
Where love comes alive™

Every day is

A Mother's Day

in this heartwarming anthology
celebrating motherhood and romance!

Featuring the classic story "Nobody's Child" by Emilie Richards
He had come to a child's rescue, and now Officer Farrell Riley was
suddenly sharing parenthood with beautiful Gemma Hancock.
But would their ready-made family last forever?

Plus two brand-new romances:

"Baby on the Way" by Marie Ferrarella
Single and pregnant, Madeline Reed found the perfect husband in the
handsome cop who helped bring her infant son into the world. But did his
dutiful role in the surprise delivery make J. T. Walker a daddy?

"A Daddy for Her Daughters" by Elizabeth Bevarly
When confronted with spirited Naomi Carmichael and her brood of girls,
bachelor Sloan Sullivan realized he had a lot to learn about women!
Especially if he hoped to win this sexy single mom's heart....

Available this April from Silhouette Books!

Where love comes alive™

*Silhouette presents an exciting
new continuity series:*

**When a royal family rolls out the red carpet
for love, power and deception, will their
lives change forever?**

The saga begins in April 2002 with:

The Princess Is Pregnant!

by Laurie Paige (SE #1459)

**May: THE PRINCESS AND THE DUKE by Allison Leigh
(SE #1465)**

**June: ROYAL PROTOCOL by Christine Flynn
(SE #1471)**

Be sure to catch all nine Crown and Glory stories: the first three appear in
Silhouette Special Edition, the next three continue in Silhouette Romance
and the saga concludes with three books in Silhouette Desire.

————————————

And be sure not to miss more royal stories,
from Silhouette Intimate Moments'

Romancing
the Crown,

running January through December.

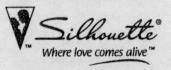

Where love comes alive™

*Available at
your favorite
retail outlet*